Night Rising

Mantle of the Gods

Quest for Truth

Unmasking Truth

Truth Revealed

Night Rising

Anthologies

Discovering Truth

Night Rising

Tricia Sparks

NIGHT RISING, Book 4 of the A *MANTLE OF THE GODS*

This is a work of fiction. All characters and events portrayed are fictional, and any resemblance to real people or incidents is purely coincidental.

Cover Design by Doris Ross

A Trinity Gateways LLC Publication
www.TrinityGateways.net

ISBN: 1941426115
ISBN-13: 978-1-941426-11-1

PROLOGUE

TEL AVIV
SUNDAY
7AM

Sam moved into the bathroom needing to get away from the others. His mind and spirit troubled. He turned on the faucet and threw cold water in his face. As his eyes fell shut the image of a black dragon in the heavens filled his mind. His thoughts rushing back to the battle he'd been fighting only moments before.

Dragon's fire poured down around him and his allies. Their efforts to bring it down were proving fruitless. He could see they were doing damage but it wasn't lasting. The Fallen's power was undoing their work too quickly. They'd soon run out of ammo and have nothing to show for their efforts, as the beast was still coming.

"Terra!"

"Yeah."

"Get your sister and the boy out of here!"

"Aye!"

He watched as the Rogue retreated from the field to see to Anna and the child. At least they would live through this, he reasoned as he fired a rocket from his bazooka. Sam watched as the beasts side ripped open; a gaping hole that had the dragon falling abruptly. He closed his eyes and drew a breath, hands shaking.

Eye lids lifted hoping that this time he'd see the reptilian form on a collision course for the earth bellow. He cursed as the smoke cloud split and the dragon rose in the heavens once more. The damage he'd created mended before his eyes. How was Ares sword going to fare any better against such power, he wondered, as fire fell from the heavens yet again. The homes around them burst into flames. Half of

Jerusalem was burning and there wasn't a damn thing they could do to stop it; so long as Hades was there to undo the injury to his beast.

Sam lifted his head. His eyes opened to settle on his reflection. At his side, his hands coiled into a fist as he cursed. He'd been desperate enough to stop the beast, he'd even tried challenging the god of the underworld directly to no avail.

"Come out and fight us like a man," Sam challenged. "Your host was a more worthy opponent," he taunted jabbing Zaharrah's knife deeper in the fallen one's sense of pride. Hoping her blade was well aimed.

A cloud of green smoke erupted between Sam and the others surrounding him. Cutting him off and blinding him to the world beyond.

"That mortal was a FOOL! I led him about by the nose like an ASS. Every step toward power he took was at MY urging. Magnus Halden was NOTHING without ME!" Hades hissed in rage as his hands wrapped around Sam's neck. "I played him like the PAWN he was just as I'VE played YOU. I gave you a chance to get out before it was through but you refused; now I'LL CRUSH you and when I'M done I'LL destroy EVERYTHING you care for, ANYTHING you love starting with your precious ANNA," Hades mocked as he squeezed the life from Sam.

"No," Sam gasped as he tore at Hades hands and fought to survive.

The truth of the matter was if not for Lance, he'd be dead and the rest of them with him. They'd survived for now but at what cost. Lance had used Ares sword.

"You've LOST," Ares voice mocked, as the man Lance walked through the flames, sword drawn ready to fight.

"Detective Roman I see Ares managed to get his claws in you after all. Consider carefully your next step for it will have a price. You know who I am, do you really want to make me your enemy? ALL you know, ANYTHNG you care for, WHATEVER you love, I'LL tear it apart. NOT even your beloved DANA is beyond MY REACH," Hades hissed.

"HE'S bluffing detective, so long as ZEUS'S crown is beyond him, his power is sealed. HE can't take anyone before their ordained time," Ares answered.

"I can if they've heeded MY CALL. Your SERENITY is within MY reach. WE both know she's not much further from the EDGE that the lovely DANA was," Hades warned.

"She can be protected. I'LL show you how," Ares vowed.

"Why do you interfere WAR god? We have ALWAYS been allies," Hades snarled.

"I'M through being YOUR puppet HADES," Ares answered, as the man Lance swung his sword cutting through scaly hide, muscle, sinew, flesh and bone; separating the reptilian head from the long serpentine neck.

Hades roared in fury, as his beast passed from existence to the underworld, and vanished in a cloud of smoke aware that Ares would not hesitate to turn that sword on him as well.

The detective trembled where he stood as sweat dripped from his brow. He drew a deep breath and blew it out as the sword in his grip flashed with power and the flames around him died out. He looked down at the blade he held tight in his hands and the carcass of the fallen beast.

He'd just killed a dragon.

"With my help," Ares reminded.

"Okay, fair enough," Lance muttered. He felt the press of the war god's power around him now in a way he'd not before and wondered why. "You vowed not to press me," he grumbled reminding Ares of their deal feeling uneasy.

"I'm not. I'm still out here," Ares assured him.

"But, you're more pronounced," Lance muttered.

"A side effect from the dragon's blood, it increases our strength," Ares explained.

Lance looked up at the sound of Zaharrah's voice. "Why did you have me put the blade in the fire?"

"To clean it," Ares answered.

"Lance put the sword in the scabbard!" he heard his comrade shout but the cry was muffled as if from far away.

"Why?" he shouted back but she gave no reply as if she'd not heard him.

"WE have to move NOW," Ares commanded.

"Why?"

"YOU heard HADES. HIS threat was not an IDEL ONE. HE will strike back at YOU through CATHARINE and HE'LL do it swiftly."

"You told me she could be protected."

"SHE can. If YOU want to KEEP HER safe YOU'LL need to hold onto MY sword a bit LONGER. I MUST obtain MY true power."

"If you're not going to go back on our deal how can you do that?"

"I'LL TEACH YOU," Ares vowed.

Lance drew a breath to quiet his mind, feeling Ares power wrap around him tighter. He put the blade in its scabbard as Zaharrah had instructed and felt the power dissipate. He blew out his breath with relief. He needed time to think, plan and most of all rest. He'd made too many hasty choices of late and it didn't sit well with him.

Crossing the field he moved to Sam's side and helped his friend to his feet.

"What happened?" Sam asked groggy.

"The beast fell. Hades fled," Lance stated.

"How?"

"I cut off its head."

"That worked?" Sam asked with disbelief.

"Yeah."

"How are you?"

"Fine," Lance assured him.

Now Sam wondered if it was true, Anna's words from a moment ago played back in his mind.

"Ares is getting stronger. We've got to get Lance to get rid of that sword," she whispered.

Sam counted their losses and felt frustration become despair. "We failed," he muttered with regret. His head fell in shame with defeat.

"Why is it you humans look at any set back as a failure?" An all too familiar voice questioned with exasperation. The words came from nowhere and everywhere.

"Three of the fallen are walking the earth, another is riding my friend in there waiting to take him over. How is that not failure?" Sam questioned with annoyance as he looked up at the mirror. On it he found the reflection of the angelic figure that seemed to be watching him and the others at every turn.

"Lance's fate is not yet sealed, another might still become war."

"Then that will be four of them in all."

"True, but have you considered the possibility that you were never meant to stop them all," the angel asked.

Sam turned to face the messenger with disbelief. "But you said..."

"I told you that you were to prevent the mantels from falling into human hands and those that were not already found you did. The whip, the gauntlets, the bow and even the crown will never get the chance to corrupt a mortal."

"But the others...."

"Were not within your power to contain, I never said you had to hold back all the fallen. Just to keep the mantles out of mortal hands."

"If we couldn't hold them all back then why did we bother to try?"

"Four is more easily managed than nine."

"Why put us through all this?"

"Consider what has changed Sam Abrams since you began your journey. Anna who once sought knowledge at every turn now looks for truth and she will find more of it than she ever dared to dream of. Detective Lance Roman who once hunted monsters, until the day one nearly consumed him, is now reinvested in his life's call. Serenity, Catharine, Jade Collins who had hidden herself behind lies, fearing she was a monster, has taken back her name and seen herself through the Creator's eyes as a writer, her work will now fill the world with light and hope rather than darkness and despair. Zaharrah Lynch who abandoned her life and the call upon it due to Hades torment has embraced her existence and returned to the life she left with Gunnar. His fear that he was unlovable has been silenced and the anger and despair washed away. The Ancient huntress's loyalty has turned from the fallen she served to that of men. In time she will be given a choice as you were and will take her place in the war to come."

"And me?" Sam asked, afraid to hear what the angel would say and yet unable to hold back the question.

"Sam, you who were a great warrior have taken up your fight once more. The love you thought was yours in your youth that was lost has been given to you anew," the angel answered with a smile.

Sam shook his head as the winged messenger's word sank in. "Okay, maybe my measuring stick for success is a little off," he muttered.

"Each of your lives has been brought full circle and set on the path the Father chose for you before you were born."

"So you're saying that Hermes, Ares, Dionysus and Hades were meant to be unleashed. Why? What sense does it make to turn these monsters with their power over humans loose in this world?"

"It was prophesied long before you were born that four would one day walk the earth. What the Father says will come to pass, for his word is true."

"Then times up?" Sam asked with disbelief.

"No, no man will know the appointed day or hour of His coming. But that doesn't stop the enemy from trying to set it in motion early, in a vain attempt to change the outcome."

"Okay, so if this is one such attempt then what comes next?"

"Now the four will battle for the crown of Zeus. In the process the last mantle, the scroll of Chaos will be brought to light. Only one can rule; it is the way of them. Artemis has slowed their accent to power but not for long."

"Where do we fit in?"

"Your steps will be dogged by these fallen as you possess something they seek. Guard well the keys you hold and seek answers in the pages of the Black Hand. Hold true to each other as you begin this new leg of your journey."

Sam cursed as the angelic messenger vanished with his final words. He really wished the guy would stop doing that. Despite his irritation at the abrupt end to the conversation he found his spirit renewed and his mind eased. So maybe they hadn't failed as he'd believed moments ago. Whatever lay ahead of them, he intended to be ready for it?

1

Sam stepped out of the bathroom and back into the main room of their hotel. His mind free of turmoil, it was time to discuss their next move.

"You okay?" Anna asked as he reemerged.

"Yeah, I just needed a minute to clear my head," he assured her.

"What's our next move?" She asked as he reached her side. Rather than answer her, he drew her into his arms and held her close for a moment, brushing her forehead with a light kiss. When he drew back, his eyes locked with hazel ones that had turned gray.

"Are you okay?" he asked seeing her fear.

"Yeah, I just went a round with Ares," she muttered.

At the words Sam let her go and looked her over for injury. "What happened?"

"It wasn't like that. He's just taunting me. Making it pretty clear that despite whatever deal he made with Lance, he has designs for Catharine still." Anna explained.

"Yeah I'm not surprised there; I figured that a deal made with a fallen wouldn't end well," Sam grumbled.

"What are we going to do?" Anna asked.

"We'll deal with Lance in a minute, first we need to get people on their way and figure out what we can do to stop these four want-to-be gods from jump starting the apocalypse," Sam whispered.

Anna nodded her understanding as Sam drew her back to his side. He watched as the others in the room moved away from each other and in his direction, all but Lance, he stayed at Catharine's side. That was just fine by Sam, he didn't want Ares privy to whatever plans they set in motion.

"All right yank quiet times over, what are we gonna do?" Terra demanded, her green eyes sharp and cold.

"You and your Mr. Fenton are going to get back to the states and monitor the movements of these fallen. The second any of them pops up on your radar I want to know about it."

"But..." Terra began in protest.

"Will do," Vince answered, stalling his wife's protests.

"Thanks. Zaharrah you and Gunnar take your kid and run; after what Lance did earlier today I have a feeling Hades undivided attention will be on him and Miss Nichols..."

"I can't do that; there are artifacts still at those digs, I can't let them find. As a member of the order it's my duty..." Zaharrah began with objection.

"You said it yourself the order is done." Gunnar stated.

"Anna and I know what to look for, we'll see to it Hermes doesn't locate any more," Sam assured her.

"But..."

"You gave up five years for this, it's time to walk away. Your family needs you," Anna reasoned.

Zaharrah nodded. "I'm going to go back to the library, see if anything useful survived the fire," She muttered.

"We Will. If we come up with anything I'll let you know," Gunnar corrected.

"Fine," Sam answered.

"Not fine, do ya expect me ta sit by and watch while ya go gallivantin about with mi sister, with those fallen chasin ya," Terra snapped in objection.

"Do you think I'd risk taking her if I didn't have to? Believe me, I'd like nothing better than to put her on a plane with you; but whether we like it or not she's a part of this. Has been from the start and nothing we say or do can take her out of the middle of it," Sam stated.

"So we do nothin Mr. Abrams?'

"No, you keep your eyes on their movements, let us know when they're closing in on us and trust me to protect my fiancé by doing my job," Sam corrected.

"I don't like this," Terra muttered.

"Well, I do not like your trying to step in and run my life. Sam is right, if I go back with you I'm in more danger than out here with him," Anna stated.

"I liked ya better when ya were obedient," Terra muttered.

"Tough, miss prim, proper and responsible grew up," Anna snapped.

"I think ya best let this go Terra-Ann, my love," Vince said amused.

"Laugh it up Mr. Fenton, when we get home ya'll be paying for it later," Terra grumbled. "What about him?" she questioned pointing over at Lance.

"I'll be going to LA with Catharine. I've no intention of leaving her unwatched with Mr. Hardagen or unprotected from Hades reach," Lance declared in answer to the question.

"Well, then, it would seem we're splitting up again," Sam stated.

"Right, good luck Sam," Lance offered.

"Thanks, be careful detective," Sam replied. "I suggest we get moving, it won't take long for Hades to find us here."

Gunnar nodded and Zaharrah lifted her son into her arms and moved for the door.

"Stay safe," Anna urged.

"You too." Zaharrah answered before the family of three walked out.

Sam looked back to where his friend sat and watched as the detective leaned over and brushed a kiss on CJ Nichols forehead. The pretty writer's lashes fluttered and she looked up at him with question in her blues eyes.

"Sorry, Catharine, time to go home," he murmured.

"Home?" she asked groggy.

"Back to LA," he elaborated, before gathering her into his arms. Catharine snuggled close to him and closed her eyes.

"Be careful and stay in touch," Anna entreated.

"We will," Lance assured her before he walked out.

"Well, if we're gonna be watchin your gods for ya we'll be needin a list of names," Terra muttered.

"Magnus Halden, Ian Broody, and James Hardagen…"

"The actor," Vince asked with disbelief interrupting him.

"Right," Anna replied.

"Do I even want to know?" Terra asked.

"You got a glimpse of him when we rescued her," Sam stated.

"Do ya want us to keep an eye on your cop friend as well?" Vince asked.

Sam hesitated unsure of how to answer the question. He wanted to believe he could trust his friend's word that he was fine but his gut told him not to. Before he could respond, Anna spoke.

"He'll be in the same area as James, only if he leaves abruptly do you need to worry about monitoring him," she stated.

Vince nodded. "Come along Terra, my love, it's time we were off as well. Say good-bye to your sister."

Terra drew Anna into her arms and gave her a hug before brushing a kiss on her cheek. "So long Annalynn, ya keep your head down as best ya can," she requested before letting her go.

The Rogue then took Sam's hand in hers and shook it. "Good-bye Mr. Abrams ya take care of mi baby sister. If anythin happens to her I'll be holdin ya responsible," Terra stated.

"I will," Sam assured her as he shook her hand. He watched as Vince took Anna's hand in his and kissed her knuckles.

"Farewell Annalynn, it was an honor to finally meet ya."

"It was nice to meet you also. I want to hear how you two met next time I see you."

"It's a deal," he assured her before turning his attention to Sam.

"Sam, it's been interesting," Vince muttered.

"Yep. Hopefully next time we meet it won't be to fight a dragon," Sam stated with a grin.

"Or if we do, it won't have a god mending it back together," Vince chuckled.

"After this little adventure I imagine getting back to normal operations will seem dull by comparison," Sam said amused.

"I'm looking forward to the everyday run of the mill terrorist threat and a normal night's sleep," Vince stated.

"I'll bet."

"We'll be in touch, hopefully the next time we meet will be under less dire straits. Perhaps even for a celebration," Vince speculated.

"That would be nice," Sam answered thinking about his recent proposal to Anna and their future ahead; if they lived long enough to get there.

"Good luck," Vince offered before he took Terra by the shoulder and guided her toward the door.

The door opened and a moment later it closed a third time leaving him alone in the room with Anna.

"Where are we going to go?" Anna asked curious.

"I don't know."

2 UNKNOWN, HADES FORTRESS

Hades roared, as he appeared in his self-styled throne room. His well laid plans had been ruined. Ares would pay dearly for the intrusion. His host detective Roman would suffer for his part in the affair. His dragon had been planned as the first wave of his vengeance upon men. That the war god had dared to raise his blade against it – or even threatened to use it against him was unacceptable.

The sword's true power had been sealed after Zeus fell, to prevent its use against another god again. When Ares cut off the dragon's head, he'd not only declared war against him but the act had broken Hade's seal upon the sword. It wouldn't be long before Ares began pressing his host to seek out the sea king's seal as well.

A fully awakened Ares was the one scenario Hades had hoped to avoid. The war god in his power was a force even he feared. The lord of the underworld's desire to unleash his wrath upon mankind would have to wait now. Before he could move against Ares or the others he needed to obtain his full power. He needed Zeus's crown.

"PAMELA," he called in temper.

"My lord," she answered as she emerged from the chamber she and his other women were housed.

"FETCH MY SAND," he demanded his green eyes gleamed with barely controlled power.

"Yes my lord," she whispered before she rushed away.

Hades smiled pleased by her fear. It seemed she'd accepted her place in his ranks. The lord of the underworld turned his focus to the world map laid out on his desk as he wondered where his troublesome niece might have hidden her father's crown.

He watched as Pamela returned carrying an earthen jar filled with sand. She set it at his feet and drawing upon his power, he lifted the grains from within. Spreading them over the map.

"May I go now, my lord?" she questioned.

"Not yet," he muttered. His long slender fingers skimmed over the sand making it glow green. "TELL ME WHERE THE CROWN WAITS," Hades commanded of the dust. He watched as the sand's light dimmed all but the small grains that lay upon the isle where Atlantis was located.

Hades cursed and Pamela flinched. It seemed Artemis had sealed his brother's crown inside Chaos's door. That would make obtaining it a bit trickier than he'd anticipated but he'd manage. The huntress knew much of their secrets but not all and her ignorance would cost her this time. He'd pursue the crown from a different angle. "PAMELA I NEED YOU TO GO BACK OUT TO LA AND KEEP AN EYE ON DETECTIVE ROMAN FOR ME."

"My lord?"

"I WANT TO KNOW EVERY MOVE ARES MAKES," Hades hissed.

"Understood."

"FAILURE WILL HAVE A HIGH PRICE," he warned.

She nodded. "Anything else you desire?"

"YES, KEEP THE WINE GOD AWAY FROM MISS NICHOLS. I DON'T WANT ARES GETTING EVEN A TASTE OF HIS WOULD BE BRIDE. SHE WILL SUFFER FOR HIS ARROGANCE. IF YOU HAVE TO, RETURN EMILY TO HIM FOR HER."

"As you will," Pamela answered with a bow.

"GO." Hades commanded and he watched with satisfaction as she departed to carry out his bidding. Once she was gone he picked up the sand and as it ran through his fingers back into the jar, whispered a name," GAIL, BLACKWOOD," he watched as the sand grains became red as blood. "WHERE ARE YOU?" he questioned, as he drew upon his hold over the mortal woman that Ares puppet Kurt had tortured nearly to death.

3 Atlantis, Somewhere in the Bermuda Triangle

Hecate stood before the door that would lead her to where Zeus's crown lay in wait for her. As she lifted the key to the lock she felt the hairs on her host's flesh rise as Hades icy fingers pulled at the chains he held upon her, seeking her location and cursed Serenity's refusal of her. By taking the woman Gail as her host, she'd left herself vulnerable to Hades influence.

She didn't dare claim the king's crown now as she was; by doing so, she'd be handing it over to the lord of the underworld on a silver platter. No she'd need another host one whose heart would feed her power and bend to her will. Someone who held as much hate for the fallen as herself.

Drawing upon the power her lord had entrusted her, Hecate sought a suitable host and the name burned upon her brain like a brand. As the image of the woman came into focus in her mind's eye Hecate laughed before departing the throne room. Once she was well away from the lost city, she released her hold on Gail's mind, allowing the woman to answer Hades call, if she had any chance of pulling off what she was plotting, she'd have to keep him and his brethren blind to her movements.

4 UNKNOWN, HADES FORTRESS

Hades cursed as he waited for the woman Gail's reply to his call. It shouldn't be taking this long if it was it could mean only one thing Hecate was up to something and didn't want him to see it. The old witches' secrecy was troublesome and frustrating. She knew things the rest of them were missing.

He wondered what game she was playing but dismissed it as unimportant, nothing mattered now but finding the key.

5 Athens, Greece

Hermes blood boiled at the sight of what had once been his grand palace. Now only a few of the graven statues of his brethren remained standing in a mass of rubble. Hades would pay dearly for this humiliation. Drawing upon his power the god of knowledge worked to reconstruct his dwelling to make it livable until he could establish a new palace. As he worked, a hawk descended to land upon his arm, the beast cried out and when it did the image of all it had seen filled Hermes mind.

The god laughed with pleasure as he was informed Hades grand scheme had gone up in smoke. Artemis had brought the great serpent to the ground and Ares had finished it off with a swing of his sword. Now he too knew the shame of failure at the hand of these upstart mortals. Now the only clear path to the throne lay with Zeus's crown.

He was no longer out of the race to claim the title; King of the gods. All he'd need was a way beyond the door and here in the stone tablets he'd collected; would lay the answer. He needed only to find it but first he'd complete the set. It was time he headed over to the dig site for Zeboim and retrieved the last tablet of the Black Hand.

6

Cairo, Egypt

Gunnar pulled the SUV up to a curb near the wreckage of the library that had until the day before housed the secret base of the order of the Black Hand. He watched as his wife got out of the car and made her way toward the ruins. Gunnar checked that Caleb was secure before getting out of the car and following after her.

The pair moved through charred rubble with care and once they were past the main room, found that the sealed corridor he entered with her the day before was still intact. "I guess Hades couldn't break past the seal," Zaharrah said surprised.

"What seal?" Gunnar asked curious.

"The order's seal."

"Maybe it's some sort of god protection," Gunnar muttered.

"Could be."

"Where's the archive?"

"It’s this way, follow me," Zaharrah murmured as she started down the hall in the direction of the archival vault, she hoped as she went that more than just the hall had survived.

7 Los Angeles, California

Artemis walked through the gates onto the grounds of James Hardagen's home. As she stepped up to the door it swung open and Dionysus grabbed he by the wrist and drew her to him.

"WELCOME HOME MY PRINCESS," he breathed before he lifted her chin and captured her lips in a hungry kiss. Artemis gasped at the contact as the taste of him hit her system like a strong drink that left her reeling and hungry.

Hands sank in her hair fisting, pulling her head back to the razor edge between pleasure and pain. Teeth nipped drawing blood. When his lips parted hers, she was drunk with passion and her body ached for him in a way that shamed her.

She knew him. He'd claimed her as his bride but he was the god of debauchery, incapable of devotion, his thirst for wine and sex was insatiable. He'd used his cup in the past to enslave more women to his cult of pleasure than even her father had bedded. He'd bound her to his damn cult with their first coupling.

"My lord," she breathed when she found her voice.

"I TRUST YOUR TRIP WAS SUCCESSFUL," Dionysus whispered, even as his hands raked over her body making her burn for him.

"The beast was broken," she answered struggling to focus on their discussion. She wouldn't give into his spell; here in the open, for anyone to see.

"THAT'S WONDERFUL," Dionysus stated, as he drew her flush against him, so that not an inch separated their bodies. His eyes glowed red as he ground himself against her eliciting a moan. "I MISSED YOU ON THE PLANE."

"I'm sorry my lord," she breathed as her eyes fell shut.

"I HAD SUCH PLANS FOR YOU HUNTRESS, MY HUNGER

IS UNBEARABLE," he groaned.

"I'm here now, let's go inside and," she began.

"I'LL NOT WAIT A MOMENT LONGER, "the wine god growled before his fangs sank in her throat taking the thing he craved most of her. The intoxicating taste of power filled blood.

Artemis cried out as the bizarre mix of pleasure and pain sent her body crashing over the edge into ecstasy. She came alive in his grasp tearing at his clothes seeking his flesh desperate now to have him. He dragged her in the door and it slammed shut behind them. She felt the bite of wood at her back as he pressed her against it and began to ravage her.

8 Cairo, Egypt

Gunnar stared at the vast collection of writing within the archival vault with silent disbelief. There were pieces here from around the world. He wondered what secrets they held, where they were from and just how old they were. He looked over to where his wife stood studying one of the glass cases and wondered what she was studying.

Seeing her here in the midst of this was an eye opening experience. When they'd met, he'd thought of her as a simple librarian and now he understood that there was nothing simple about his wife. How many ancient languages could she read? What sort of hand to hand had she studied, what weapons training did she possess?

"Got anything?" he asked uncomfortable with the quiet around them.

"Not yet."

"When we get done here where are we going to go Zaharrah the house is gone."

"I have a place," she assured him.

"Oh?' Gunnar asked curious.

"It's nice and will accommodate us until we get settled somewhere else," she assured him before falling silent once more.

"Sounds good," Gunnar said. He had a million questions he wanted to ask her but she seemed less than willing to talk just yet. He'd let it go for now, let her focus on the task at hand and once she had her answers, they'd talk at length about the last five years, starting with just who Magnus Halden was and why the man felt he'd had the right to touch her.

9 Los Angeles, California

Artemis's golden lashes fluttered and blue eyes popped open to find herself staring at a reflection of her laying naked upon crimson silk sheets, the wine god lay at her side, his arm wrapped around her slender waist, his leg tangled with that of her own.

She felt the heat of his flesh pressed against her and her breath caught in her throat with the realization that his passion had not cooled. She wondered how she'd gotten there but figured he'd carried her at some point.

"SO MY BLUSHING BRIDE IS AWAKE AT LAST," he teased as his fingers skimmed down her body rousing her slowly, making her heart race with need for him.

"I am," she replied. Stretching like a cat under his caress, her flesh begging for more.

"YOU'RE A TREASURE MY DEAR," he whispered as he leaned over her enjoying the sight of her. His touch upon her became more insistent, with her body now awake to his influence, he took her pleasant sense of desire and built it up to a gnawing hunger. She responded instinctually, drawing him to her, teeth sinking into his shoulder, drawing his blood she lapped at the wound losing herself in the crimson elixir getting drunk on his passion.

He hissed at the sensation and thrilled in the response. She was further along in the change than even Emily had been. Already well on her way to being one of his Bacchae. He eased back from her and she growled in protest at the loss of his blood. Her blue eyes gleamed red with bloodlust.

“SHH, NOT TOO FAST LITTLE HUNTRESS, IT'S BETTER IF YOU GO SLOWLY," he whispered as his hands played over her feminine parts teasing her with the promise of the pleasure to come."

"I'm thirsty Bacchus," she hissed in frustration.

"I KNOW PRINCESS AND YOU'LL DRINK AGAIN SOON," he assured her, as he played her body like an instrument, bending her to his will taking her right up to the edge of bliss but not letting her fall over into the drunken sea of ecstasy beyond.

"BACCHUS," she cried his name, desperate; wind tore through the room ruffling the sheets around them and rain began to pelt the windows as her control snapped and her power surged. Dionysus sank his fangs into her left breast drinking directly from her lust filled heart. She cried out, overwhelmed as the mark threw her violently into release. Her teeth sank into his shoulder once more and he allowed her to feed for a moment before drawing her back once more. She roared in irritation and he laughed. "YOU'LL HAVE MORE HUNTRESS WHEN I GET WHAT I WANT," he growled in temper at her challenging his authority here.

"What do you want of me my husband?" she asked her voice desperate to please him, her eyes red as his had been when he greeted her at the door.

"BE MY SERENITY," he requested.

"Of course," she vowed, willing to play the role in his damn film if it would give her another taste of his blood. The drink made it easier to accept his embrace, made the pleasure he gave her greater. Made her feel stronger somehow.

"THANK YOU, PRINCESS," he whispered as he nuzzled her belly he licked her navel and drew a breath then nipped playfully at her midsection. She gasped and his eyes met with hers. "RELAX MY QUEEN I'D NOT DRINK HERE WHAT LAYS BENEATH IS FAR TOO PRECIOUS A GEM TO HARM," he whispered before his lips moved over to her hip.

"My lord?' she asked dazed, his kiss moving to the inside of her thigh.

"OUR CHILD," he breathed, before his fangs pierced her skin and sent her trembling. As she lay lost in the rapture of his spel,l he lifted his head and moved back over her till his lips hovered over her jugular once more.

As his fangs pierced the delicate column of her throat he surged forward and his aroused flesh filled her body making them one. He didn’t hesitate once he’d gained entrance he began to move inside of her immensely pleased, when her teeth pierced his flesh and she began to drink again. Things were going better with the huntress than he'd dared to hope.

She'd agreed to his demand of her without hesitation and every chance she got here, she tasted his blood. With each drop she had, his power over her grew. It wouldn't be long before she'd do anything he bid her to satisfy the hunger clawing in her belly. Even give him her father's crown.

10 Zeboim, somewhere in the Jordan Desert

Hermes stepped out of Ian Broody's car and onto the hot sand that covered the ruins of what had once been the queen's city. He drew upon his power and cleared the sand away to reveal the ancient city. Walking through the gate, he made his way in the direction of the temple.

As with the other lost cities he descended the stairs into the hidden chamber below. He opened the stone chest and drew out the cuneiform within. Turning, he made his way back out of the temple and headed back to the car. At last he had the final piece of the Black Hands' text.

Now maybe he could figure out his best plan of attack in the battle to claim Zeus's crown.

11 Cairo Egypt

"Damn," Zaharrah swore as she looked up from the current scroll shed been skimming over.

"That doesn't sound good," Gunnar muttered.

"It's not."

"I take it you found something."

"Yes, it seems the key I had in my keeping is not the only one nor is the door we've located the only one."

"Is that bad?" Gunnar asked not understanding the significance of the news.

"Yeah the damn doors lead straight into the depths of hell."

"Wonderful," Gunnar groused.

"Do we have a duffel still?"

"Yeah, why?" her husband questioned.

"Go get it," I want to pack up as much of this as possible and take it with us. It's not safe here."

Gunnar nodded and moved to collect a bag. He returned soon after and helped her to load up what she could before escorting her back to the car. Once they were on the road Zaharrah pulled out her phone and punched in Anna's number to pass on the bad news.

12 Somewhere over the Atlantic

Sam sat beside his fiancé trying to relax but his mind kept wandering to the storm building around him Three of the fallen had come into their true power, a fourth, the one who'd named himself the god of war, had a hold on his friend. Hours earlier he'd been overwhelmed with despair thinking they failed, now he felt oddly reenergized. He didn't know what task lay ahead of them now but he was ready for it. He figured he owed the attitude adjustment to their winged friend.

Thinking of the angelic messenger, Sam glanced over at his seat mate and noted she was miles from him. Lost in her own thoughts and from the worry lines creasing her brow, he figured she was back in the motel alone, Ares orange eyes gleaming at her from within detective Lance Roman's face.

It occurred to Sam that if he let her dwell on that fear, she might somehow reach the same pit he'd crawled out of. Given how Lance got mixed up in the mantle mess, she might feel that his precarious state was her fault. He couldn't let her go there.

"Doc," he whispered to draw her out of her thoughts.

"Yes," she answered as she turned to look at him.

"I'm sorry about leaving you by yourself with Lance earlier, but I needed a minute, I felt like I'd failed."

"It's hard not to. I mean look at what's happened… "

"Yes, a lot has happened and on the surface it looks like failure; but it's not."

"How can you say that? Three of the Fallen are loose another has his claws in Lance…"

"His fate isn't sealed yet Anna."

"How can you say that ,you saw what happened to Ian, to James, even to Magnus, anyone who comes to hold a mantle is lost."

"I can say it because when I was in that bathroom I got a visit from our…" Sam began, but his words were cut off by the ringing of Anna's phone.

13

Anna heard Sam curse, as she turned her attention to the offending object. Whatever he'd been about to say; he wasn't happy about being interrupted. Well, the truth was she wasn't either but with everything going on she couldn't afford to ignore an incoming call. It could be news pertaining to the others.

Hazel eyes looked at the caller id before pressing the talk button and lifting it to her ear.

"Hello Zaharrah, what can I do for you," Anna asked.

"Anna, we found something at the library."

"What is it?" Anna asked as she leaned forward on the edge of her seat. Beside her Sam sat up straight, his blue eyes alert and filled with questions.

"There are three other keys out there each with its own lock."

"What?"

"According to the archives fours key were forged. One for each of the four great generals. The brother gods. Hades, Poseidon, Zeus and Chaos. Each one has his own direct passage to their prince."

"Wait are you saying those doors lead into hell?"

"Afraid so. From the looks of it the key you found was Zeus's ,his was capable of opening all the doors. The one at Atlantis is Chaos's passage."

"Shit. Okay I don't suppose your reading says where to locate the other keys."

"Nothing yet. I've got everything that was salvageable with me, the minute I find anything I'll let you know."

"Thanks."

"You're welcome Anna."

"Be safe Zaharrah."

"You too," the other woman countered before breaking the call.

Anna pulled the phone away from her ear and held it in stunned silence for a moment until she felt Sam's hand squeeze her own. She blinked then looked over at him.

"What's wrong?"

"Apparently there's more than one way to get inside that door at Atlantis."

"Another way to enter hell," Sam muttered with disgust having overheard her end of the conversation.

"Yes. There were four doors, each one has a key."

"Judging by the look on your face I'm guessing that Zaharrah said they don't know where the other three keys or doors are," Sam stated.

Anna nodded.

"Damn it."

"Sam if there's more than one way into that passage and Hades or the others find it before we can…"

"Hush doc, don't go borrowing trouble, it'll be okay," Sam assured her before brushing a kiss on her forehead.

"I'm sorry, it's just this is all so overwhelming. I can't help but feel at times, like this is my fault….if I hadn't…" Anna began with regret.

"Don't go there Anna. I understand how you feel; like I was saying before, I was there earlier until our winged friend turned up and talked some sense into me," Sam said.

"What did he say?"

"He said that we humans have a messed up way of measuring success and failure."

"What does that mean? How can you look at this situation and not conclude we failed? We were supposed to…" Anna began with exasperation.

"We were supposed to keep the mantles from falling into human hands and we did."

"How can you say that and not burst into flame? Four of them are in the hands of men. Ian held The Horn of Hermes, James Hardagen has the Cup of Dionysus, Magnus Halden has the Candle of Hades and the Sword of Ares right now is in our friends hands. All four of them are in human hands!" Anna snapped in outrage.

"True but they were already in human hands before we were given that task. There was nothing we could do to stop that. We kept the other six from finding their way into mortal hands. We're not being chased by ten gods just contending with four. Four that were always meant to roam this world again," Sam argued.

Anna blinked dumbstruck her anger fizzling out. “I take it your visitor said the same to you.”

“Right.”

“So why get us involved at all if we couldn’t…”

“The journey changed us for the better, it prepared us for what’s still to come. We know what we’re up against and we are better prepared to defend against it.”

“What about Lance?”

“His fate isn’t sealed yet; someone else could still come to possess the sword. So don’t go blaming yourself for his current plight. It’s not your fault even if you hadn’t come back, odds are his path would have crossed the sword. His connection to the Fury Killer, its first wielder were going to bring him into its path anyway.”

Anna nodded knowing he was right. “Thank you.”

“No need, like I said I was there earlier, I don’t want to see you there either. Guilt is useless and worry is worse. Let it go and get some rest, once we land we’ll start trying to figure out where these other keys are.”

“Okay,” Anna murmured before she put her phone away. She sank back in her chair beside Sam and rested her head on his shoulder. Closing her eyes she soon dozed off.

14

Sam blew out the breath he'd been holding as he urged Anna to rest, grateful she'd done so. As he sat alone in the silence of the cabin, he admitted to himself that Anna's news was troubling indeed. Her fears that Hades or one of the others might learn the news was a legitimate one.

As he played out the worst case scenario in his mind, he wondered if Artemis was aware of the other doors and figured she wasn't. Her move of stealing the crown from its resting place and locking it within the passage had been in a bid to keep the fallen from claiming her father's crown.

Sam had no doubt that if she'd been aware of the other keys the huntress would never have hidden the crown there. Her desire to keep it from the others was genuine. Her hatred of the fallen was obvious. She told Ares that her wrath would come swiftly to any who pursued the crown.

The real question, at this point, was did Hades know where his key was? Sam figured he didn't. If he was aware of the keys location he'd have it already. But it wouldn't take a lot of work for him to discover it. Based on what he'd witnessed in Athens it seemed that Hades had some kind of power over the land itself. It had given up its secrets to the lord of the underworld once already. Hades would use that power to gain the location of his key and its corresponding door as well. That made the god of the dead a real threat as a potential candidate to becoming the king of the gods.

Burt what of the others? How much of a danger were they?

Did Hermes or Dionysus know anything of the other keys? Sam considered the question and shook his head. He was willing to bet that only the four knew of the keys existence. Dionysus and Hermes would have been kept out of the loop to keep them in check.

However if there was anything Sam had learned about the god of knowledge, it was that it wouldn't take Hermes long to find out. He figured somewhere in those cuneiform tablets they'd unearthed at Sodom, the knowledge would be kept. Hermes would be hot on the trail of the keys as well.

As for Dionysus, while he may not know of the keys, he didn't need another route to get to the crown; he had a hold on Artemis, after all, as a result of her efforts to protect Anna. Sam had been witness to what the wine god's influence could do to a person. He'd watched Anna go mad with lust from Dionysus's touching her mind. He'd nearly broken her in a week. Given the strength of his hold on Artemis it was likely he'd be able to get her to give him the crown if given enough time.

All three were dangerous to them and they were just the obvious threats. Where Ares fit into this or even Hecate for the matter Sam couldn't know for sure. All he knew was that they'd have to move fast if they had any chance of stopping the fallen from getting ahold of that crown.

15

Anna felt a chill wash over her skin as she descended from the hall of feasting into the cursed throne room below. As she entered the chamber she found that the candles were lit with various flames of unnatural glow: blue, green, purple, aqua, orange and gold, they lined the room. Green being the most predominant, orange the faintest. Before the throne the image of three of the gods stood in rank and line Hermes, Poseidon, and at the end Dionysus.

She blinked what was the sea king doing here where was Hades? Poseidon wasn't awake. The question faded as she noted their eyes were focused upon the altar below. Turning she looked to see what had their attention and gasped. There below the dark crystalline image of their king, Lance and Ares were locked in a duel for control.

Catharine lay on the stone floor garbed in an orange toga her wrist bound one to the other by a golden chain that kept her tethered to the altar where she was to be sacrificed when Ares won. A golden chain hung from her neck, following it with her eyes Anna trembled as she spotted Hades lurking in the shadows waiting. In one hand he held his scythe, in the other he held the end of the chain ready to make his claim, the second the battle ended.

Anna turned from the image to the back wall where a door to hell stood closed; she walked past the fallen to touch the wall. When she did a jolt of power shot through her. She closed her eyes involuntarily and when she did, flashes of images played out in her mind. For a second she saw herself standing upon a high mountain, looking down upon the islands of Greece. In the next moment she was deep in the heart of a volcano. The heat so intense she thought she might melt. In the next, she was plunging into the crushing deep of the sea. Surrounded by blackness. She fell for what felt like hours, the burning heat chased away by an icy cold as she went deeper. When she hit bottom she found a door waiting there.

Anna opened her eyes and her attention moved to where the key had lain. Understanding now why she was here again. She was being shown more truth. The images of the gods reflected the games a foot and who was in play.

Touching the door had shown her the others. When she touched the place Zeus's key had lain in wait to be discovered it would show her where the other keys were, so that she could get to them before the fallen could. Anna crossed the floor, descended the steps to kneel where the disk had once been; as she reached to touch it. she was pulled violently away from it. Her vision clouded and when it cleared she was no longer in the throne room but in a vast desert; she lay in the dust bleeding and naked. Hades loomed over her, his green eyes gleamed with power, on his lips a satisfied smirk.

"Release me Fallen you've no right to drag me here," Anna roared in fury.

"FOOLISH WOMAN, I HAVE EVERY RIGHT, YOU CAME HERE OF YOUR OWN VOLITION AND TRADED PLACES WITH ZAHARRAH. YOU LET ME TOUCH YOU AND IN DOING SO GAVE ME A DOOR TO FIND YOU HERE."

"No," Anna said with disbelief.

"SAVE YOUR PROTEST MISS GALLAGHER THEY'RE POINTLESS. I'M HERE NOW AND YOU'RE MIND IS MINE TO DO WITH AS I PLEASE."

"That can't be," Anna gasped with dismay.

"YOU'RE A SMART WOMAN ANNA, I'M SURE YOU RECALL THE TALE OF PERSEPHONE, BY LETTING ME TOUCH YOU ONCE, YOU'VE EATEN HALF OF THE POMEGRANATE, HERE IN DREAMS YOU ARE MINE AS SHE WAS," Hades whispered as he knelt down at her side and brushed his hand against her cheek. She flinched at his icy touch. But said nothing more.

"THAT'S BETTER," he murmured pleased by her silence. "

"I don't want this," she breathed.

"I'LL SPARE YOU MY TORMENT IF YOU TELL ME ALL THAT YOU KNOW," he offered.

"I won't help you," Anna hissed in refusal.

"SO BE IT!" Hades roared in fury and as soon as the words had passed his lips, her torment began.

16 WASHINGTON DC, VIRGINIA

Terra moved through the secret headquarters that belonged to her employers and made her way to the cyber division. She gave her best man the list of targets to track before moving down the hall to the conference room to debrief. She wasn't looking forward to the meet, she'd not been put in the position of lying to the agency in five years and the prospect of it now was unpleasant.

She'd been an outsider. A target marked for capture until she and Vince met up again on the isle of Kauai. She'd toed the line since being given a second chance. Now she found herself in a position she'd hoped to never be again. An outsider with her own agenda. If she revealed to the agency what she'd been witness to, they'd think her section eight.

She couldn't afford that.

Anna needed to be aware of where the gods were at all times, on her own that wasn't possible. She needed her big sister to watch her back and she'd be damned if she was going to let her down.

17 Somewhere over the continental US
Sunday
7pm

Lance Roman looked out the window at the land below at the site of the Rockies he pulled out his cell phone. They were nearing their destination, it was time he made the proper arrangements.

Lanced punched in the number for his boss and waited for the older man to pick up.

"Hello."

"Chief,"

"Detective, how's your friend doing?"

"Better. We're headed back out to LA."

"I take it you're using up your vacation time?"

"Yes, if that's all right."

"It's fine. You're due."

"Thanks chief."

"No problem. Enjoy your time off," his boss answered before hanging up.

"You didn't have to do that, Bryan's gone I'll be fine."

"I know, but I am staying," Lance stated.

"Why?'

"For one Hades is still out there and he will come after you, for another I'm not too thrilled with the idea of leaving you alone around the wine god, just because he let you go doesn't mean that he won't try to mess with you again," Lance muttered.

"You can't play body guard forever," she grumbled.

"Is that what you think I'm doing?" he asked with annoyance his blue eyes flashed orange for a moment and then dimmed back to their natural color.

"Isn't it?" she challenged not caring for his tone.

"No, I'm not here working," he corrected.

"If not that, then why?"

"I'm here because I care what happens to you Serenity," he whispered as he brushed her hair away from her eyes.

"Lance..." she began uneasy with his closeness. She'd just seen ice blue go orange a harsh reminder that Ares was lingering here as well and might at any moment be the one in control.

"You invited me to visit you before the movie was done and I plan to do so now; as long as the offer still stands," he whispered as his fingers slid into her hair.

"It does," she assured him as she leaned into his caress, liking the feel of it.

"I'm here because I want to be," he murmured before he closed the last few inches between them and kissed her. His hands fisted in her hair pulling lightly, tilting her head back so he could get a better taste.

Catharine gasped startled and eased back. He looked at her his blue eyes held questions and confusion. "I'm sorry Lance, I just..." she began unable to explain the mix of emotions running riot inside her. She saw flashes of memory from before and blushed at the thought of how reckless she'd been while under Dionysus's spell.

"Too fast," he whispered with understanding. She nodded sheepishly. "It's okay, it's not your fault," he assured her before he kissed her brow and let her go.

18 Los Angeles California

Artemis crawled out of Dionysus's bed. Her blue eyes glanced back at him and was relieved to find him asleep. She needed a minute to herself. She was tired and sore from their exertions and understood that she'd have little time when she wasn't in his bed. It was the curse of being his bride. His hunger never abated and his power made her crave him.

As she wrapped her gown about her, she felt her skin respond to its caress and hissed. Even now as he slept his power worked its will upon her, readying her for when he woke. The huntress crept with stealth and care from the room out of the house past the pool and through the grounds, toward the distant sound of crashing waves.

As she stepped out onto the sand she drew upon her power to call the waves up to meet her. She snarled, frustrated when it did not answer. Trudging on toward the cool water of the Pacific, even as she wondered why the tide had not heeded her summons. She figured the blame lay at her husband's feet. He'd fed upon her more times than she could count while they mated and it had probably left her weak.

When she reached the surf Artemis shed her clothes and dove into the salty waters. She felt the hunger that clawed at her recede and her mind eased. The huntress sighed with relief at the change. Muscles began to relax as her body recovered.

But her peace was short lived, as her husband soon stood on the shore before her naked and without shame of it. His eyes gleaming red with thirst of her and she felt a jolt of lust sweep through her that left her shaking with want of him.

"SO HERE YOU ARE MY PRINCESS," he breathed amused as he stepped into the surf. He had her in his arms within moments, his fangs poised to pierce the ivory column that was her throat and she turned away.

"Please don't I'm weak enough as it is..." She began in protest.

"WHAT DO YOU MEAN?" Dionysus asked puzzled.

"Your feeding it's left me unable to call the sea," she said upset.

"MY DEAR HUNTRESS MY FEEDING CANNOT DRAIN YOUR POWER. EACH TIME YOU TASTE MY BLOOD IT STRENGTHENS YOU WHEN I DRINK I MAKE THE MAGIC YOU POSSESS THE MORE DOMINATE IN YOUR BLOOD."

"Then why won't the sea heed my call," Artemis asked confused.

Dionysus pricked her skin tasting her blood and hissed. "THE POWER HAS BEEN SEALED. IT SEEMS YOUR UNCLE POSEIDON IS BACK," he said with disappointment before he sank his fangs in her flesh once more this time to feed. She cried out with pleasure at the sensation lost to its spell. She bit him in kind feeding as he joined their bodies' one to the other and began to mate once more.

19

Artemis opened her eyes to find she was once more laying in Dionysus's bed. How had she gotten there, she couldn't recall. Everything after his bite was a blur. Where was he? She wondered and looking up watched as he strolled out of the closet dressed.

"AH GOOD YOUR AWAKE, HURRY UP AND GET DRESSED WE HAVE COMPANY COMING," Dionysus said amused.

Artemis blinked but did as he bid. Once clad she headed for the door a powerful arm wrapped around hers at the elbow and turned her so she faced him. Dionysus drew her close and kissed her his hands skimming along her dress altering it to his liking.

Splitting the skirt open along seams giving him view of her legs as she walked. Parting the front into layers that would allow him to gain access to her easily. Splitting the bodice with a deep and wide v--neck that gave him both a tantalizing view of her breasts and made it easy for him to touch her. The back fell away leaving her exposed to his touch.

"THAT'S BETTER," he whispered before he drew her to his side. His hand slid under the thin fabric in the back to grab her ass. She hissed in response to the bite of his nails and he smiled as he felt her lust awaken once more. "COME, PRINCESS WE DON'T WANT TO KEEP OUR GUESTS WAITING."

20 SUNDAY 8PM

Lance lifted his hand to knock on the door that had once belonged to James Hardagen well aware that the man who dwelled within was no longer the former actor turned director or even human, he was one of the fallen. The god of wine and debauchery. Dionysus was the name the Greeks had given him in days past.

"MISS NICHOLS, DETECTIVE, IT'S GOOD TO SEE YOU AGAIN. I BELIEVE YOU KNOW MY WIFE, ARTEMIS," he said with amusement as he stepped aside to let them in. The demi goddess at his side nodded but said nothing.

"Hello," Catharine said politely but nervous.

"ARTEMIS HERE WILL BE PLAYING SERENITY FOR US IN THE FILM, WON'T YOU PRINCESS," Dionysus stated as he pulled her closer to his side. She stiffened and Lance wondered at it but the huntress nodded.

"COME, WE'LL TALK BUSINESS OUT BY THE POOL," the wind god suggested as he turned to head in that direction.

Lance blinked at the sight before him. Artemis's back lay exposed for him to see and he understood her flinch at the sight of Dionysus's hand under the fabric. He was playing with her under their noses. Lance wondered why the wine god had revealed his game as he followed him toward the pool.

Lance felt Catharine's hand grab his own and cursed with understanding the move had not been intended for him it was for Catharine. A warning and a reminder of what his power was, a silent threat of what he might do to her if she crossed him.

Lance gave her hand a light squeeze to assure her he was there as they sat down at the table. He listened with interest as Catharine began to lay out what she had in mind for Dark Heart.

"IT SOUNDS WONDERFUL, CJ YOU'VE OUTDONE

YOURSELF," Dionysus said pleased.

"It will be the perfect end to the series if I could just get it done," Catharine said annoyed.

"YOU'LL WORK HERE; I INSIST. HADES WILL NOT DARE INTRUDE HERE."

"Agreed," Lance stated before she could respond.

"But..." Catharine began in protest.

"He's right you're beyond Hades reach here at least for now," Artemis stated.

"Good," Lance said pleased.

"IT'S SETTLED THEN, ARTEMIS MY DARLING SHOW SERENITY TO HER ROOM," Dionysus commanded.

Artemis nodded and without a word led Catharine from the room. Lance watched as the pair walked away and in his mind's eye he saw Catharine in a similar gown of orange and blinked. His eyes shifted to Dionysus and he glared at the wine god with fury, his own eyes beginning to gleam orange.

"Don't!" He snapped outraged.

"CALM YOURSELF DETECTIVE, IT WAS MERELY A JEST. I HAVE NO DESIGNS FOR YOUR PRETTY WRITER," the wine god assured him.

"We'll stay; cup bearer, so long as you respect her privacy," Lance hissed in warning as his fingers wrapped around the hilt of the sword at his hip.

"COME NOW ARES, NO NEED FOR THREATS; I'VE GOT THE HUNTRESS WHAT NEED HAVE I OF YOUR MORTAL BRIDE," Dionysus snapped in temper.

"IF YOU BETRAY ME TO OUR BROTHER, CUP BEARER, I WILL RIP YOUR FANGS FROM YOUR HEAD AND SEE YOU STARVE TO DEATH," Ares hissed before he let go of the sword.

"I'VE NO INTEREST IN SEEING THE LORD OF THE UNDERWORLD BECOME OUR NEW KING. I'M A DRUNK, NOT A FOOL. IF HE TAKES CONTROL, THERE WILL BE NO MORE MORTALS TO PLAY WITH, AND WHEN HE'S DONE WITH THEM; WE'LL FOLLOW. AS I SAID YOU'RE SAFE HERE."

"SEE IT STAYS SO," Ares commanded before the orange glow in the detectives eyes faded. Lance blinked. "If you mess with her..."

"I'VE NO INTENTION OF TROUBLING YOUR SERENITY, DETECTIVE, I WANT HER TO FINISH HER BOOK," Dionysus assured him. The wine god handed over the key that connected his room to Catharine's along with the camera that had previously occupied it. Satisfied Lance turned and headed in the direction of the stairs.

21

Artemis opened the door to Catharine's room and showed her inside. She bit her lip nervously as she debated on her next move. There were things happening around her that left unchecked could lead to trouble. But she wasn't sure if she should risk speaking of them. She felt a mental nudge from her husband to proceed and drew a breath. It seemed the wine god had no interest in helping his brethren.

"MISS NICHOLS THERE'S SOMETHING I WANT YOU TO PASS ALONG TO OUR MUTUAL FRIENDS."

"What is it?" Catharine asked curious.

"THE SEA STIRS, ITS KING WAKES," Artemis whispered before she turned and left heading back to her own room compelled by the life growing inside of her to feed.

22

Catharine watched as the huntress retreated down the hall in the direction of Dionysus's chambers, her blue eyes having begun to gleam red and shuddered involuntarily. Understanding that if the wine god had gotten what he wanted it would have been her racing down the hall to seek him out.

"You okay?" Lance's voice questioned startling her. When had he gotten there?

"Yeah. Need to call Anna though," she muttered.

"Why?"

"Artemis said that Poseidon is moving," Catharine stated.

"Perfect, just what we don't need right now another god crawling out of the wood work," Lance groused.

"I know, I'll call Anna and..."

"No, I've got the message I'll pass it along you focus on the book," Lance stated.

"Why?"

"So long as you're producing results, Dionysus will stay away from you, he needs that book to secure his power," Lance stated.

Catharine nodded her understanding. "You okay?"

"I'm fine," he assured her before he opened the door to his room and stepped inside. Catharine closed her door and locked it before crossing to the desk and flipping on her laptop to get started.

23 Somewhere over the Atlantic Coast

Anna woke with a jolt to the sound of Sam's voice. She blinked as she tried to shake free of the lingering images of her nightmare. She bit her lip at the sensation of icy hands on her skin and repressed a curse, it seemed Hades was still lingering in the dream realm to torment her here.

Sam's blue eyes settled on her as he became aware of her gaze and he looked at her with concern.

"You okay doc?"

"Yes, I'm fine just a bad dream," she assured him with a smile that didn't quiet reach her eyes.

"Anna, don't lie to me," Sam requested.

"It was nothing. I just had a vision is all," she explained.

"A vision?"

"Yes, I was back in the throne room."

"Tell me everything," Sam demanded hating that place more than any other he knew of.

"Hermes, Poseidon, and Dionysus stood at the top of the steps looking on as Ares and Lance battled it out over who would claim Catharine. She was chained to the altar to be a sacrifice. But another chain hung from her neck. I followed it to find Hades lingering in the shadows waiting for the outcome of the fight. To take on the victor."

"They're just watching."

"For now. I turned from the spectacle to the door. When I touched it I was transported to three other locations..."

"The places where the other doors are," Sam said with understanding.

"Yes, one was on Mount Olympus, another was in a volcano somewhere and the third was at the bottom of the Marinas Trench. After I came back to the moment I moved down the steps to touch the floor where the key had lain."

"Did you see where they are as well?" Sam asked.

"No, I was interrupted."

"Interrupted?" Sam questioned.

"Yes I heard your phone, it drew me out. Was that Lance you were talking to?" Anna questioned.

"Yes, it was. It seems that Poseidon is moving."

"How?"

"Apparently when Artemis broke the scepter it didn't seal his power as she'd hoped."

"Okay, so we'll need to figure out who Poseidon has possessed and try to break his control over them, along with hunting up these keys, that shouldn't be too hard," Anna muttered."

"Right, we just need to get landed," Sam replied as he eyed her with suspicion and she swallowed nervously.

"Right."

"He interrupted your vision didn't he?"

"Who?'

"Hades."

"Sam…"

Answer me doc."

"It's nothing."

"I doubt that."

"Let it go Sam. I don't remember it."

"Damn it Anna, Why do you keep lying to me where he's concerned."

"Because I'm not going to be the sword he uses to kill you," Anna snapped.

"What?"

"Nothing, forget it and him. I'm fine, Mr. Abrams" Anna muttered as she crossed her arms over her chest and sat back in her seat turning her attention away from him.

Sam groaned at the response and grabbed her by the arm turning her so that she faced him once more. "Don't start that again, doc we're long past it," he muttered before he kissed her.

Anna melted in his grasp, kissing him back. He was right they were well beyond her playing at prim and proper, she'd agreed to marry him after all. At the thought she eased back.

"I'm sorry, Sam you're right, I just don't want to talk about him," Anna whispered.

"Why?"

"I don't want to dwell on him while I'm awake," Anna answered before she kissed him again.

Anna felt Sam sink into her kiss and knew he'd decided to let the matter go and was grateful; she didn't want him to ever know what Hades had done to her on the other side.

24 Zeboim, somewhere in the desert of Jordan

Fox Elwood looked out the passenger window of the team van at the desert beyond with disbelief. Where yesterday there had been nothing but sand; today there were the ruins of the city to see. He blinked, how was that possible?

As he wondered at it, the van pulled to a stop and the team began to unload. Fox got out of the van and made his way into the ruins. "Any idea how this happened?" he muttered to the one member of the team whom he wanted most to talk to him but thus far had been unresponsive. Robin, he'd hoped that the close proximity with her would have given him the chance to mend old bridges he'd burned, with no luck. The lady wasn't giving him an inch.

"I heard there was a freak windstorm last night," she answered her violet eyes gleamed with excitement.

Fox smiled at Robin's enthusiasm as he made his way toward the temple. It was the most exciting thing that had happened since they started working the dig.

He'd joined Dr. Broody's team because the experience would meet his final requirements for his doctorate. It didn't hurt either that Broody's projects had a way of becoming famous.

Beyond that Fox had seen her name on the list and been unable to pass on the opportunity to be around her long term. He'd missed her in the nights since they parted ways, found he thought of little else. It had irritated him and then unnerved him to find himself comparing other women with her secretly and then he'd finally just admitted to himself that one taste of the pretty doctor had not been enough to satisfy him. He still wanted her.

So far the dig had been a bust.

Nothing remotely dangerous had happened and he'd had no access to the more interesting artifacts. As for Robin she'd ignored him from day one, acting as if she didn't remember him. It had pricked his ego and only made him want her more. Fox groaned as he turned his thoughts away from her and his failures. He considered just giving up on the whole damn thing.

As a kid he'd grown up on images of Indiana Jones and the Goonies. He'd dreamed of being a treasure hunter and had pursued that dream by studying archeology, wanting to be knowledgeable in his chosen field. Now that he was closing in on his doctorate, he was frustrated, the work was boring.

Fox was learning fast that the archeology game was not grand adventures in foreign settings as he'd dreamed of but a lot of long days in remote locations, sifting through dirt and rubble to study the mundane. His grand delusions of locating the lost Ark or the cup of Christ had gone up in a cloud of sand and any notions of getting out of this damn sandbox were looking bleak. Dr. Broody didn't seem too keen on sharing.

Fox had heard rumors of another site somewhere outside of the desert. Heard that the lead working that dig Dr. Gallagher had been pulled for some reason and brought back here, then left. Dr. Lynch had replaced her. He'd been optimistic then that maybe he'd get out of this hot sun and over to the main site, now he wasn't so sure. The tomb raider had taken off along with any chance of fame or fortune.

As Fox moved into the temple he was surprised to find it was different from the one near the Dead Sea. Beside the main chamber there was a second room, a library. Fox moved into the chamber and began to sift through the texts if there was any hope of salvaging his ideas of a grand adventure it was here. There was no telling what long forgotten secrets the text might contain.

25 Tel Aviv

Gunnar stared at the corner flat across the way with disbelief.

"You were staying here?"

Zaharrah nodded and Gunnar laughed to know his missing wife had been but an hours travel from their home.

"You never left," he breathed with understanding.

"No, I couldn't not after Caleb was born, I had to know you were both safe, but I couldn't risk coming back. Hades threat was a real one. If I'd stayed…"

"Hush Zaharrah, I understand…" he assured her as he gathered their son in his arms and stepped out of the car to follow her into her home.

He watched with interest as Zaharrah unlocked the door and stepped inside. He heard the familiar sound of a gun's safety being flipped followed by a wire being cut before she opened the door to let him in.

"Traps?" he questioned with disbelief.

"To ensure no one came in without me knowing it," she explained as she made her way into the main room. The sight of an album cover laying on the floor had her freezing midstride.

"What is it?" Gunnar asked.

"We can't stay here," she muttered.

"Why not?"

"Someone's been here," she replied with irritation. Gunnar watched as her eyes closed and her finger tips skimmed over the surface of the discarded album cover. "Hecate," she hissed the name with disgust. "Move," she commanded as she turned toward the door.

"Now what?"

"We get out of the country. If Hecate found this place, Hades will soon enough, it's not safe," Zaharrah said with regret as she got back in the car.

Gunnar loaded their son in the back seat and slid into the passenger seat. “I’ll pull some strings to get us away from here,” Gunnar assured her before pulling out his phone. Zaharrah nodded as she sped away from her flat in the direction of the airport.

26 Zeboim, somewhere in the desert of Jordan

Fox laughed as his green eyes locked onto a reference he'd have never expected to find within the library. In the text was described a golden city built upon a hill ruled by a wise man who held in his keeping a sword of great power.

Camelot. How something related to a tale that was centuries older was here; Fox didn't know nor did he care. As a child there had been one tale that had drawn him. One legend he'd desired to prove and that had been the existence of Arthur's city. Now before his eyes was a reference to the fabled place. Fox scribbled down notes of the reference with the intent to investigate it later, for now he had a job to do. He'd not been at it long before one of the security team entered the room.

"Mr. Elwood," the man muttered as he eyed him with disinterest.

"Yes," Fox answered as he lifted his head.

"Dr. Broody wishes a word," the man stated before he turned to go expecting Fox to follow him. Fox stretched stiff muscles before getting to his feet. He dusted off the knees of his slacks then followed the other man wondering what his employer wanted now.

27

Hermes sat behind Ian's desk waiting for the arrival of his intern. As he waited his eyes skimmed over the series of cuneiform tablets he'd collected from the lost cities and he smiled, within the lines of the text were the answers he'd been searching for. It spelled out how he and his brethren had come to be imprisoned within cold stone.

The records spoke of his bride being given a stone chest, within it had been the mantles she'd gifted him with. The objects had been cursed. The moment Dionysus had given his cup to one of his followers in exchange for his daughter, they'd been stripped of their mortal form and sealed away.

The revelation was both fascinating and sobering. It meant two things, one that their power was not absolute as he'd once believed. It could be taken again if their mantel fell into a mortal's hands and two; he needn't fight his brothers for Zeus's crown, he needed only to strip them of their flesh again and keep his own. A feat that according to the tablet was possible if he could just get ahold of his horn.

28

Fox watched as the security agent knocked on the door leading into the space that served as Ian Broody's office out here at the dig and swallowed nervously as he realized it was the first contact he'd had with his employer since he left the desert for the undisclosed second dig site.

"Dr. Broody, I've brought him," the man stated before he turned to go.

"EXCELLENT, SEND HIM IN," Ian Broody's voice commanded from the other side and Fox couldn't get over the sensation that the voice had changed somehow. It held more authority than before and intimidated. He wondered at the phenomenon but dismissed it as his nerves before opening the door.

As he stepped in the room the professor rose from his seat and rounded the desk to meet him.

"Fox my boy, thank you for coming. I realize you must be busy but there are changes taking place now that I felt you should know about."

"Changes? Fox questioned as he studied the other man. He blinked, wondering if his eyes were playing tricks on him. Dr. Broody seemed younger than when they last met. His dark hair no longer flecked with gray, the age lines in his face having faded.

"Yes, Dr. Lynch has left the project here."

"What? She was all gung ho to get started on the fourth city but a few days ago," Fox stated confused.

"She's had family matters come up and can no longer linger here. I'm placing you in charge,"

"Me?"

"Yes, you are my senior intern and are more than qualified to run the team here."

"Thank you sir."

"How goes the research within the library?" Dr. Broody asked curious.

"It's remarkable really," Fox said with excitement.

"How so?" Ian pressed.

"I found a text earlier that references Camelot," Fox blurted out; then blinked. He'd had no intention of mentioning the find to anyone and wondered why he'd been unable to keep it from Dr. Broody.

"I see that is fascinating. It definitely takes precedent over the current project here. I want you to go look into the matter take a team of your choosing and see if you can find Arthur's city. If you come across anything of note let me know," Ian demanded.

"Of course," Fox answered with excitement before he left the office. As he went, his thoughts drifted back to the news that Dr. Zaharrah Lynch had left the project. First Dr. Gallagher and now the tomb raider; it was odd that his new job seemed to have such a high turnover rate.

The position was the sort that made a career and he wondered why after investing so much time in the project they'd just walked away. He made a mental note to contact his predecessors and speak with them later but for now it was time to celebrate. With this thought in mind Fox smiled, he knew just who he wanted to party with. Fox whistled to himself picturing the gleam of excitement he'd seen earlier in Robin's violet eyes. He finally had a way to get around the pretty doctors refusal to join him for a drink. She'd not be able to resist the news of Camelot.

It was one of the things that had drawn them together in the first place. Her knowledge of the Arthurian legend was beyond even his. He'd been given the right to select his team and she was going to be part of it. With this thought in mind he headed back to the dig to seek her out. A smirk curled his lips as he went knowing that tonight Robin Chase would be within his reach.

29

Robin cursed as Fox Elwood emerged from Dr. Broody's tent and started across the ruins in her general direction. His lips were curved in that wicked smirk she knew well and she bit her lower lip in a show of nerves. His green eyes gleamed with excitement as he stalked towards her.

She wondered what he wanted now even as she scolded herself for answering his question earlier. Since learning of his inclusion on the team she'd been careful to avoid giving him the time of day, knowing how he operated. When he'd greeted her that first day she acted as if she didn't remember him. She'd seen the shock in his green eyes and had been pleased, but it had been just that an act.

Robin had been trying to forget him since she woke up a year earlier to find herself alone. Trouble was the man wouldn't take a hint, she'd been giving him the cold shoulder since that day and he still continued to try and get past her defenses. What did the damn man want?

"Robin."

Robin ignored him, refusing to answer his informal greeting. She wasn't going to give him an inch because she knew when he got it he'd take a mile instead. He'd draw her in until he had whatever it was he wanted from her and then vanish leaving her alone again. She'd been warned by a friend before and been foolish enough to give him the benefit of the doubt; not again.

"Dr. Chase, a word please," he requested.

She blinked at the formality of the request, whatever it was, it was big and despite herself she lifted her head from her work. Violet locked with green and she felt the same jolt of longing tear through her that always followed at the sight of him. "What do you want Mr. Elwood, I'm busy," she said her voice cool, crisp and edged with impatience. The sooner he said his piece and moved on the better, she reasoned, as she got to her feet. She hated it when he stood over her like that it made him seem bigger than he was.

"I've found something in the temple you have to see, something that will get us out of this damn sandbox," Fox muttered.

"What is it?" she asked curious.

"Just come and see," he requested.

"Mr. Elwood..." she began in refusal.

"It will be worth the trip," he promised.

Robin gave a nod and turned to follow him. As she walked, she cracked her stiff neck and shoulders wondering just what would lay within the temple. Berating herself for even caring.

30

Fox walked ahead of Robin pleased she'd followed, at least he'd gotten past her argument. As he stepped through the main chamber into the library, he noted her gasp at the sight of the additional chamber.

"It's over here," he called as he stopped in front of the text he'd been reading earlier that morning. He moved aside allowing her to stand in front of the scroll and waited as she read in silence.

His green eyes skimmed over the library trying to understand how anything pertaining to the Arthurian legend could be there. Camelot was a medieval tale. The city of Zeboim had been lost long before then…

"That's not possible," Robin whispered her voice full of wonder.

"I know, but there it is clear as day, Camelot's location," Fox assured her. "Broody put me in charge of investigating the claim. I want you on the team."

"Mr. Elwood…"

"Come on Robin, this is it; the dream hunt," he whispered shocked she'd even try to pass on it.

"Why are you in charge, I thought Dr. Lynch was calling the shots," Robin said with suspicion.

"Dr. Lynch left, Broody promoted me…"

"He did, Fox, that's great…"

Fox smiled at her use of his first name, it was the first time she'd called him that in over a year. "I want to celebrate Robin, both the promotion and the find," he stated.

"Of course, you should it's a big deal…"

"Come with me, have a drink…"

"Fox…"

"We can talk about Arthur and speculate what this means."

Robin cursed inwardly knowing she couldn't refuse him as she knew she should.

"All right, one drink,' she relented.

Fox smiled it was going to be a good night.

31 GREAT FALLS, MONTANA

Anna stared out the window, of the quaint Bed and Breakfast they'd settled in after arriving, at the green valley lined by mountains in the distance as far as her eyes could see. It was a beautiful place, too bad she'd not get to enjoy it.

Anna sighed as she turned from the window back to the laptop in front of her. She was in the midst of typing up notes on the images she'd seen in her vision trying to determine where the third door, Hades Door might be located while Sam finished ensuring their security.

She groaned as any notion about locating the volcano based on the glimpse of the cavern she'd seen erupted, every image of volcanic caverns looked the same. Nothing stood out. The only thing she was sure of was it had to be located somewhere in the ring of fire.

"No luck?" Sam questioned as he joined her in the main room.

"Afraid not, it all looks the same," She admitted.

"It was worth a try," Sam assured her.

"I know it's just…"

"Frustrating I get it. But stressing over it won't get you an answer. Set it aside for now, we'll look at it again later. For now let's look at the question of who Poseidon might be," Sam suggested.

Anna nodded and after saving her notes closed the laptop and moved to join him on the couch.

"I spent the rest of the flight reading over the tale, Lance and Catharine located on the location, of the crown and found something." Anna stated.

"What was it?"

"It seems that the king's bride was a true beauty, one of such magnitude, she captured the eye of the sea king. He gave her his scepter as a gift to woo her. Honored by his gift and not understanding its nature the king had a beautiful city built for it and her."

"Zeboim," Sam said with understanding.

"Right so the scepter lay in wait there. In order to figure out who has it now we only need to get its location from Zaharrah and then call Terra, see about getting satellite images, see who else has been at that dig."

"Okay then, let's make some calls," Sam said with excitement, it seemed like they were finally starting to catch a few breaks.

32 Somewhere over the Mediterranean Sea

Zaharrah sat on a cargo plane westward bound. It wouldn't be long before they were over the Atlantic. Gunnar sat beside her, their son between them still slumbered. She was grateful of the fact. She didn't want him to hear anything about the Black Hand or the god they had unknowingly served.

The trio had fled their home but Zaharrah wondered if it would do them any good; if Hades wanted to find them he would. She hoped Sam was right in his assumption that Hades focus would be turned to the detective and the war god who traveled with him.

Almost as if thinking the name had conjured him, Zaharrah's phone pulsed with notice of an incoming message. Drawing the thing from her pocket she found a text from Mr. Abrams requesting the location of the city of Zeboim. She typed in the quadrants and tried not to worry about why he needed them, it was no longer her concern. Her days as an agent for the Black Hand were over. Her part in the mantels fate had come to end. She had more important things to see to, Zaharrah reasoned as she looked to the boy sleeping at her side and then to his father. Gunnar took her hand in his and kissed it letting her know he was there for her and she smiled. She'd missed him more than he could understand and was glad he'd welcomed her back. She'd no intention of jeopardizing their marriage again.

33 Great Falls, Montana

Sam studied the quadrants Zaharrah had sent back and passed them on to the Rogue requesting satellite images for the past week. He hoped Anna's idea panned out. She was restless now and he didn't understand why but figured it had something to do with the nightmare on the plane. Hades was messing with her somehow and Sam didn't care for it.

He wondered if there was anything he could do to help her but figured not if she wasn't willing to discuss it, he couldn't fight it. Sam looked back over to the table where Anna sat once more in front of her laptop pouring over her notes, she'd turned her attention to going back through her files looking for some clue on the location of the other keys.

They both knew it was a waste of time but she'd insisted on doing something until they heard back from the others. He'd suggested a film or a book and had been shot down. Anna wasn't about to quit yet, not with the world at stake. Sam smiled, her dedication to the task was admirable.

He'd turned his focus back to the book of Greek myth looking for more insight into their enemy. But as he read he couldn't help but wish it was her reading the text aloud to him as she had in their hotel in Nottingham while they were tracking down Eros's bow.

34 Washington DC, Virginia

Terra blew out a breath as she exited the conference room. She was exhausted after hours of questioning but much to her relief her employers seemed to be satisfied with her answers. Now she was headed back to her work station to check in on the status of her current task. As she walked, her phone pulsed signaling an incoming message. She pulled it from the holster at her hip and read the text with irritation.

Mr. Abrams and his project were really starting to get on her nerves. She'd see about his Intel but only because what he needed would ensure her sister's safety, as soon as it was sent she was heading down to the Brickskeller for a drink with Mr. Fenton. After which she was going to demand the bloody yank take her to bed.

35 Jerusalem, Israel

Fox Elwood sat in a local bar beside the lovely Robin. She shifted nervously on her stool beside him, when her violet eyes met his gaze she gave him an anxious smile. At least she was there, he'd gotten past her objections and could tell she was rethinking her acceptance of the invite, having found they were alone.

Before she could bolt, he called for the bar keep and ordered her favorite drink and one for himself.

"One drink," she reminded.

Fox nodded though he knew better. Once they started talking about Camelot she'd lighten up.

"One drink," he agreed and he clanked his glass against hers. "To Camelot," he whispered.

"To your promotion," she answered.

Fox threw back his shot and watched as Robin sipped at her drink. She blinked as the liquor hit her system and set down the glass. Before he began the discussion of topic, he watched with satisfaction as she settled into her seat and drank her drink, it wasn't long before the bar tender took the glass away only to replace it.

Robin drank it down having forgotten her pretense of one drink and her smile changed from uneasy to the sweet one he'd known a year ago. Her violet eyes shined with the influence of the liquor they'd shared.

"Would you like to dance?" he asked her, recalling that she'd enjoyed doing so when they'd dated.

"One dance," she muttered.

He nodded and the pair left their stools heading out to the dance floor. She was careful to maintain her distance and when the song ended, moved in the direction of a table wanting to sit. The pair finished their drinks as they talked further. Fox was careful to keep the conversation on the dig though he wanted to ask her a million questions about what she'd been up to since he left and why she'd acted as if she didn't know him.

They danced again later, Robin no longer held herself out of his reach, and it was clear to him it was time he got her back to the hotel. She wasn't drunk but was definitely buzzed. He laid down money for their drinks and got up from his seat. "Come on Robin time to get back," he entreated.

"Okay, Fox," she answered allowing him to lead her out. They got a cab back to the hotel and Robin headed for the elevator. Fox cursed not ready for the night to end. It was the closest they'd been in weeks.

"Robin?"

"What do you want Mr. Elwood?" she asked with annoyance at his stopping her retreat.

"Would you care to join me for a cup of coffee and maybe a bite of desert?"

"Fox..."

"No ulterior motives I promise," he assured her, though they both knew he was lying.

"One cup," she relented. Fox smiled as she stepped on the elevator. He joined her inside the car and pressed the button for his floor, as soon as the doors were shut he grabbed her by the arm and drew her against him. She melted into him without protest and when his lips found hers they answered with a wild passion he'd missed more than he cared to admit.

His lips parted hers letting them both up for air and he laughed with satisfaction. She hadn't forgotten him. When the elevator door slid open Robin hesitated for a moment to get off. Fox brushed his hand against her back as he took hold of her waist and nudged her out of the car. She turned and watched as the doors slid shut before laying her head on his shoulder. Giving up the fight.

36

Robin watched as the door to Fox Elwood's suite slid open and swallowed nervously as she asked her fuzzy brain if she was really going to walk through the door. He'd offered coffee and desert without ulterior motive but she knew better after the kiss in the elevator she had no illusions, the minute she walked in that door Mr. Elwood's mouth would be on hers again and she'd be lost to his spell.

Robin blinked and sighed knowing she didn't care, she wanted this, wanted him. She walked past him into the darkened hall and heard him follow her. His hand wrapped around her wrist and he drew her against him again. His mouth crashed into hers, demanding she yield to him as the door behind her slammed shut.

She jolted at the sound, then gasped, stunned as he pressed her back against it. His hands were everywhere stirring her body with a hunger she'd been denying for months. She felt his hands fist around her shirt and pull it loose of her jeans. Felt the heat of his skin as they slid under her shirt reaching for her. His lips parted hers to taste her skin and she whispered his name. He growled in frustration as his attempts to explore her without seeing her was thwarted by a lacy barrier in the form of her bra. His hands slid out of her clothes and fingers worked to unbutton her silky green blouse. He managed the first two buttons but fumbled with the awkward tiny things.

Impatient he grabbed the green fabric and tore the two pieces apart. Threads snapped and buttons popped, the sound of the plastic hitting the floor and rolling registered in her mind but Robin couldn't find the will to care, not when he was looking at her like that. His green eyes gleaming with excitement at the sight of her.

Knowing he wanted her as much as she'd wanted him was a strong drug that went right to her head. The smooth and controlled Fox Elwood was anything but, he was in a rush, and out of control.

He was going to have her right there against the door and damn him, the idea thrilled her. She moaned as he folded the cups of her bra down and put his hands on her. Lifting her breasts for him to taste. His mouth closed around a straining peak and she moaned with delight as her fingers fisted in his long red hair urging him on.

His hands left her chest unclasping her bra, the lacy garment fell to the floor as his hand slid down her hips to paw at the lower part of her over her jeans. Robin's head fell back against the wall at the mix of sensations as he overwhelmed her. It wasn't long before she felt one of those hands under the denim brushing over her panties. She could feel the heat of his skin through the thin layer but it wasn't enough, she wanted him to touch her.

His eyes opened to meet with hers as he lifted his head from her breast.

"Robin…" he breathed her name his tongue darted out to lick his lips.

"Relax Fox, I'm not too drunk to say no," she assured him before she turned her focus to unbuttoning his shirt wanting to touch him.

37

Fox kissed her again, relieved to know she was clear headed enough to know what was happening, he didn't want this if she wasn't going to remember it. Didn't want to wake in the morning to hurt or hostility. Satisfied she knew what was happening, his fingers slid beneath the silky fabric he'd been brushing against to find her. She was warm and her body strained to get closer at his intimate caress. His finger slipped inside her to find her wet and ready. Her body tightened around him with instant release and he groaned with disbelief.

"You've been waiting for this to happen," he breathed with wonder before he drew out of her and slid back in building her up toward her next peak. She cried out with wanton need and he lost himself in her pleasured sounds but soon just touching her was not enough to satisfy him.

His hand slid free of her clothes he pulled at her waistband releasing the snap of her jeans before peeling off the denim layer keeping her from him. He freed himself from his own confinement and drove his straining arousal inside her claiming that which he'd been longing for. He lost himself in the mad rush as he raced to join her in bliss.

The restrained and reserved beauty met his wild pace and begged for more, lost in the storm of passion he'd unleashed, her violet eyes were sightless, now her mind had receded and he knew all she could do was feel.

He lost himself in the wave thrilling in the bite of her nails on his skin as she spurred him on. He kissed her, losing himself in the taste of her, fighting to hold on wanting the moment to last. His control snapped as she fell over the edge again, her body trembling in his arms as she fell into the sea of passion. Fox followed after her unable to hold on. His head fell against the door his body spent.

38

Robin drew a shaky breath as reality began to settle in around her. Her heart was pounding wildly in her breast from her physical exertions. Her bangs were damp with sweat. She once more became aware of the fact she was pressed against a cold door. Her back began to ache and she shifted beneath Fox trying to ease her discomfort.

Fox hissed at her movement as it had her body pressing against his, stirring him again before he was ready. Robin opened her eyes to look at her lover and tried not to think about what she'd just done.

She watched as his brow lifted from the wall and green eyes opened. In their depths was disbelief and mortification as it sank in that he still had her pressed against the door and neither of them were even out of their clothes.

"Damn, Robin, I'm…"

"Don't, you were…that was…"

"Come on I think we'll try it again in the bed, or at least the couch," he muttered, before he kissed her and drew her against him once more.

Robin wrapped her legs around him and he carried her away from the door and in the direction of the bed. Robin reveled in the feel of his touch, the taste of his kiss and lost herself in the reality of being in his arms again. She'd missed this; missed him, missed them.

He was right, she'd wanted this from the moment she laid eyes on him again. Had been lost in the memories of their shared night of passion a year ago. Dreamed of it and him more than she cared to admit. He was amazing better than she remembered but she knew not to look for too much. It wouldn't last, she'd learned it the hard way.

39

Los Angeles, California
Monday
9AM

Lance stepped onto the set of Heart of Clay with mixed emotions. He was glad to be there with Catharine but it was also strange and unsettling to think that less than a week ago a woman had been murdered there. One that had been used to fill in as a substitute for Catharine.

As he studied the set Ares whispered the reminder that Catharine might still be killed here if Hades had his way. The god of the underworld would find the way to hurt him the most. If Hades should gain access to his nightmares he would use it to destroy him. The god of the dead would not hesitate to hurt her in such a way if it gave him an advantage over the detective.

"I won't let that happen," Lance muttered to the war god as he moved to take a seat beside Catharine.

"YOU'RE NO MATCH FOR HIM AS YOU ARE NOW," Ares mocked.

"Maybe I'm not but the fact remains I won't let him touch her without a fight," Lance stated as the actors took their position on set and James called for quiet.

"HE'LL CUT YOU DOWN IN A MINUTE AND THEN WHAT?" Ares countered.

"I suppose you've got a better chance," Lance groused with irritation.

"NOT AS I AM, BUT WITH MY FULL POWER…" Ares began.

"I suppose you want me to just step aside and let you take control so you can get it…do you think I was born yesterday," Lance snapped.

"NO, I DON'T NOR AM I LOOKING FOR CONTROL HAVING IT WILL NOT RESOLVE THE LACK OF MY POWER,"

Ares stated.

"Then what is it you're going on about," Lance demanded with impatience.

"I'LL FILL YOU IN LATER DETECTIVE FOR NOW WE BEST HOLD OUR DISCUSSION. I BELIEVE THE SHOOT HAS STARTED AND YOU NEED TO BE QUIET WHILE THEY WORK OR DIONYSUS WILL HAVE AN EXCUSE TO HAVE US THROWN OUT," Ares stated.

Lance relented the point and sank back in his seat to watch as James called action and Artemis began the scene.

40

Catharine watched Artemis work with satisfaction, the woman was good. She understood Serenity's character in a way that even Kim hadn't. Her portrayal was exactly as Catharine had envisioned her. She figured it didn't hurt that Artemis understood the situation. After all she didn't see the huntress as one who would wed the wine god under normal circumstances.

As James called cut to end the scene Catharine smiled and rose from her seat. With her mind at ease over Artemis's ability to play the role she moved onto her office space to finish the project. She was aware of Lance moving to follow her but paid him no mind. If she was going to complete her work she couldn't let him distract her.

She was finding the task to be difficult so far. She'd caught him muttering to himself earlier and had worried, understanding it wasn't himself he was talking to, but Ares. The Fallen's influence had grown since he slayed the dragon. Catharine drew a breath and blew it out trying to quiet her fears. She reasoned Lance wasn't showing any outward signs of change; that he was in deed in control as he claimed and with that thought in mind she put her fingers to the keyboard and began to work.

41

Lance lost himself in the steady and rhythmical sound of Catharine's fingers on the keyboard as she worked. The writer was lost in her own world. He was glad she seemed to be recovering from her recent ordeal but disappointed to be forgotten at least for the moment. There wasn't much he could do here to pass the time. Catharine had tried to convince him to stay at the house but he'd been unwilling to risk leaving her alone.

Now he wished he'd listened to her. At the moment he was alone as no one on set paid him any mind. As he sat, his thoughts drifted back to his earlier conversation with the war god and he figured now that he was out of hearing range they could finish their chat.

"What is it you mean by taking over won't resolve your lack of power?" Lance muttered.

"AFTER HERMES KILLED ZEUS WITH MY SWORD, HIS BROTHERS HADES AND POSEIDON SEALED MY POWER TO PREVENT ME FROM SEIZING CONTROL. UNTIL THOSE SEALS ARE BROKEN I AM NOT CAPABLE OF WIELDING MY TRUE POWER."

"The dragon was the first seal," Lance said with understanding.

"YES."

"And the second?" Lance questioned.

"THE SEA KING REMOVED A GEM FROM THE POMMEL OF THE SWORD AND HID IT. UNTIL IT IS RECOVERED I AM NO MATCH FOR MY BROTHERS," Ares replied.

"So, if this gem is recovered you'll be better able to protect us?" Lance muttered.

"YES."

"And your hold on me grows," Lance stated with understanding.

"A SMALL RISK FOR ENSURING HER SAFETY," Ares

stated.

"So you say, but if I do this as you're asking I'm stepping up to be your puppet and I'm not okay with that," Lance grumbled.

"I GAVE YOU MY WORD..."

"Yeah, I know but I'm figuring all deals are off the minute this seal breaks," Lance stated with disgust. "No, we'll do this my way for now," he stated effectively ending the discussion.

42

Ares cursed as the key he'd been trying in the lock of detectives mind broke. He'd been close. The mortals mind was smarter than he'd anticipated. It was a risk he knew existed, he'd always had to contend with one of two mind types where his mantle was concerned. His hosts were either cunning men or madmen. Kurt Dryden had been the latter, while the detective was shaping into the former.

The story he'd told the detective was true but not complete. When Poseidon sealed his power he'd stripped the blade of all its gems. Ares had used each man who possessed the blade to restore it until Arthur. The king like Lance had seen the danger inherent in the blade and had driven it into the cursed stone to seal him away for good.

That upstart order of self-appointed guardians had guarded the cave for centuries to ensure his blade never saw the light of day again, but they'd failed. Kurt Dryden had wandered into the cave. He'd heard his call and drawn him free of his prison. He'd soon learned the man's mind was lost. Had known he'd need to find another to finish the task as Kurt was too easily influenced by the witch.

He'd seen the man he could use to finish the job in that candle lit basement. The raw emotion he'd felt in that moment around the detective had been so potent he'd known no other would match him. That Lance was fighting with him was no matter, given time he like those that had come before would soon move to seek the missing gem of the sword and after centuries of waiting Ares power would be free once more.

43 JERUSALEM, ISRAEL

Fox lay in bed awake studying the beauty sleeping beside him. Robin. He'd missed her more than he'd ever care to admit. Had thought of little else but her, here with him, in the past year. As he lay there he wondered what he'd been thinking when he left her. He'd never found anything he liked better.

He hoped that when morning came they could put the past behind them and look at the night before as the start of something new between them. Because for the first time in his life Fox wanted more than just one night with a woman and he wanted that more with Robin.

Fox brushed a strand of her auburn hair away from her face, tucking it behind her ear and brushed a kiss on her forehead. He watched as her lips curved into a smile and wondered what she was dreaming about, he hoped it was pleasant. Sinking back on his pillow Fox let sleep take him and drifted into dreamless sleep.

44

Robin woke to the brush of a familiar sea breeze and the sound of waves crashing in the distance. She opened her eyes to find herself swaying in her favorite hammock. Sitting up she stretched her body before climbing down, bare feet sank into warm sand and she sighed at the sensation.

She heard the cry of seabirds and smiled to find herself in her favorite dream. The peaceful haven was one she often sheltered in on nights when she wasn't dreaming of Fox over the last year. Her own little slice of paradise. The sea called and she moved to answer making her way across the sand toward the crashing waves.

Her violet eyes moved to the heavens and she watched as the sun finished setting and the moon began to rise. Her steps carried her unerringly to the patio of her friend's dwelling. She stopped beside the pool and splashed clean water in her face wiping away the grit of sleep from her eyes.

When she lifted her head, she studied her reflection. Her auburn hair was pulled back and tamed, pinned in place by various combs of gold adorned by dolphins, the gold bejeweled with pearl and lapis, the combs had matching jewelry, earrings, and necklace.

Rather than her normal everyday attire Robin was dressed for the beach. But the suit she wore was not one she owned or had ever seen. It was an aquamarine two piece that showed off her figure. She'd made it more modest with a white sheer scarf draped about her shoulders and down her arms with a bathing suit skirt cover-up with a lapis bead fringe at the bottom and a golden chain with a dolphin at her waist. She shivered as the ocean air grew colder and a pair of powerful arms took hold of her shoulders and rubbed them gently through the beaded scarf.

"THE TEMPERATURES DROPPING, I THINK YOU'D

BETTER PUT THESE ON BEFORE THE PATIO GETS TOO COLD TO STAND ON," a familiar voice murmured, before her companion brushed a kiss on her temple.

Robin took the offered shoes and slipped them on her feet. The golden sandals with the same design were a perfect fit and warm from laying in the afternoon sun. She then turned to greet her friend. Her violet eyes settled on the mysterious man who'd begun to turn up in her dreams shortly after Fox ran off on her.

His blue-green eyes gleamed with excitement at the sight of her before him. The sea breeze whipped through his golden bangs, the humidity made the wild strands curl at his ears. The shoulder length mane was spikey and wild in its many layers; reminding her of a wild animals, it framed his golden sun kissed skin.

"Hello, Sei," she whispered before she wrapped her arms around him and hugged him in greeting.

Not for the first time Robin felt a spark of desire at the feel of his warm skin against her own.

"ROBIN, HOW ARE YOU MY DEAR?" he asked as he led her over to one of the deck chairs to stretch out.

"I'm okay," she said with a shrug. Robin sank down on the chair as she played with the dolphin charm on her necklace in a nervous display she'd not shown in some time.

"WHAT'S WRONG," the man Sei asked as he sat down behind her.

Robin leaned back against his chest accepting the comfort he offered. "I slipped up," she confessed.

"HOW SO?" Sei asked as he wrapped his arms around her shoulders holding her close.

"I'm with Mr. Elwood…"

"ROBIN, YOU WERE DOING SO WELL. WHY WOULD YOU LET HIM IN NOW, AFTER THE LAST TIME?"

"I don't know, I just…"

"DO YOU REMEMBER HOW BROKEN YOU WERE WHEN WE MET? I DON'T WANT TO SEE YOU GET HURT LIKE THAT AGAIN," Sei murmured as he rubbed her arms offering her warmth against the chill in the air, and soothing old pain away.

"I remember. I tried to stay away from him, but…"

"HE DOESN'T LOVE YOU MY DEAR YOU HAVE TO LEAVE HIM BEFORE HE HURTS YOU AGAIN," Sei whispered and he brushed a kiss on her cheek.

Robin closed her eyes at the advice and lost herself in his gentle ministrations. "You're right, Sei I'm sorry if I've disappointed you," she breathed.

"I'M NOT DISAPPOINTED MY FRIEND," Sei assured her before he kissed her shoulder.

"I'm glad, I like seeing you here like this, sometimes I wish..." Robin let the words trail off leaving them unsaid feeling foolish.

"WHAT DO YOU WISH?" Sei questioned as his hands moved from her arms to her shoulders and began to work out the tension in her muscles.

"That you were a real person and not just a dream," she answered with a blush.

"IF I WERE REAL MY LADY I'D LOVE YOU, AS YOU DESERVE. IF I WERE REAL WOULD YOU LOVE ME?" Sei asked as his hands kneaded the muscles of her lower back.

"Yes, I think I would," she admitted.

"PRETTY ROBIN, WILL YOU LET ME LOVE YOU HERE?" He asked.

"Sei..." Robin began in denial as she drew away from him.

"ANOTHER NIGHT, PERHAPS," he relented before he brushed a kiss on her back between her shoulder blades.

"Another night," she agreed as she sank back against him.

"THANK YOU," he whispered before he placed a kiss on her other shoulder.

"You're welcome," she murmured as she closed her eyes.

"DO SOMETHING FOR ME LADY," Sei requested.

"What?"

"PROMISE ME WHEN YOU WAKE YOU'LL LEAVE HIM," he requested before he brushed a kiss on her other temple.

"Sei..."

"I DON'T WANT TO HEAR YOU WEEP AGAIN OVER HIM ROBIN IT WILL BREAK MY HEART," Sei explained.

"I promise," she relented as his hands returned to her arms. His fingers stroked down her skin lulling her to sleep.

45

Robin's eyelashes fluttered and she smiled as she rose from dreaming to consciousness. She felt better than she had in days until she shifted to find se was not in her bed but Fox Elwood's. Glancing at the bed side clock she noted it was a little after two and cursed. She needed to get out of there before it got any later. With care she slid out from under the blankets and in the cover of darkness gathered her clothes. She dressed tying her ruined blouse closed and scribbled a quick note before making her way out of the hotel room and heading back down to her own.

She'd pack and be gone before he woke. With luck they'd not see each other again until the next day at the dig and be too busy to talk about this horrendous mistake.

46

Fox rolled over in his sleep to reach for Robin only to find the place beside him empty. His eyes flew open and looked about dazed and confused.

"Where was she?"

He rose from the bed wrapping a sheet about him and moved through the room to find her. He checked the bathroom and found it dark and empty.

"Robin?" he called his voice still groggy with sleep. No answer came. "What the hell?" he muttered displeased as he headed back to the bed. He spotted a piece of paper on the pillow and picked it up.

'Fox,

Wanted to get an early start see you in Scotland.

R.'

"Early start?" Fox looked over at the clock and noted it was a little after 5am. His temper flared at the notion she'd crawled out of his bed in the middle of the night then cooled and he felt like a heel as he realized he treated her no better last time around. At least she'd left a note.

Laying back down he closed his eyes, when he got out to the new site they were going to talk. He figured he owed her an apology.

47 Scottish Highlands

Fox Elwood stood upon the top of a green hill staring out at the Atlantic smashing against the rocky cliffs below. He drew in the smell of the salty air and smiled. It was good to get out of the desert, though he'd have to admit his last night there had been both enjoyable and a memorable one.

Robin.

The pretty doctor had proven to be far more entertaining than even Fox had remembered. So much so he'd nearly missed his flight out. He'd hoped to speak with her when he got here but so far she'd been avoiding him. He'd have to rectify that later but for now she was right, they couldn't afford any distractions.

"Let's set up here the ruins should be just over there," Fox stated as he pointed to the middle of the hill top."

He watched with satisfaction as the four man crew began to do as told. Robin looked out at the sea below as if under a spell and Fox smiled. So the pretty Robin loved the sea. He'd have to make sure to take advantage of that. But for now it was time to get to work.

With a little luck they'd find something to substantiate the find in Zeboim and somewhere within the ruins he'd find Arthur Pendragon's sword.

48 Unknown

Hades stood next to his workspace where the map of the world lay. He reached into his earthen jar filled with sand and covered the map once more. Drawing upon his power he whispered a request for it to show him the resting place of his key. He smiled as the sand shifted and the green glow dimmed everywhere but over the city of Cairo.

Satisfied he released his hold on the land and departed knowing exactly where he'd find the key that would open his door to the underworld.

HIS KEY.

49 Great Falls, Montana

Anna sighed as she came to the end of her notes. There was nothing there about the keys. Wherever they were the knowledge of it was not hidden anywhere within the information she'd gathered. She was willing to bet it was somewhere within those cuneiform tablets Sam had discovered and knew that was a bad thing, because it meant Hermes had it.

Anna silently berated Hades for intruding upon her vision as he had, knowing if he'd waited but a few moments she'd have seen first-hand where the other keys were.

"Okay, I've had enough," she relented as she saved her notes and rose from her seat. Sam set his book aside and looked up at her.

"No luck?"

"Not even a bread crumb," she grumbled. "I figure the answers are…"

"With Hermes, yeah I figured as much as well," Sam admitted.

"You're still reading that book?" Anna asked amused seeing the book of Greek myth.

"Yeah, I told you I have a hard time with the names," Sam reminded.

"Right, did you…" Anna was interrupted by the ringing of his phone.

"Hold that thought doc," he requested as he picked up the cell and seeing the caller ID connected the line putting it on speaker.

"Hello, Rogue," he said in greeting. Anna looked at him in question as to whom Rogue was until she heard her sister's voice respond.

"Mr. Abrams. I thought ya should know Magnus Halden just surfaced on the grid."

"Where's he headed?" Sam questioned.

"Looks like Cairo, Egypt," her sister replied.

"Thanks Sis."

"You're welcome Annalynn. Mr. Abrams I'll be in touch," Terra stated before she broke the call.

"If he's headed to Cairo it can mean only one thing," Sam muttered.

"He's located his key," Anna s stated with dread.

"There's nothing we can do about it now doc, all we can do now is get to that door before he does," Sam stated. Anna nodded and then rest her head on his shoulder weary. Understanding now why Hades had interrupted her vision. He'd done so to ensure that he reach the key first. It was her last conscious thought before she slipped into sleep.

50

Cairo, Egypt

Hades stared with pleasure upon the ruin he'd wrought only a few days earlier. The library that had once housed the order of the Black Hand was no more. The men who had resided within its walls wiped out. Any that might still be lingering in the area he'd soon deal with as well. But for now he had a goal to achieve while there.

Hades stepped into the wreckage and moved along the hidden corridors his power led him unerringly to where his key lay in wait. The disk of metal and stone was identical to that of his brothers in appearance, the sole difference was the button that triggered its release. The lord of the underworld held it up like a compass and bid it show him the lock. He hissed in irritation when nothing happened.

It seemed that the council had sealed his power over it. No matter, there was another way to find the door. Dr. Gallagher had seen it, he needed only to pressure her to reveal the secret. Hades slipped the key inside the pocket of his suit coat then departed.

51

Anna blinked as her eyes settled once more upon the interior of the throne room beneath the temple in Atlantis. As she looked about she noted that the image had changed. Where three gods had stood upon the steps looking down at the altar now only Poseidon remained.

Hermes was nowhere to be seen within the chamber. She wondered what he was up to but let the mater go knowing if it was for her to know she would be shown.

Her eyes moved to the altar and she trembled at the sight before her. Catharine no longer was bound to the base but laid out upon the altar. Ares and Lance were locked in battle and behind the detective was Dionysus whispering in his ear. Anna saw the chain leading into the shadows where Hades still lurked but avoided eye contact.

Turning instead to the door. She rest her hand upon it for a moment, she was in the throne room and then in the next she was standing at the edge of a rocky sea coast. The other door was in a volcanic cavern near a sea coast somewhere.

With the image locked in her mind Anna moved once more to the base of the stairs where the first key had lain in wait. When she touched it she saw the door there slide open and moving down the passage she soon found a key laying within. Then the image changed and she saw the key she'd discovered in Artemis's hands. Dionysus stood at her side, his eyes fixed on the key, gleamed with hunger.

She blinked and when her lashes lifted once more she was plunging through the depths of cold dark water to the sea floor below. Power radiated through the blackness and the key hiding there began to glow. Anna shuddered with disquiet to know that lock and key were so close to each other but figured it was safer down there than on dry land where anyone could reach it.

The image faded and was quickly replaced with that of Hades standing over a map, eyes fixed on grains of sand laid on it. His key laid in front of him. Anna stared at the image trying to understand what she was seeing.

Green eyes lifted from the map to lock with her hazel ones as he became aware of her presence there. Anna screamed as she was dragged once more away from the vision and into his dream realm.

52 Scottish Highlands

Robin Chase wiped sweat from her brow as the last light of the sun's rays began to fade. As she looked up the failing light touched the soil near where Fox stood and the ground shone brightly as the light reflected off something. "Fox at your feet," she called. She watched as he knelt back down and dusted the earth aside where the light shown to reveal the tip of a knife and he smiled.

Digging around it he soon found a shard of a broken plate and goblet as well. Cleaning the broken fragment he saw something.

"Robin look at this," he called and reluctantly she crossed to his side to take a look at what he held out for her. Robin blinked as she studied part of a sigil. A delighted laugh bubbled up out of her with recognition. "It's…"

"Yeah, I know, looks like the text at Zeboim was right. This is indeed the place where the ruins of Arthur's castle existed."

"How can that be Camelot wasn't built until…" Robin began confused.

"I don't know Robin but here somewhere in the rubble below us are the answers to that question as well as to what became of the king's sword."

"Excalibur," Robin breathed with wonder, then blinked realizing they were too close. She took a step back. "We'll, dig here tomorrow, she muttered before she turned to head back for the van leaving Fox alone on the hill with the rest of the team.

53 Los Angeles, California

Dionysus smiled with pleasure as he led his wife and guests into his private dining hall. The shoot that day had been a great success. Artemis had been perfect in her portrayal of Serenity and the crew was reinvested in project. The shoot was back on schedule and even the overly critical Miss Nichols was on board with the decision. He couldn't have asked for a better first day back.

54

Artemis walked behind the wine god in quiet musing. Her day as Serenity had been both strange and wonderful all at once. Her gaze moved from her husband's back to that of the woman who had created the role. Catharine.

She seemed to be doing well given all that had transpired around her. She had given her approval of the casting then moved off to work at completing the tale which she had begun. She'd been glad to see that so far Dionysus was leaving her be. The same however could not be said of their other guest.

The detective. She'd felt the press of the wine gods power and had seen the flash image of Catharine in a gown like her own. The wine god was messing with the mortal currently in possession of Ares mantel. He'd nudged at Lance Roman's mind on several occasions during the day and the man was showing signs of agitation as a result.

Artemis wasn't sure what her husband was up to where the detective was concerned but she intended to find out and if necessary put a stop to the wine god's games.

55 MONDAY 8PM

Lance sat and ate his meal in an awkward and near unbearable silence. A strange and disheartening quiet had settled in around him, one that he didn't seem able to shake off. Since his conversation with Ares earlier that day, he'd not heard another word out of the war god or Catharine. His hostess had been watching him which was a bit unsettling given the fact the last man to possess Ares mantle she'd killed with an extreme vengeance.

He didn't sense any hostility from her but he was not one to trust appearances when it came to the fallen or their children. He'd thought Dionysus harmless his first visit here and had learned the hard way how wrong he'd been. Lance groaned at the thought of the wine god.

When Ares had made his deal to get Lance to take the sword to slay the dragon he'd stipulated the wine god release Catharine from his hold and he had, however it hadn't occurred to him he needed to make the same request of his own mind and he was now paying for the error. Dionysus had been nudging at his mind all day with thoughts of her. He didn't know what the fallen was playing at but once Catharine was out of ear shot he intended to get his host to back off. Because feeling the lust the fallen was stirring in him and knowing it was one-sided was a slow form of torture.

He was grateful that Catharine was safe, nothing mattered more to him than that at the moment. It was why he'd listened to Ares prompting in regard to the mantel that and to ensure the war god's influence on him didn't get any stronger. Lance had no intention of hunting down the missing gem from the Fallen's sword. He was not interested in being turned into War's puppet.

Despite his need to ensure Catharine's safety a part of him was beginning to wish she still wanted him as he desired her. He wanted to feel her in his arms again as she'd been, trembling with need of him; her body straining for more, mouth hot, and hungry demanding.

Lance blinked as his hand clinched into a fist at his side with frustration as the wine god once more pressed against his mind.

56

Catharine picked at her food self-consciously keenly aware that in that moment she was the center of attention and not caring for it. She'd felt the wine god's attention settle on her as they moved into the dining hall. His gaze made her edgy after their last encounter in this place. While she was currently free of his influence she had no illusions where Dionysus was concerned.

The wine god was not a harmless distraction, nor was he less of a threat than his brethren as myth depicted. His power was the ability to manipulate mind and body. He'd made her burn with desire, tried to enslave her to her lusts. If he wanted to he'd do it again without a second's hesitation despite Ares request.

The next set of eyes she felt settle in on her were that of her hostess, Artemis. The huntress had begun to study her just before they settled into eat. Catharine wasn't sure of the reasons behind the other woman's scrutiny nor did she care to find out. All she knew for sure was that when those blue eyes had come to rest upon her that all three of her companions in that moment had come to be staring at her.

Lance's gaze had fixed in on her the moment she emerged from her work space and had not left her once. As she sat in silence and pretended to eat Catharine was careful not to meet the eyes of any of her watchers, but she avoided Lance's in particular. She'd met his gaze in the limo and had felt her mouth go dry.

The heat of his stare had been so intense she'd have sworn in that moment, she felt his hands on her. Catharine had trembled involuntarily in response and a smile curled his lips. Ice blue eyes gleamed orange for an instant and the war god had spoken without words. "I'LL HAVE YOUR SURRENDER," he boasted before those unnatural eyes had skimmed over her body from head to toe;

undressing her for his enjoyment.

Orange had faded as Lance returned but the war god's departure had not brought an end to the detective's roaming eye. If anything it had grown more bold; a harsh reminder that Lance was a man still under the wine god's power. She'd wondered the night they met what it would be like to have the detective desire her as he'd looked upon Anna and now that he did she wished the controlled man was there instead.

Weary and restless Catharine rose from the table and headed for her room. She muttered an apology as she went. Aware her host probably wanted to celebrate the day's success but she wasn't in the mood. As Serenity's world seemed to be taking shape Catharine's felt like it was spinning out of control and she feared that it might never stop.

57

Lance waited until Catharine was clear of the room and out of ear shot before speaking. "I thought I made it clear I didn't want you messing with her," Lance snapped with irritation.

"DETECTIVE WHILE I APPRECIATE YOUR FRUSTRATION AT MISS NICHOLS DISTANCE, I WILL NOT ALLOW YOU TO IMPUGNED MY HONOR. I'VE IN NO WAY HARASSED HER. I REFRAINED FROM SUGGESTING A CELEBRATION THIS EVENING AWARE THAT SHE WOULD NOT BE COMFORTABLE. I'VE GONE OUT OF MY WAY TO ACCOMMODATE HER NEEDS AND RESPECT YOUR WISHES," Dionysus challenged with temper.

"Then stop messing with me as well," Lance demanded.

"THAT WASN'T OUR DEAL DETECTIVE. ARES REQUESTED HER MIND BE RELEASED AND I HAVE DONE SO, YOURS WAS NEVER BROUGHT INTO THE DISCUSSION, IT IS MINE TO WANDER THROUGH AS I PLEASE, WHAT YOU SEE AND FEEL AS A RESULT IS NOT MY DOING IT'S SIMPLY A REFLECTION OR AMPLIFICATION OF WHAT YOU ALREADY FEEL."

"Let me go," Lance requested.

"NO, I WON'T BE TASTING WATER AGAIN THIS WEEK DETECTIVE. I'VE GREATLY REDUCED MY POWER BY RELEASING BOTH DR. GALLAGHER AND YOUR MISS NICHOLS, I'M NOT WILLING TO CUT THAT POWER FURTHER WITH HADES ROAMING UNCHECKED. I NEED THAT POWER TO MAINTAIN THE SECURITY OF MY PALACE," Dionysus stated.

Lance cursed and the wine god smiled. "IF YOU DON'T LIKE FEELING AS YOU DO AND HER NOT RECIPROCATING

THERE ARE A COUPLE OF REMEDIES. ONE OF COURSE WOULD BE FOR ME TO REAWAKEN HER FOR YOU."

"Not an option," Lance hissed.

"THE OTHER WOULD BE FOR YOU TO REDIRECT THAT DESIRE ELSEWHERE," Dionysus suggested. Before he rose from his chair to go. "COME MY LADY WE SHALL CELEBRATE THE SUCCESS OF THE DAY," he prompted as he took her by the hand. She rose from her seat and he drew her into his arms kissing her passionately. She moaned with want of her lover before her teeth pierced his neck, as his hands took liberties with her body for the detective to see.

Lance closed his eyes as he felt his body react to the wine god's power and cursed as in his mind's eye he pictured grabbing Catharine in a similar fashion. His memory filled in the image with the taste of her kiss and the sound of her own cries of desperate need.

Lance took slow deliberate breaths trying to regain some semblance of control. As he fought for calm the wine god's parting comment echoed in his mind and unbidden the image shifted the woman in his arms changing to a stunning blonde with whisky eyes he knew all too well.

Lance snarled in outrage at the image and the audacity of the wine god to press her into his thoughts. He wasn't interested in the troublesome reporter. Her interest was as fake as her smile. He wanted something real; he wanted his faerie.

At the thought Lance's mind fell for a moment back into the bizarre fantasy his mind had been indulging in of late and he found himself once more in the embrace of his faerie queen. Lance groaned as he slid further into the dream feeling much like a man caught in quicksand. He clenched his hands at his side into fists and felt a twinge of pain as his nails dug into his palms drawing blood.

Opening his eyes Lance found he was alone in the room and growled as he wondered how long he'd been sitting there lost in the fantasy. Rising from the table he made his way up to his room wanting a cold shower. As he stepped in the room he felt the key in his pocket burn against his hip and looked to the door that joined his room with Catharine's. He'd forgotten to give it to her earlier. He should take it to her now he reasoned best to be rid of the temptation to use it.

As soon as the thought had finished he felt a new wave of Dionysus's power sweep over him. He blinked and reality melted away as once more he fell into lust driven fantasy. In his mind he pictured crossing the floor to the door sliding the key in the lock and opening the door that joined his room with Catharine's. He saw her sitting in front of her laptop lost; oblivious to his presence lost in her story.

Not for long. She'd ignored him too long that day already, Lance told himself as he crossed to stand behind her. He reached over her and closed the screen with a snap. She turned her blue eyes full of irritation and outrage. Lance silenced her objection to his action by drawing her out of her chair and into his arms. His mouth slanted over hers claiming it with demand.

Her lips came alive under his answering his intensity with a hunger all her own. Her arms wrapped around his neck and he eased his grasp upon her indulging in the need to touch her. She gasped startled and then moaned with delight as she arched toward him her body craving more.

"Yeah, now I've got your attention," he breathed before he kissed her again. His hands fisted in her clothes and he drew back heart pounding wildly. "Tell me to go now Serenity," he murmured aware if she didn't he wouldn't be able to draw back later.

"I don't want you to go detective," she whispered before she grabbed him by the shirt and drew his mouth back to hers and kissed him.

Lance's hands tore her shirt off of her tossing it aside with disinterest before moving to remove her slacks. He wanted her naked in his arms. Wanted to see the body he'd been dreaming of.

Lance blinked as reality crashed in on him once more to find he was standing beside the door. His skin burned with desire for the woman on the other side. He wanted to open it to go to her. Wanted the dream... He heard Ares whisper to do it assuring him that if he did his Serenity would yield to him.

Lance pressed a heated cheek against the wooden door, cooling his flesh as he fought against the impulse to take the key out of his pocket and open the door; to take the woman on the other side. Despite his own need and Ares nudging Lance turned from the door and crawled into bed choosing to sleep off the effects of Dionysus's influence; aware that his dreams would most likely run riot with fantasy of the blissfully unaware writer next door or her alter ego the enchanting faerie queen that had been tormenting him since they met.

58

Catharine's head snapped up from its focus on her laptop her mind falling out of the scene she'd been working on as she heard the sound of Lance's door open and shut. She blinked unnerved by her sudden over alertness to his movements. She dismissed it as merely an extension of the fallout from what had happened with Bryan and tried to settle back into her work only to fail miserably.

Within a few moments of her fingers returning to the keys she found herself distracted once more by the sound of his every step as he started across the room. She put in one earphone her intent to block out the sound until she noted his footfalls were closer. He seemed to be pacing now by the door that connected their rooms. She wondered if he was going to knock and waited as his movement stopped and silence settled in once more.

She'd turned back to her work wondering what he was waiting for and it was in that moment she recalled that their last stay in this place Dionysus had given him a key to her room. A key he most likely had in his pocket even now. Catharine felt her mouth go dry with the knowledge as she lifted her fingers from the keys and turned to look at the door. She watched the knob for movement unblinking for several minutes before she muttered a curse. This was crazy Lance would never open the door uninvited she assured herself.

Serenity laughed at her in a corner of her mind calling her a fool; reminding her that Davrik was based on him and that the damphirs had not hesitated to claim what was his when she'd forced his hand. Did she think the man would fare any better when he was being toyed with by a pair of gods.

Catharine groaned knowing the words were accurate, she'd been aware of Dionysus toying with him throughout the day. Figured he was messing with him now. Could all too easily imagine what might be rolling around in his fevered mind given her own experience with the wine god's games.

She wondered if the detective was okay. He'd been silent and tense since he kissed her the night before, was aware she hurt him when she drew back. She'd felt bad for his discomfort and for the prick to his ego, aware that days earlier she'd been more than willing to follow where he was leading. It must have been confusing to have her interest cool so suddenly when his had not.

She'd come to that realization earlier in the day when she'd felt him watching her on the set. His gaze never straying from her had unnerved her. She'd retreated to her work space hoping for a reprieve that had never come.

He'd followed her.

Her detective had stood outside her door a silent sentinel on guard against any who dared to disrupt her. Trouble was, he'd done so; as he was now. She'd found her senses heightened around him. She'd heard him first moving about beyond the door; then when he'd stilled she'd heard him breathing. Rough breaths that spoke of agitation and she'd even heard him muttering to himself a few times as Ares worked to strengthen his hold on him.

Catharine had found it difficult to focus on the book, aware that he was struggling against both the wine god's influence and war's. His close proximity had also affected her. She'd felt a longing inside her for him to step through the door and talk to her. As well as anxiety at the idea of him invading her space with the intent to act upon his lust filled dreams.

Or worse that when he did it would be a pair of unnatural orange eyes that looked back at her as he took her. As a result of this mix of emotions inside her Catharine had been hyper aware of his presence near her at all times as the day went on.

He was holding on to control for now. She assured herself even as she got to her feet and crossed to the door. She considered talking with him but was concerned that by breaking the silence that had settled in between them she might be giving his troubled mind an invitation to play out whatever dreams were running riot through him.

Catharine wondered what she could do if he did decide to come in. There was nowhere to retreat to. The bathroom door didn't lock. She considered moving the dresser in front of the door to bar his way but dismissed the notion. Lance was a good man, he wouldn't hurt her; he just needed to quiet the noise in his head, she assured herself as she pressed her hand against the door and whispered a prayer for his peace.

When she touched the door she'd seen him for a moment on the other side. A hand in his pocket playing with the key. He gritted his teeth and hands fisted as he fought for control. The image broke for a moment as she heard something bump into the door.

She bit her lip as she felt Ares presence emanating from the other side.

"No, Lance. Don't listen," her mind whispered; silently urging him to be strong. Her eyes fell shut as she willed him to hear her and once more she saw him. He stood a fist against the wood as if he'd hit it, knuckles cracked. He had a cheek pressed against the door where her hand was in front of her.

Catharine felt a jolt as something passed between them and her body weakened. Dizzy she rested her forehead against the door as she felt Ares presence dissipate.

Her fear abated knowing that for the moment Lance was still holding the war god at bay. She blinked as she lifted her head from where it was pressed against the door that connected her room to Lance's. Aware the danger was not done yet. Dionysus's power still held him and it was not so easily cast off.

As she lifted her head it occurred to her what it might look like to the detective if he did open the door to find her there and by extension how he might react. As the possible scenario played out in her over active imagination she felt a rush of conflicting emotions tear through her.

Her body stirred with anticipation as it reminded her that it had enjoyed his touch. Dread woke as well as her mind reminded her that men in general had a history of hurting her and her heart protested she wasn't ready to leap so soon after all that had happened.

Catharine's spirit simply urged her to have faith.

She wanted to scream at the inner conflict and found herself wishing that for once all the different parts of her being would agree on how to handle the situation. As if to mock her; mind, body and heart all ordered her to run, he was a danger she dare not risk, but her spirit warned if she did Ares would consume him. Catharine's teeth released her lower lip and her tongue wet it, nervously as she considered the matter.

Every fiber of her soul screamed at her to flee. So long as she was near him she was in grave danger not just from him and the gods' who tormented him but from Hades as well. She wanted to run because while under the wine god's influence she'd spoken words she vowed never to say again. Had felt things she wanted no part of.

Every second spent with the detective was a risk she wasn't sure she wanted to take, but despite all these reasons to go Catharine found she couldn't. She didn't want to see him wind up lost to Ares power. He was a good man and she cared what happened to him.

Serenity laughed at her and called her a fool warning that if not that night then soon her detective would open the door to take what he wanted just as Davrik had in Heart of Clay. That when he did she wouldn't be able to refuse him and anything that came after would be on her. Catharine ignored her telling herself she didn't care as she watched the door and waited to see if it would open.

Several minutes passed and at last she heard him stir. Catharine drew in a breath as she waited to see what he'd decided. She blew it out as she heard his footsteps retreat from the door, crossing back in the direction of the bed. She heard the sound of him flopping down on the bed and backed away from the door as all the tension in her body seeped out.

He'd walked away and with that truth she knew that for now she was safe.

59

Anna lay upon the cracked parched ground of the dead wood in the Fallen's dream realm. The sun beat down on her bare flesh, scorching it as the lord of the underworld struck her yet again with a lash. She hissed in pain her voice having left her earlier.

"Please stop," she breathed knowing if this went on much longer she'd not survive it.

"PRETTY ANNA, YOU WISH THE PAIN TO END," he questioned as he lifted her chin with the whip so that her hazel eyes met his green ones.

"Yes," she answered voice desperate.

"IT'LL ALL STOP WHEN YOU TELL ME WHAT I WANT TO KNOW," he vowed.

"Never. I won't help you claim you brother's crown," Anna snapped with more spirit than she'd known was left in her.

"OH ANNA, YOU'RE GOING TO REGRET THAT," he taunted as his fingers released the whip and coiled in her hair instead. He yanked her up off the dusty earth exposing her to his wrath filled gaze.

Anna trembled knowing what he was threatening and he smiled pleased with her fear. "LET'S START WITH SOMETHING EASIER," he breathed as he eased his grip on her blonde locks.

Anna blinked as she wondered what he was playing at now.

"TELL ME WHERE YOU ARE," he requested as his hands skimmed over her battered flesh.

"No," she answered weakly and at the word his touch grew rougher and more invasive.

"COME NOW DOCTOR, WE BOTH KNOW I CAN FIND OUT IF I WANT WITHOUT ANY KIND OF DIFFICULTY; THE GROUND ITSELF SPIES FOR ME. WHAT HARM IS THERE IN

ANSWERING ME?" He argued as his hands slid down her belly.

Anna hissed as his nails raked over her hips and slid inward toward her pelvis. “I won't help you fallen one," she answered knowing not to listen to him. Once she gave him access to any part of what she knew it would be easy enough for him to sink inside her mind and find the rest.

For her refusal she was punished further. His icy hands parting her legs so that clawed nails could tear through course feminine curls as he sought the part of her he delighted in abusing most when she was here.

"OH ANNA, YOU ARE SUCH A FOOLISH WOMAN TO DEFY ME. DO YOU THINK THAT YOUR SILENCE HERE CAN STOP ME FROM FINDING YOU, OR THE CROWN?" he asked amused. “DO YOU THINK YOUR SILENCE CAN KEEP SAM FROM DISCOVERING THE TRUTH OF WHAT HAPPENS HERE? I THOUGHT HIM THE ARROGANT ONE BUT PERHAPS YOU ARE? WITH TIME DOCTOR YOU WILL GIVE ME ALL I DESIRE INCLUDING YOUR MR. ABRAMS HEART AND SOUL," Hades hissed in her ear as he began the next phase of her torment.

60

Dionysus lifted his head from the huntress's breast where it had lain and slipped out of her body aware that the security of his inner sanctum had been breached. As his bride began to stir he lifted her wrist to his lips and pricked the skin licking the injury he elicited a gasp before he began to drink.

He watched as her body trembled in response, desperate for him and smiled. He bit his lip and brushed a bloody kiss against hers. Her tongue darted out to taste the crimson elixir her body craved and he looked on as she sank back into lust filled dreams her thirst quenched for now.

The wine god wrapped a silk robe about him as he rose from the bed and moved to greet his guest. No sooner had he entered his work space then Miss Walsh stepped in off the balcony.

"PAMELA, TO WHAT DO I OWE THE PLEASURE OF YOUR VISIT," he asked amused as he crossed to her side to greet her with a kiss on each cheek.

"Hades sent me," Pamela stated.

"INDEED AND WHAT IS IT THE LORD OF THE UNDERWORLD DESIRES?" Dionysus asked as he sank into his chair and picked up his cup swirling its contents. He drew in the aroma and smiled as he lost himself in the tempting scent of its currents draught.

"Hades bid me make it clear that if while he is under your roof Ares should be permitted a taste of his chosen bride he will be greatly displeased." Pamela replied.

"I SEE. YOU CAN ASSURE THE LORD OF DEATH THAT I'VE NOT NOR DO I INTEND TO MESS WITH MISS NICHOL'S MIND AGAIN. IF ARES DOES GET A TASTE OF THE WOMAN IT WON'T BE THROUGH MY INFLUENCE. THE WAR GOD'S

POWER GROWS STRONGER WITH EACH DAY THAT PASSES BUT HE'S NOT YET IN CONTROL OF THE DETECTIVE." Dionysus whispered before he took a sip from the cup he held. His eyes fell shut involuntarily at the potency of its taste and when his lids lifted it was to reveal violet eyes ringed in red.

"Thank you, Hades will be most pleased," Pamela murmured as she moved to leave. "You'll keep me in the loop if things change?" she requested as she stepped out on to the balcony.

Dionysus grabbed her by the arm halting her departure, his violet eyes gleaming red with his rising hunger. "OF COURSE, SO LONG AS YOU KEEP ME AWARE OF WHAT YOUR MASTER IS UP TO," Dionysus breathed as he drew her against him. He watched amused as whiskey colored eyes widened with alarm, aware of the danger at doing as he requested. He didn't give her a chance to deny him. Drawing upon his power over her he coerced the answer he sought of her past those blood red lips before he kissed her giving her a taste of that which she craved most.

She was his spy whether she liked it or not and despite what it might cost her she would tell him all if only to cool the fire he'd woken in her blood when she drank from his cup. Once more his fangs pierced her neck. He swallowed down the rest of the liquid in his cup and bit his own wrist allowing his life's blood to drip in the chalice and gave it to her.

He watched with amusement as she drank it and her body went wild as the taste sent her crashing into an all-consuming ecstasy that had her crying tears of blood as it tore through her.

"WHEN NEXT YOU DESIRE TO SPEAK WITH ME LADY YOU NEED ONLY POUR YOURSELF A GLASS OF WINE AND ADD A FEW DROPS OF BLOOD, DRINK AND I'LL BE WITH YOU," he whispered as he brushed the pad of his thumb over her lower lip bruising it and reveling in the feel of her fangs protruding, seeking another taste.

"My lord," she groaned in frustration and need as he denied her the taste as well as his flesh.

"YOU'LL GET WHAT YOU WANT WHEN I HAVE WHAT I'VE ASKED," he assured her. He watched with delight as she bowed and withdrew to do as he'd bid. Moving back inside he returned to his bed where Artemis was awake once more. Her blue eyes watched as he disrobed and sank down into the bed with her once more. His nearness clouded her senses and that pleasant sense of inhibition that came along with the intoxication brought on by his power began to wrap around her. Dionysus pawed at his wife's body drawing her deeper under his spell needing her passion.

The night of Bacchus was fast approaching and his hunger was growing by the minute. Soon she wouldn't be enough to satisfy him, the thirst would have him drawing others. His mark would draw those he'd already tasted back to him but he'd crave more always did. He'd need the blood of one yet untasted. He pressed the thought from his mind, careful to conceal it from his pretty princess for now, by the time the night was upon them she'd not interfere in the ritual, she'd be too lost to the thirst to object.

61

Artemis fought against her lord's drugging kisses and his skilled touch, she had questions she wanted answered, had since they left the dining hall and was not going to let him side track her from them again. She bit her lip trying to fight for control of her mind and her eyes shot open as his wicked hands sent her blindly into bliss, when her vision cleared it was to see the reflection of herself cast in the mirror above.

She was horrified to see the woman it reflected. She arched into the wine god's touch desperate for more, her blue eyes glowed faintly red and her lips parted begging for him to give her more. She felt her stomach role with disgust as she wondered how he'd turned her into this mindless mass of wanton flesh. Her flesh burned and she ached with need of his passion.

When she tried to stop him so that they could speak she found the raw hunger tearing through her system for him only intensified painfully. Rather than fight him she gave herself over to her desires. Her teeth sank into his flesh and she tasted his blood drinking greedily.

"OH, YOU'RE GOING TO PAY FOR THAT," he growled in warning at her impatience. She laughed, drunk on the taste of him. "Don't play with me wine god you'll not drive my mind from me forever," she warned.

"WHAT DO YOU WANT TO KNOW LITTLE HUNTRESS?"

"What do you want with the detective," she questioned.

"I NEED HIM TO DO AS ARES IS PRESSING HIM. TO GO SEEK THE SEAL THAT WILL RESTORE HIS POWER. HE'S THE ONLY ONE WHO STANDS A CHANCE AGAINST YOUR UNCLE."

"Why press his desire for the woman?"

"BECAUSE ARES IS RIGHT, THE KEY TO GAINING THE DETECTIVE'S ACCEPTANCE OF HIM IS THROUGH THE WOMAN SO LONG AS HE BELIEVES SHE IS IN DANGER HE WILL YIELD TO THE WAR GOD'S POWER."

"Why do you hesitate to re-enslave her I can see you desire her?"

"DOES THAT HURT YOU MY DEAR, KNOWING THAT I CAN DESIRE ANOTHER?"

"No, I've no illusions here that you'll be faithful. This is a political union," Artemis replied.

"YOU ALWAYS WERE LEVEL HEADED, I'VE NOT TOUCHED HER BECAUSE TO DO SO WILL INVITE WAR'S WRATH. I'M NOT FOOL ENOUGH TO PURSUE HIS BRIDE A SECOND TIME."

"Yet you mess with uncle's whore."

"HE'S NO INTEREST IN HER."

"And you, what do you want wine god," she asked.

"I WANT YOU TO CONSIDER THE POSSIBILITY THAT MY CLAIMING YOUR FATHER'S CROWN IS A BETTER OUTCOME THAN THE LORD OF THE UNDERWORLD GETTING IT," Dionysus whispered before he kissed her ,silencing her objections, drawing her once more under his spell. Reveling in the feel of her desperation to get her next taste of ecstasy whatever its source.

62

Ares spirit slid out of the sword where it had been residing and moved through the room to where his host lay lost in fitful sleep. He sank into the mortals flesh and crept towards his mind. The self-named god of war felt Dionysus's power pulse behind the door he'd been attempting to get past and smiled.

He could feel the inner conflict of the man struggling against the wine god's power, could feel the raw power he craved radiating from the other-side. Ares reached out to the source of strife and touched it. When he did the door before him shifted to include a window; allowing the war god to see inside.

Once more the detective stood in his room, his mind crowded with memories and fantasies of his lust filled encounters with the pretty writer. The wine god pressing him to give into his desires and unlock the door that separated him from his sweet Serenity. Dionysus was playing games with his host and that would give him a way past the gate.

Ares pressed his power against the window focusing it on the conflict within. The war god felt the glass crack and his power sank into the detective's mind. As it did he focused his thoughts on Hades warning and smiled as the man latched onto the image slipping from lust driven fantasy to nightmare. The typing on the other side of the door stopped as the woman screamed.

Ares looked on as Lance shoved the key in the lock opening the door without hesitation. As he stepped through the door the image faded and darkness surrounded him as the wine god changed the stage and the game.

63

Lance blinked dazed as he found himself not in Catharine's room but instead in a dense wood.

"I'm dreaming," he whispered with understanding. Dionysus was still toying with him. Catharine was fine, the scream a ploy to get him to open the door. Well, now that he'd walked through it, Lance wondered what it was the wine god intended for him here.

He moved through the trees down a broken path until his eyes fell upon a familiar clearing. Water lay ahead, the moon light poured down from above illuminating the lake. As he looked upon it the water broke as a golden head rose out of the depths. Water cascaded down her body as she emerged from below.

Blond and beautiful she looked every inch the part of the goddess who had descended from heaven to enjoy the secret pleasure of a private bath.

His Serenity. He smiled at the thought as he crept closer knowing it was true she'd told him as much. He was Davrik. As he drew nearer a voice whispered here was a fantasy he could indulge in, one that was not betrayal or intrusion. It's path already written and embraced. He need only take those last few steps and begin it. But as he moved something inside him shifted. This was not what he wanted. He didn't want the tragic heroine and he didn't want her as the damphirs her creator had set on the page, he wanted his faerie.

Lance turned to retreat and watched with stunned disbelief as his shadow rose from the ground and took shape. Becoming like that of the character he'd brushed off. As he turned to seek out his love, the woods behind him closed as the goddess surrendered to the embrace of his shadow.

Lance raced back down the path until he found himself in the garden grove of his faerie queen. She smiled at him, pleased to see him, her blue eyes lit with excitement and mischief. “Here you are then,” he breathed as he moved closer.

“I do hope the wood did not lead you too far astray,” she whispered as she ducked behind a tree keeping distance between them.

“It took me to her,” he admitted as he moved closer resting a hand upon hers.

“I see,” she said with disappointment.

“I did not surrender to her call,” he assured her as he drew his faerie toward him.

“You didn’t,” she asked her blue eyes wide with wonder.

“I don’t want her my queen, it is you that hold my heart,” he murmured. He pressed a kiss on her brow as his other hand took hold of her hip and molded her against him so that there wasn’t even an inch between them. She melted into him, her head lifting to meet his kiss.

Lance’s hand holding her arm released his fingers sinking into her long flowing mane of fiery silk. His hands fisted one pulling upon red locks as he kissed her deeply while the other had nails biting her hip marking peaches and cream skin he couldn’t wait to see, touch; taste. Here was his fantasy, she was his dream. His mind whispered as he lost himself in his hunger for her.

64

Ares watched with both amusement and a growing sense of desire as he watched the mortal get swept away in his lust filled pleasures. He had to hand it to the wine god, Dionysus had done a master stroke here taking the dream from where Ares had tried to lead it and steering it back to the course he desired. Filling the other god's cup with the taste he craved most.

Let the fool drink. Ares wasn't done yet. The war god again pressed his power against the cracked window and watched as it passed through the narrow opening to seep down in the man's brain. As it did Ares breathed one word "Hades" and watched with pleasure as his host reacted.

Out of the shadows of the wood the villain came like an angry spirit. He tore the lovers apart and threw the man aside with such force he struck a tree and saw stars. The pretty Faerie screamed with horror as the lord of the underworld grabbed her by the arm and drew her naked body against him.

"HUSH, CATHARINE YOU KNOW ME," he breathed as he skimmed his fingers against her temple. "YOU'VE CALLED MY NAME MORE TIMES THAN I CAN REMEMBER," he whispered as his fingers slid down her face. Tears fell from blue eyes as she tried to turn away from him.

His host struggled to get to his feet as the image around him shifted, it was no longer the wood he was in but that of Catharine's room and the woman in Hades grip was not the faerie queen of his dreams but Catharine. She was naked and trembling terrified of the man who held her prisoner.

No sooner had Lance regained his feet then Hades sent him flying again, this time he crashed into the wall on the opposite side of the room. Lance groaned as he fought to remain conscious aware that as he was he was no match for the god of the dead. Ares watched with delight as the mortal reached for his sword only to find it missing from the dream. The man cursed. “Ares damn you; help me,” the man roared in rage as he watched Hades touch his Serenity.

The glass window shattered at the utterance and the war god’s form shifted from man to Serpent. The fiery snake slithered through the open path to where the mortal lay upon the floor losing the battle to get back up. When he reached the man’s side Ares sank his fangs in the man’s hand and the human cursed. The serpent coiled around the limb constricting about it as he poured his venom into his host.

65

Lance roared as the serpent's fangs pierced his flesh and he grabbed the tail to rip the beast away in instinct.

"BE STILL FOOL," Ares hissed as he released his bite and uncoiled from around his arm. Lance froze and watched as the serpent slithered up his arm and to his ear. "YOU ASKED FOR AID; YOU HAVE IT. FOCUS YOUR MIND ON MY SWORD NOW AND IT WILL BE IN YOUR HAND," Ares whispered.

Lance blinked, he closed his eyes doing as the war god bade when he opened his eyes they were no longer blue but orange and the sword he'd been thinking of indeed was in his hand ready to strike.

"RELEASE HER BROTHER," Ares hissed, his words coming out of the mortal's lips. Hades turned to face the challenger and laughed.

"ARES, YOU DARE CHALLENGE ME WEAK AS YOU ARE," The god of the underworld questioned with disbelief.

"I DO," the war god answered.

"VERY WELL, THIS WILL PROVE AN AMUSING DISTRACTION AND WHEN I DEFEAT YOUR HOST, I'LL ENJOY MAKING YOU BOTH WATCH AS I CLAIM YOUR PRECIOUS SERENITY," Hades stated before the candle he held changed into his scythe.

Ares rose from the floor and sword drawn advanced on the lord of the underworld. The two crossed blades and the battle was on.

Ares was good, he had access to centuries of battle strategy, but despite this distinct advantage he was no match for the lord of the underworld. Hades power was stronger, older. Limited as he was Ares was no match for the lord of the dead.

66

"Damn it, Ares you're supposed to help us," Lance roared in frustration as Hades scythe marked his face.

"I CAN ONLY DO SO MUCH, DETECTIVE. MY POWER IS STILL PARTIALLY SEALED," Ares hissed.

"Enough, war lord I've had enough of your excuses if you won't help her I will. I'm not about to..."

"DO YOU THINK THAT I WANT TO SIT BY AND WATCH AS THAT MONSTER HARMS HER?"

"You're fallen you care nothing..."

"OH YOU FOOLISH MAN YOU THINK THAT BECAUSE I AM ONE OF THE FALLEN I DON'T CARE WHAT BECOMES OF HER. YOU ARE SORELY MISTAKEN. I'D RATHER SEE HER DEAD THEN WIND UP WITH THE LIKES OF HIM. I KNOW HADES AND HIS HUNGERS BETTER THAN YOU COULD EVER UNDERSTAND. I'VE NO DESIRE TO SEE OUR SERENITY FALL VICTIM TO THE LIKES OF HIM," Ares snapped with outrage.

"Then help me," Lance demanded again.

"I'LL TRY," Ares muttered as he picked them up off the floor and launched himself at Hades once more. His final effort to drive back the lord of the underworld ended in failure as Hades disarmed him.

"NOW, BROTHER YOU WILL WATCH AS I TAKE YOUR BRIDE," Hades gloated as he bound Ares with a shackle forcing him and his host to look on as he threw Catharine down upon her bed and began to rape her.

Lance roared in fury his blood burning with hate as dream became nightmare.

67

Lance's eyes snapped open the pupil glowing orange as he rose from the bed and headed in the direction of his hosts room. The war god had one goal in mind find Dionysus and make him release his host's mind he was in no mood to play these games. While he'd set the nightmare in motion to teach his host a lesson the ending that had played out was not in the game. It was Dionysus's doing and he'd have no more of it.

The wine god looked up from his bed at the war lord as he invaded his chambers.

"ARES."

"NO MORE GAME'S CUP BEARER, RELEASE MY HOST."

"I CANNOT," Dionysus hissed.

"HADES!"

"I'M AFRAID SO. HE MADE IT VERY CLEAR THAT YOU ARE NOT TO BE ALLOWED EVEN A TASTE OF YOUR WOULD BE BRIDE SO LONG AS YOU ARE UNDER MY ROOF."

"UNACCEPTABLE."

"I'M SORRY BROTHER I'VE RISKED MUCH BY ALLOWING YOU TO STAY HERE BUT I'LL NOT OUTRIGHT DEFY HIM. THE DREAMS WILL CONTINUE."

"DAMN HIM."

"INDEED I HOPE YOU'LL SUCCEED IN THAT," Dionysus muttered.

"YOUR LACK OF LOYALTY ASTOUNDS ME BROTHER," Hermes quipped as he slunk out of the shadows with Dionysus's cup in his hand.

"MESSENGER WHAT BUSINESS HAVE YOU HERE, SHOULD MY BRIDE WAKE TO SEE YOU..."

"SOON SHE'LL FORGET YOU AND MY TRANSGRESSION," Hermes quipped as he held the goblet. With a brazen boldness that startled Ares; Hermes tipped back the cup and drank.

"HOW DARE YOU," Dionysus hissed his violet eyes gleamed red with thirst in his rage.

"I DARE BECAUSE I KNOW ITS SECRETS. I KNOW ITS POWER AND SOON IT TOO WILL BE MINE," Hermes stated as he moved to leave.

"I THINK NOT," Ares snapped as he drew his sword and moved to stop the lord of knowledge.

"ARES, NO MATTER. I WILL JUST BE TAKING YOUR SWORD AS WELL."

"I MAY BE DIMINISHED THANKS TO MY BROTHER'S WORK BUT I'LL BE DAMNED IF I'M GOING TO STAND BY AND TAKE SHIT FROM AN UPSTART MESSENGER LIKE YOU," Ares hissed as he attacked the intruder.

Hermes roared as the blow took his hand clean off and the cup with it.

"THIS IS FAR FROM OVER WAR LORD. MAKE NO MISTAKE I WILL HAVE WHAT I CAME FOR AND MORE," Hermes hissed before he vanished aware that Ares power had grown.

"THANK YOU," Dionysus breathed as he picked up his cup.

"DON'T THANK ME WINE GOD, I DIDN'T DO THAT FOR YOU. IF HERMES WANTED YOUR CUP IT'S GOT TO BE A BAD THING."

"I must agree," Artemis stated as her eyes opened.

"I SUGGEST WE FIGURE OUT WHAT HE WAS UP TO," Ares stated before he put his sword away and headed back to his hosts room.

He sank back down on the bed and his host once more took control. Lance blinked as images of what just happened played out in his mind. Okay so maybe Ares wasn't exaggerating about his power being limited. He'd have to look into it, but first he was going to warn Sam of the latest turn of events here. Though he was unsure about the war lord's words on many things one thing he was sure of, if Hermes wanted the cup then it couldn't be good for them.

68 Great Falls, Montana

Sam sat reading his book in an unbearable silence. Anna had slipped into sleep sometime earlier and he found himself restless. Her dreams were not peaceful ones. Her body stiff and tense like that of an animal with its hackles raised. She was trapped somewhere in the dream realm with Hades and there was nothing he could do to help her. All he could do was wait and pray.

He'd shifted her from his shoulder to where her head lay against his chest. Her ear over his beating heart. He hoped somehow the sound might reach her wherever she was and lead her back. When she surfaced he was going to find out what was going on.

He didn't care for the idea that any time she slipped away into sleep she might be drawn away by the lord of the underworld. What did it mean? Had he miscalculated was Hades focus now on her? That didn't make any sense Ares was a greater threat to the fallen than he was. So what was the deal?

As Sam tried to make sense of it his phone rang breaking the silence and shaking him out of his morose thoughts.

"Hello."

"Sam."

"Lance, what's up?"

"Thought you should know Hermes turned up here in LA he tried to steal Dionysus's cup?"

"What, why? It holds no power anymore…"

"Apparently it's not as useless as we thought, he said something about knowing its secrets and its power soon being his before I stopped him."

"You stopped him?"

"With a little help from Ares," Lance muttered.

"Lance…"

"Save your breath Sam I'm not about to put the sword down right now not until I'm sure Catharine is beyond Hades reach."

"She may not even be in harm's way," Sam muttered.

"Why would you think that?"

"Because Anna's asleep right now and I'm pretty sure she's enduring her second round with the lord of the dead," Sam said with disgust.

"That doesn't make sense…"

"I know that, but it's happening," Sam snapped.

"Damn. I'm sorry man…"

"Don't be it's not your fault, I just wish I knew why it was happening and what is going on in there, she won't talk about it. Said something about not being his sword…"

"Ares says if he targeted her it's because she has something he wants…"

"The location of his door or the other keys," Sam muttered.

"Other Keys?" Lance asked curious.

Sam cursed realizing he'd just inadvertently shared knowledge he held with Ares. But he was also aware that Artemis needed to know that her father's crown was not as secure as she believed. Weighing his choices he drew a breath before explaining what he knew.

"You need to tell Artemis the crown is not secure," Sam stated.

"Will do. Ares says you need to respect Anna's wish to keep hidden her dreams it is for your own good."

"What does that mean?" Sam groused.

"I don't know."

"I wish you'd stop listening to Ares."

"Just following your golden rule," Lance defended.

"Meaning?"

"Keep your enemy close," Lance stated.

"This is different Lance keeping him close could end really badly." Sam stated.

"I'll take that chance. If things were reversed and it was you and Anna in this spot what would you do?"

Sam cursed. "Probably the same thing. Just be careful you're playing with fire."

"I know. You need to find out what Hermes is up to."

"I'm on it. Thank you for the tip," Sam answered before he hung up. He turned his attention back to the sleeping woman in his arms. He kissed her forehead and as Lance's question played in his mind he admitted that if their roles were reversed he'd have kept the sword as well.

He'd be hunting down the bastard fallen who was tormenting the beauty in his arms to ensure he never messed with her again. That was why Lance held the blade now and not him. Lance looked only to defend where he would go on the attack.

He'd be unable to resist Ares voice. He was a warrior.

69 Los Angeles, California

Hermes stared at Dionysus's opulent palace with envy. The wine god was doing well in this new world Hades had let him settle in. Hermes hadn't been so fortunate. His palace was in ruins and his court shredded for now. Once he had Zeus's crown he'd rebuild. He'd take the bride he'd set his eye on from the start.

Anna.

She'd not escape him this time around. He knew the means by which to capture her. But first he had to obtain that crown. The safest way to do so was to eliminate his competition. That had been what brought him here. He'd failed in his first venture to capture Dionysus's cup. His efforts were thwarted by Ares. It was no matter. He'd try again. The wine god's power wasn't the only one he could steal.

But first he needed to get his mantle back from Anna before the others figured out what he was up to and tried to take his power instead.

70

Hecate smiled as Hermes fumed over his recent failure. Watching him fall further from power thrilled her. She was looking forward to the day when he groveled at her feet. He and his brethren would all kneel before her and when they begged for their freedom she'd crush them under her heels.

None of them would ever dare try to touch her again when she was done with them. They'd know her pain as their own. Hermes had just handed her the final piece to the game.

Thanks to his stunt she now had her opening to meet with Pamela and Artemis as well. Hades and Dionysus both would pay well for the news she now held. It was time to collect.

71 Great Falls, Montana

Anna jolted awake as the nightmare faded to the dark recesses of her mind. Her panic quieted as Sam wrapped his arms around her tighter.

"Sam," she whispered his name with relief and he brushed her forehead with a kiss.

"Shh, it's over now doc," he assured her as he brushed her golden hair away from her eyes.

"I had another vision," Anna whispered recalling where the dream had begun.

"I'm listening."

"I was in the throne room again."

"Were the gods still there?"

"Yes, but they'd moved. Only Poseidon was still standing by watching the games. Lance and Ares were still battling over Catharine but she was on the altar. Dionysus was behind Lance egging him on. Hermes was nowhere to be seen. Hades was still lingering in the shadows. I moved past them to the door and then I got another glimpse of where Hades door was." Anna stated.

"What did you see?"

"A rocky sea coast."

"Okay so a volcanic cave near a rocky seacoast that should help to thin the possible locations."

"There was more. I touched the place where the key was and I saw them all. Artemis has her father's key, Dionysus is drooling over it. Chaos's key is already in the passage. Hades has his and Poseidon's key is with the door at the bottom of the Atlantic," Anna revealed.

"So we just need to worry about Hade's door for now," Sam said with understanding.

"Yes."

"He interrupted you again didn't he?"

"Sam…"

"Are you okay?"

"Yeah, I just don't understand why…"

"Ares claims you have something he wants," Sam muttered.

"Ares?"

"I spoke with Lance while you were sleeping. He said Hermes tried to steal Dionysus's cup."

"What? Why?"

"I don't know, but whatever the reason it can't be good."

"Great. I guess that means we'll need to be more careful in our watch over the horn," Anna muttered.

"Yeah, and you need to be on guard against telling Hades anything when you're lost in the dream realm."

"Right."

"Anna…"

"I know you want me to tell you about the nightmare Sam trust me when I say it's better if you don't know."

"Why do you think I can't handle it?"

"No, the truth is I don't know if I can," she admitted.

"Is it bad?"

"Yes."

"I'm sorry," he whispered as he tucked her head under his chin.

"Why? This isn't your fault."

"He's lashing out at you because he knows it's my weakness. He used it before…"

"With Pamela," Anna said in understanding.

"Yeah."

"I invited this Sam when I helped Zaharrah," Anna corrected.

"No, I don't believe that and I don't want to hear you say that again," Sam said as he gave her another tight squeeze.

Anna nodded and snuggled closer to him.

"Will you tell me?"

"I'm not ready Sam," she murmured.

"Okay, no more about it then, so will you do something for me?" Sam asked.

"What do you want Mr. Abrams," she asked playfully using miss proper to tease him.

"Anna…" Sam groaned in warning.

"I'm sorry…"

"Read to me?" he requested holding out his book.

Anna laughed before taking the copy of Greek myths and flipping it open to where he'd left off. She noted he'd not gotten very far since last time, before she began to read.

72 Cayman Islands, Hades Fortress

Pamela stepped through the guarded door into the heart of Hades inner chambers. As she made her way to his throne room the lord of the underworld emerged from within to meet her.

"MISS WALSH I TRUST YOU HAVE WHAT I REQUESTED?"

"Yes. Dionysus has given his word that Ares will not be allowed to even taste of his would be bride. He said that Ares power has grown but he's not yet gained control of the detective."

"Excellent, you've done well my dear," he whispered as he caressed her cheek.

She trembled under his touch and he kissed her brow.

"Thank you my lord," she whispered relieved to have gained his praise, aware that where he was concerned she was on dangerous ground if he was displeased.

"NO, THANK YOU," Hades answered as his magic touched her, his power turning back the clock giving her the thing she desired most, her youth.

Pamela gasped as her reflection changed before her. "My lord?"

"A GIFT FOR YOUR GOOD WORK, ENJOY IT."

"Thank you."

"YOU MAY GO." Hades muttered before he turned and left her; headed back to his chambers.

Pamela moved down the hall in the direction of her chambers and tried to sort out her next move.

73

"Lord Hades," a feminine voice called from somewhere in the shadows ahead of him.

"HECATE, WHAT A PLEASANT SURPRISE, I SEE YOU MANAGED TO SLIP PAST THE GUARD WHILE I WAS BUSY WITH MISS WALSH," he muttered displeased to find her lingering in his personal quarters.

"Forgive the intrusion but I have news which you'll want to hear," she whispered, as she emerged from the shadows to bow before him.

The lord of the underworld took her by the hand and brought her to her feet kissing her fingers.

"WHAT NEWS HAVE YOU MY LADY AND WHAT DO YOU DESIRE IN RETURN FOR IT?"

"The news I bring is in regard to the fallen you stripped of all. He now seeks to do the same to you. What I'd ask for this knowledge, is the right to meet with Miss Walsh."

"YOU'LL HAVE IT. NOW TELL ME, WHAT IS THIS UPSTART PLAYING AT?"

"He's discovered the secret of the mantles powers, he will try to strip you and the others of their power by forcing one of you to give your mantle to a mortal. When it happens, you will all be sealed away again."

"NEVER! I SHALL NOT GO BACK IN THAT STONE PRISON. IF IT WOULD IMPRISON US ALL, THEN HE MUST KNOW A WAY TO PREVENT IT FROM HAPPENING. DO YOU KNOW THIS AS WELL?"

"I do, my lord," she assured him.

"CLEVER LADY, TELL ME THIS SECRET AND I WILL GIVE YOU ALL YOU SEEK," Hades vowed as he brushed a kiss on her cheek. Hecate leaned closer and whispered the answer in his ear. She watched as his green eyes flamed with fascination and excitement.

“THANK YOU, MY LADY,” he murmured before he kissed her brow. Hecate turned her back to him denying him the right to touch her further. “YOUR LADY IS IN HER CHAMBERS,” he stated, displeased and watched as the old witch departed.

74

Once Hecate was gone Hades cursed; her news was grim. With his efforts at locating his door to the underworld thus far failing and Anna's refusal to answer him, despite her torment he was left with little choice. The crown still being beyond his reach thanks to his troublesome niece; he had to change his focus.

His attempts to break Anna would wait, for now. He had to break the curse over his mantle first. To ensure that he never wound up trapped within a stone image again, but more so to prevent Hermes from finding a way to rise to power again. He'd crushed the upstart messenger once for trying to rise beyond his station, he had no interest in doing so again. If Hermes came at him again, this time he'd not hesitate to destroy him.

75

Hecate moved down the corridor in the opposite direction of the lord of the underworld and smiled as she felt his disquiet grow. Good she'd shaken him with her warning. It gave her such pleasure to see these posturing fallen reduced from would be gods to the fearful dogs they truly were.

Let him stew over what her ex was up to, she didn't care. All there posturing and chest thumping would get them nowhere. Zeus's crown and his throne would never be filled by one of them. She'd see to it.

As the vengeful spirit stepped inside the woman Pamela's chambers the pretty blond lifted her head eyes full of alarm. Almost as if she were expecting trouble to be coming. Hecate wondered why and tapping in to her power could understand the woman was fearful that the master of the fortress had already discovered her little agreement with the wine god.

"Be at, ease lady, no harm do I bring," she assured her.

"Hecate?"

"Yes."

"Pamela eyed the other woman with mistrust. "What do you want?"

"What I want is irrelevant. What is it you want?" Hecate asked as she crossed the room to stand beside the broken woman hiding in shadows. She drew upon her power flooding the chamber with light.

"I…" Pamela stammered as she shielded her eyes.

"Look at you cowering here in the dark waiting for death's wrath to come. Trembling with a desire that won't fade, lost to the wine god's influence. Abandoned by your husband at the first sign of danger. A prisoner of you husbands enemy.

Cast off, spurned, abused by their power, lower than a dog. You, who were to have been queen of all reduced to Hades whore."

"Enough witch!" Pamela roared in outrage to be insulted so.

"Ah, there, see," Hecate murmured pleased as she reached out and lifted Pamela's chin so that whiskey eyes met with black. "You still have fight left in you good. Now, tell me what is it you want?" Hecate demanded as she brushed unruly strands of blond hair out of Pamela's eyes her touch like that of a mother to comfort a troubled child.

"I want everything promised me," Pamela hissed in fury.

"If you wish it I can give you all that was promised and more," Hecate whispered as she wiped away tears from Pamela's cheeks.

"How? If I betray him…" Pamela asked frightened, curious and intrigued.

"When you tire of your lowly state, call to me and I will free you of this wretched fortress and its master. I'll give your flesh ease of the wine god's spell, I will free you of your gilded cage," Hecate whispered before she kissed Pamela on the forehead. She then turned and walked away.

76

Los Angeles, California
Tuesday
6:05am

Catharine cursed as her eyes popped open yet again to stare at the alarm clock beside her bed. She'd not slept well that night, kept waking at odd moments tossing and turning, waiting though for what she wasn't sure.

Seeing the clock now, said it was after 6am, she gave up on the notion of going back to sleep and stretched before climbing out of bed. She looked to the laptop and shook her head, she wasn't ready to tackle work yet. She needed a few minutes to quiet her nerves.

Crossing to the dresser she pulled out her bathing suit and stepped into the bathroom to change, a swim was just what she needed and at this hour, with a little luck, she might just get a few minutes all to herself.

77

Lance paced his room nervously waiting for Catharine to get up. He didn't recall everything that had happened since he woke, but one image was branded in his brain and shook his confidence in the wine god's ability to keep Catharine beyond Hades' reach. Hermes had been here, he tried to take Dionysus's cup. He wasn't sure what it meant but it boded ill.

Ares voice was a constant one now pressing for him to go get the missing piece of his mantle. Warning him that without it he couldn't possibly hope to keep her safe from the lord of the underworld's wrath. Lance didn't know if that was true or not but he was sure of one thing with this newest wrinkle, he wanted Catharine out of LA.

Lance heard the sounds of her moving about next door and waited for her to emerge, even as Ares pressed him to forget waiting and just open the door. Lance crossed the room to the door and lifted his hand to knock as the sound of the outer door opening and closing sounded. He stepped out in the hall in time to watch her disappear down the stairs.

Lance blinked. What was she up to that had her roaming about Dionysus's palace alone before dawn he wondered as he moved to follow her?

78

Catharine shed her outer clothes and set her towel down on a deck chair before she dove into the deep end of the pool. She cut through the water like a fish surfacing at the other end. Her fingers pressed against the wall before she turned and started back in the opposite direction. As she went she turned her thoughts to the book and where she was taking it from the scene she'd left off in.

Davrik and Syvarin were about to have a face-off over Serenity but how was that going to end, where was the story driving to? How did she give the pair their happily ever after, keep Syvarin alive and tie up the rest of the threads she'd started? She didn't know but more troubling was she wasn't even sure how to write Davrik. Where had he been all those years since the lovers parted? What had he been doing? What effect had the cloak had on him during his time of despair?

As Catharine's mind began to wander she became aware of the fact she was no longer alone. She paused mid stroke and lifted her head. Opening her eyes she found Lance waiting at the other end of the pool.

"Good morning detective."

"Morning," he muttered distracted, his voice hinted at irritation.

"Something wrong?"

"Yeah, we had a late night visitor," Lance groused.

"Who?"

"Hermes, he tried to steal our hosts cup, said something about stealing his power. I don't think you should be here, after all, it's not as safe as I thought."

"I see, well, while I appreciate your concern Lance, you know I can't leave LA."

"Damn it Catharine, I know you've got a job to do out here but I don't think seeing Dark Heart through is worth your life," Lance snapped.

"You're right, but you're forgetting if I don't finish I run the risk of bringing down both Dionysus and Hecate's wrath on me," Catharine reminded with disgust.

Lance cursed and then began to pace as he muttered to himself. Catharine tensed aware he was once again arguing with Ares. She didn't catch most of it but was aware this was about more than just Hermes visit.

"Okay, you're right but that doesn't change the fact I want you out of here," Lance stated.

"Why? What's this really about?"

"I don't like knowing that our host is playing with me," Lance admitted.

"He'll do so if you're here or not," Catharine reminded, her patience wearing thin. He was going to be honest with her if he wanted her to listen.

"I don't like him looking at you."

"You don't or Ares doesn't," Catharine challenged with temper.

"I don't," Lance snapped.

"I'm sorry, it's just…"

"I'm the one in control here Serenity, he made a deal. He won't interfere."

"I know, but I'm not convinced you can trust the word of a fallen. You're changing Lance, I can see it."

"Catharine…"

"I heard you at the door last night," Catharine blurted out cutting off his protest.

"I didn't open it."

"You wanted to and he wanted you to, I felt his presence."

"I kept my word."

"Yes, but you struggled to do so."

"And, I told Dionysus to back off this morning."

"Get rid of the sword Lance, before it gets worse."

"I can't. The minute I do Hades will take you…"

"You can't know that," Catharine snapped cutting him off again.

"You know I'm right! I won't let him hurt you."

"Lance…"

"No Serenity, I'm not letting the sword go until I'm sure you're beyond his reach," Lance argued staring down at her his blue eyes cold unwavering.

Catharine trembled aware he would not budge on the matter. She nodded. “I’m not leaving town, I’ve got too much to do and I should probably get back to it now before we head over to the film shoot.”

“Fine. I’ll go get ready.” He said curtly before he turned and walked off giving her the space she craved.

Catharine blew out a breath before she climbed out of the pool and dried off enough to put back on her clothes. She needed to get ready to go and then try to finish up the scene she’d been working on before she left. Because she figured it was going to be another long day.

79

Lance cursed as he stepped in his room, Catharine's refusal to leave trying his patience. She didn't have to be there. The shoot was going fine from what he'd seen. She could keep tabs on the project via call and fax. She could work on the book anywhere, why was she being so difficult? He was just trying to keep her safe.

"YOU CAN'T KEEP HER SAFE ON YOUR OWN LANCE," Ares reminded.

"I know, I get it but…"

"IF YOU WANT TO MAKE SURE SHE STAYS OUT OF HARM'S WAY FOR NOW, YOU'LL KEEP HER RIGHT WHERE SHE IS. BELIEVE ME I DON'T LIKE THE WINE GOD WATCHING HER EITHER BUT FOR NOW IT IS NECESSARY."

"But it's not safe here either…"

"NO IT'S NOT, IF YOU WANT TO KEEP HER BEYOND THEIR REACH THEN YOU'LL DO AS I'VE SAID AND GO GET THE FINAL PIECE OF MY MANTLE."

"I told you I'm not going to…"

"DON'T YOU GET WHAT THE MESSENGER WAS SAYING LAST NIGHT? HE THINKS HE CAN STRIP YOUR HOST OF HIS POWER. IF THAT HAPPENS THERE WILL BE NOWHERE FOR YOU TO HIDE FROM HIM OR HADES."

"Artemis…"

"THE HUNTRESS IS NO MATCH FOR THE LIKES OF THEM BESIDES WITH DIONYSUS GONE SHE'LL HAVE NO REASON TO LINGER HERE. NO, YOU'LL BE ON YOUR OWN AND YOU CAN BELIEVE THAT IF HERMES SUCCEEDS IN WHATEVER HE'S PLAYING AT, THE FIRST THING HE'LL DO IS GO SHOPPING FOR A NEW BRIDE. NOTHING WILL PLEASE HIM MORE THAN TO TAKE SOMETHING THAT

HADES WANTS FOR HIMSELF AFTER THE WAY THE LORD OF THE UNDERWORLD HUMILIATED HIM. THAT WILL MAKE CATHARINE LOOK LIKE A PRETTY INTERESTING OPTION,NOT ONLY DOES HE GET TO SWIPE AT HADES BUT HE ALSO GET TO SWIPE AT ME, NOT TO MENTION THE BONUS OF GETTING TO MESS WITH ANNA AS WELL."

"You're lying!"

"NO, DETECTIVE I'M NOT AND YOU KNOW IT. IF YOU WANT TO STAY AHEAD OF THE OTHERS TO HOLD THEM AT BAY YOU'LL DO AS I'VE SAID, YOU'LL LOOK FOR THE LAST SEAL OVER MY POWER..."

"Shit... fine I'll look into the sword that doesn't mean I'm going to go get the damn thing for you, and if I find you're lying to me I'll drive this blade so deep in the earth no one will ever be able to find it again," Lance warned.

"FAIR ENOUGH, DETECTIVE," Ares said amused as his host turned on his laptop and began the task of researching the blade he carried at his side.

80

Catharine sat and watched as Dionysus gathered the team to discuss the shoot for the day. Making sure that everyone knew which scenes were being done.

"So, what's on the board for the day?" Lance asked curious?

Catharine blinked at the question, surprised by it, the detective had shown very little interest in the shoot yesterday. "We start filming the scene where Davrik becomes aware of how his sire is controlling Ashella and we'll wrap with the lovers capture if the shoot goes well," Catharine replied.

"It's moving well then," he said knowing they were a little over half way through the novel."

"Yes, Artemis is doing great," Catharine said pleased.

"How is the book coming?"

"Not so well," she admitted.

"What's the problem I thought you'd sorted it out?"

"I had, but now that I've got Davrik and Syvarin clashing I'm not sure where to go. I can't let Davrik kill his sire but after what Savarin's done to Ashella I can't see him letting him live. I don't know how to end the scene."

"Play it true to reality," Lance suggested.

"Kovrin…"

"Yeah, the only thing that father and son share in common besides a desire to have Ashella for themselves is a need to protect her from the werewolf who desires her as well."

"Brilliant they'll have to work together. That's how I can have Syvarin walk off into the sunset at the end. Davrik owes him."

"Right."

"Thank you," Catharine said grateful before she knocked a kiss on his cheek.

"Go finish your book," he instructed.

"I will I just want to see how the first couple scenes run," Catharine assured him. Lance nodded and the two fell quiet as the crew got set to shoot.

81

Lance sat outside Catharine's office door watching as the filming continued after overseeing the first couple sequences and being satisfied with Artemis's delivery of Nivali turning Selene as well as the murder of the duke, she'd retreated into her office to finish the scene that had been giving her trouble.

He wondered how she was doing and what would come of their conversation as he watched the actors prepare for the final sequence of the day. He could picture the scene in his mind father and son locked in combat unaware of their surroundings when suddenly Ashella screams. They turn in time to see her dragged off by Kovrin. Then the hunt would be on, a race against time to catch him before it was too late.

Lance turned away from the story as flashes of a very ugly reality crashed in around him. He didn't want to go there again. Kurt was gone he'd never hurt Serenity again. Now Ashella was on her way to the same freedom with her beloved. Serenity would finally have the happy ending her fans were craving and Catharine would be free of Dark Heart.

At her name Lance's thoughts turned back to the pretty writer. In the lull around him his mind once more began to wander and he pictured her hard at work within. Head bent over her screen, fingers to the keys pressing in a fast and rhythmic pattern. As she strung letters together to form words and words into sentences. He felt his cheek warm where she'd kissed him earlier and he blinked.

His ice blue eyes fixed on the wine god with warning and Dionysus smiled amused. Lance turned his focus to the team of workers trying to ignore the wine god's power pressing at him.

"Alright people, places," Dionysus called.

The detective watched as the actors took their position.

"Quiet on the set."

"Heart of Clay scene 52 take one and action."

Lance watched as Artemis stalked the actor playing Davrik in the role on Nivali prepared to carry out the vampire lord's orders. The vampiress wanting the interloper gone. Her prey stood staring at the vampire Lord's tower. His back was to her making him an easy mark.

Nivali drew her sword and moved to attack. As fast as she was, he was faster, dodging the death blow and sliding into the shadows. He drew his own weapon as he prepared to defend himself. His green eyes held pain at facing his Sire's Nivali yet again. He wonders what Ashella had been forced to endure before she retreated from her tormenter before giving the sick bitch control.

"Did you come to rescue her, how sweet, but foolish, beyond the wall you have no power. How did you hope to stand against our Sire?" ,Nivali teased as she swung her blade to cut him down.

He blocked the strike with the flat of his own blade and looked for an opening to once more create a link and draw forth Ashella.

To his growing frustration the cloak moved with him, blocking his every advance, creating a barrier between them.

"I'd have found a way. I'll not let him have you, Ashella, without a fight. You're mine," Davrik hissed as he dodged another blow.

"Silly Dhampirs; he already has," Nivali taunted as she pressed images of what Ashella had seen and endured within the tower after his failed attempt to claim her.

Davrik roared in rage and swiped at Savarin's servant as his eyes began to shift from green to red. He fought back the blood lust, reminding himself this was not his enemy, this was Ashella he needed only to bring her back.

"Not yet, he hasn't. Ashella you are not lost yet fight my beloved," he murmured as his thoughts pressed into her mind reaching deep to find her there. Aware his fighting her was only driving Nivali's blood lust, he lowered his sword and drove the blade into the ground. He dodged her attacks and she shrieked with frustration.

"Fight me dhampirs," Nivali snarled.

"I will not fight with you Ashella," He whispered in reply.

"You can't dodge me forever half-blood, eventually I'll strike you."

"If you injure me I can endure it my love," he assured her.

"I'm not talking about injury fool I'm here for your head at our Sire's command," Nivali snapped.

"If you kill me then the Ashella I know and love is gone and I don't want to live in this world without her," Davrik murmured. He winced as the blade of her sword sliced his arm.

"I got you," she said with pleasure.

"It's only a scratch, Ashella," he assured her as the scent of his blood was carried on the evening breeze.

"Stop calling me that," Nivali hissed.

"No it is your name and who you are. You are more than this beast Syvarin seeks to make you. You are mine," he breathed as he grew still.

He watched as Nivali lifted her blade for a killing stroke that never fell. Red eyes became amber as Ashella returned.

"Davrik, please kill me before I fall, she's become too powerful I don't know how much longer I can fight her back," Ashella murmured, her voice weak and weary.

Davrik nodded he drew his sword from the earth and prepared a killing blow but the blade arches wide and he releases the hilt unable to do as she asks. "I can't, I won't."

"Davrik..."

"Ashella, listen to me, she is not the dominate mind, you are. She told me herself she cannot act in full if you do not give into your anger. She needs you to rage in order to take over. Stay with me," he entreated before reaching out to touch her, the cloak about her, lashed out piercing his hand again preventing him from getting near her.

You will not touch her again Dhampirs I'll not allow it. The spirit that dwelt within the cape hissed.

"You answer to my Father's blood. That blood flows through my veins you will answer to me this night," Davrik roared. He drew upon the power that resided within him and pressed his mind and will upon the spirit within the cloak. The spirit pressed back tendrils growing drawing more blood weakening him.

"Davrik, no stop this," Ashella cried with fear as she watched him fall to his knees. She knelt down at his side but made no effort to touch him, fearful of the cloak.

Davrik did not answer her or even acknowledge the request. His green eyes glowed with the strength of his power and the cloak gave way, tendrils retreated. His bloody hand caressed an ivory cheek wiping away her tears.

"I will not let you go," he whispered. Davrik kissed her forehead and ran his fingers through her long tresses. He kissed her lips lightly as he reached to remove the offending garment that had dared to harm her.

Once more the cloak came alive with fury, its barbs lashing out at him and her as well. While it had let him pass, it would not grant him the right to remove it. Only Syvarin himself was powerful enough to do so.

Ashella screamed in pain. "Kill me now," she demanded.

Davrik said nothing he simply refused to discuss the matter any further. He released the clasp on the cloak and the attack ended.

"Then leave me now and I shall do it myself."

Davrik closed his eyes as regret and sorrow filled him. She'd made her choice, he had to honor it even if it destroyed him to do so. "Ashella, please," he breathed as he drew her against him.

"I am yours no more. Go."

Davrik roared in rage at her denial of his claim his eyes glowed with power. "You will always be mine," he snapped before he kissed her.

Lance turned away from the scene knowing what would follow and cursed Dionysus's games. As once more his thoughts turned to the author on the other side of the door. He pictured stepping into the office closing the door and crossing to her side. Drawing her away from her work and into his arms. Kissing her as Davrik was kissing Serenity knowing that he was the dhampirs. Wanting her as she'd described in her book.

He struggled against the mental attack resisting the impulse to open the door even as the fantasy played out further in his mind.

82

Catharine froze at her keyboard as once more she felt the unsettling sensation of knowing Lance was on the other-side of the door wanting to come in. She pressed the save button and sat back in her chair. Drawing a breath, she tried to relax as she asked herself what she would do if Lance opened the door to come in.

She bit her lip as her nerves grew with the realization she didn't know. She turned in her chair to look at the door and her blues eyes settled on the lock. She had time, she could lock it. Part of her knew she should lock it, remove any opportunity for the detective to cross that line, but she didn't move. Despite the danger in her inactivity. She wanted to believe him when he said he was in control. Desired for him to prove stronger than Dionysus and Ares influences alike.

"I'm a fool," she muttered to herself before she turned back to her laptop. If he came in she'd face the consequences and trust that he'd not hurt her.

83 Camelot ruins, Scottish Highlands

Fox Elwood trembled as he found the entrance of a cave in the location the text had referenced. Stepping inside he followed the narrow passage until it deadened. A large rock rose out of the earth and a deep groove marked it where, Fox reasoned, a sword had once been sheathed. But the king's sword was missing; the mighty blade long gone, and he cursed.

Excalibur was lost and any notion of the great discovery he'd hoped for was stolen right along with it.

Camelot was nothing without the sword of legend.

Fox moved back down the passage his excitement having died out and a spirit of dejection settled over him. He moved away from the dig and headed back in the direction of his rental car.

"Where do you think you're going?" Robin's voice snapped as she moved in his direction.

"I need a drink," he muttered.

"Why?"

"Excalibur's gone."

"What?"

"I found the place the records indicated the sword was but the stone was empty."

"It could have been moved don't give up Mr. Elwood, we'll find it," Robin assured him.

"Where, how?"

"Trust me," she entreated.

Fox nodded aware that if anyone could find the sword it was her. Robin knew more about the Arthurian legend than anyone else.

"I'll get started on the research."

"Thanks," Fox said before he got in the car.

"Where are you off to?"

"I still want that drink," he said with a shrug. "Want to join me?"

"Not this time Mr. Elwood," she said her voice cool as winter's frost.

"Robin, I'm…"

"Save it Mr. Elwood, we both know that you're not the least bit sorry for before," she said, her voice held hurt and disappointment.

"Okay maybe I'm not, and why should I be, we both enjoyed ourselves."

"True."

"Why'd you run off Robin?"

"I don't know, I just figured you'd not want the awkwardness of the morning after. I remember…"

"What do you remember?"

"That you leave during the night. I didn't want to experience waking to find you gone again. Better to go myself, avoid the hurt feelings."

"I've handled the morning after poorly before I'll admit, but Robin I'd no intention of leaving. I knew you deserved better than to wake up and find me gone," he stated.

"I'm sorry, but now you know how it feels."

"Why'd you do it?"

"I got scared," she admitted as he opened his car door and got inside.

"Why? We had a great night…" Fox said confused.

"You got too close, I felt too much, I wasn't going there again. I was ashamed for letting you get that close, I promised myself…"

"Going where again? What did you promise?"

"No, no more words, go get your drink Mr. Elwood, we're not finishing this discussion, I'm not ready to let you in again," Robin muttered before she turned to walk away. Fox closed the car door and turned grabbing her by the elbow, he turned her to face him.

"I think you're a little late on that Robin," he said amused.

"Damn it Fox let me go," she snapped with irritation.

"Not until you answer me. I want to know why you walked out."

"You want, see that's the problem, all you ever think about is getting what you want. You don't stop to consider that you might be hurting anyone when you're getting it."

"Robin…"

"Go get your drink Mr. Elwood, and while you're at it find another dame to chase I don't want the job anymore," Robin snapped before she shook loose of his hold and stormed off.

Fox blinked stunned by her outburst. He contemplated going after her and calling her bluff but instead did as she bid getting in the car and driving away. He'd let her cool off and try talking to her again later.

84 Great Falls, Montana

Anna laughed with triumph and Sam looked up from the book he was reading at the unexpected end to the silence that had settled into the room.

"Got something?" he asked as he rose from where he sat. Crossing the floor he moved to her side to look over her shoulder at the laptop.

"Yes. I'm pretty sure the door Hades is searching for is somewhere in Hawaii."

"Okay so now that we know that what do we do with it?"

"We go out there, figure out which isle it is and pray we get to it before he does."

"Even if we do locate it, it's not like we can seal it."

"I know, but I still think if we can get there before him maybe we can get the key and get rid of it for good."

"How?"

"Open the door ourselves and throw it on the other side," Anna suggested.

Sam blinked, it wasn't a bad plan but he still found he didn't care for it. There were a lot of ways it could go bad. However he didn't have any better ideas and she was right about one thing they couldn't just sit and do nothing.

"All right then pack your things doc we're going to paradise," he muttered as he gave her shoulders a squeeze. He watched as Anna closed out her laptop and set to work.

Maybe now that they had a clear purpose and destination she'd relax a little. He didn't like how on edge she'd been since they left Israel. He knew it had to do with her troubling dreams, he only wished he knew what they were and that he had a way to shield her from them.

Turning his thoughts from the matter he began the task of packing, as well recalling what Lance had said, he was better off not knowing. As he worked, he wondered how Lance was doing with his own troubles with the Fallen. He hoped the detective was keeping the War God at bay. The last thing that any of them needed right now was for Ares to get any stronger.

85

Los Angeles, California
Tuesday
8pm

Lance watched as the wine god and his bride retreated up the stairs to their wing of the house, flushed with the days successful film shoot. He didn't have to speculate as to what they were up to, the wine god had been pushing images of his plans for the woman since he watched her perform the turning point moment in Heart of Clay.

Dionysus's mental assault had not let up since, at random moments he found himself reflecting on the scene and Artemis's face changing to that of Catharine's as he took the place of Davrik. He cursed as the image ran through his mind once more to torment him and wished in that moment he'd stayed naive to the fact he was the Damphirs.

His eyes moved from that of his host to his charge. She rushed up the steps, her laptop in tow headed for her room and Lance figured he'd not see her again until dinner. Her focus was on the book which was where he'd told her he wanted it but at the moment he would have preferred to have her attention. The lust the wine god was pressing upon him was maddening, when it was one-sided. He wanted her to distraction and she seemed oblivious.

"SHE'S AWARE OF YOUR INTEREST DETECTIVE," Ares assured him with amusement as he too watched the pretty writer with a growing hunger, he knew that as long as they were under the wine god's roof would be denied them both. "LET HER BE FOR NOW, WE HAVE WORK TO SEE TO AS WELL," Ares reminded.

Lance stepped in his room and closed the door. He crossed the floor to his work space and powered up the laptop. Sitting down he opened the internet and began the task of researching information on the sword in his possession.

As he read through various sites and posts pertaining to Excalibur, he hit one by a Dr. Robin Chase and Ares got excited. He pressed at Lance to contact the doctor. Not having anything else to go on Lance picked up his phone and dialed the good doctor's number, he hoped the expert on Arthurian legend would be able to shed some light on the matter.

86 Camelot ruins, Scottish Highlands

Robin set down her magnifying glass and wiped sweat from her brow as she finished the translation from the fragments of the round tables remains. She looked up and noted the rest of the crew was milling about, some working others staring and she cursed as she found herself wishing Fox hadn't wandered off.

She figured right about now he was throwing back his third shot and working his charms on some pretty local. Her mood soured at the idea even as she reminded herself she could have been there instead and had passed on the chance even going so far as to tell him to do just what she figured he was doing.

Robin stretched as she got to her feet and began the task of packing up her things for the day. As she put her tools in her bag her cell phone began to ring. She cursed figuring it was Fox checking in and told herself to ignore it. As it rang a second time she reached for it despite herself and connected the call.

"Hello."

"Dr. Chase?"

"Speaking, and you are?"

"Lance Roman, I'm doing some research on Arthurian legend and your name came up as the expert on the subject."

"I do teach a course on the subject, I don't know that I'd call myself an expert," Robin began flabbergasted by the conversation, wondering how he'd gotten her number.

"Everyone I've read so far sites you, that tells me you're the expert," Lance explained.

"How can I help you Mr. Roman?"

"I'd like to meet Dr. Chase, and discuss the legend in depth with you. I have something I think you might find interesting," the man Lance answered cryptically.

"I see, and how soon were you wanting to have this discussion?"

"Can you be in LA tomorrow?"

"Look Mr. Roman, I don't know what this is about but tomorrow isn't possible, I'm a bit busy at the moment with another project," Robin said dismissively her intent to end this bizarre call.

"Whatever it is Dr. Chase, you'll want it to wait, believe me. what I have for you will be far more fascinating," The man Lance muttered.

"I'm working on the ruins of Camelot I doubt you can beat that in priority," Robin snapped irritated. Who did this guy think he was?

"I'VE GOT EXCALIBUR," Lance Roman stated, his voice having changed suddenly to something dark and powerful that made her tremble both with fear and excitement.

"That's a bold claim, considering there have been many replicas made and other fakes," Robin answered.

"IT WAS DRAWN OUT OF A STONE IN A CAVE SOMEWHERE IN THE SCOTTISH HIGHLANDS, I'LL SEE YOU TOMORROW," Lance stated before he hung up.

Robin blinked, then cursed. She punched in a number she'd promised never to call and waited for Mr. Elwood to pick up.

87

Fox Elwood threw back his sixth shot and tried not to think. He was completely depressed and there was nothing right now that could draw him out of his funk. Not even the pretty blonde sitting at the end of the bar who'd been trying to catch his attention since she finished her second beer.

Nothing was going according to plan. They'd found Camelot but it was worthless without the King's Sword and Excalibur was gone. Lost somewhere or worse stolen. His efforts to fix things between him and Robin were proving pointless as well. She'd been avoiding him since their night together in Israel.

As the liquor burned through him, her words from earlier circled round in his brain, like a swarm of bees, stinging him.

"I still want that drink," he said with a shrug. "Want to join me?"

"Not this time Mr. Elwood," she said her voice cool as winter's frost.

"Robin, I'm…"

"Save it Mr. Elwood we both know that you're not the least bit sorry for before," she said her voice held hurt and disappointment.

Did she really think that he had no regrets for the way he behaved before? He'd dropped the apology earlier, wanting to avoid upsetting her further but damn it he'd meant it. He felt bad for his choice now.

Wished he could take it back. Was dumbfounded to think she'd done it to him this time. Why had she left it wasn't like her?

"I got scared," her vague answer echoed in his mind and he again wondered why only to receive her same muddled response.

"You got to close, I felt too much, I wasn't going there again. I was ashamed for letting you get that close…I promised myself…"

Going where again? What had she vowed after he walked away? Why was she pushing him away? When he pushed her for a reason, she'd let him have it.

"You want, see that's the problem, all you ever think about is getting what you want. You don't stop to consider that you might be hurting anyone when you're getting it."

"Robin…"

"Go get your drink Mr. Elwood, and while you're at it find another dame to chase, I don't want the job anymore," Robin snapped before she shook loose of his hold and stormed off.

Fox rubbed his temple as a headache began to build behind his eyes. Maybe he'd do just what she'd suggested forget the whole damn thing and her, he'd never been good at relationships. Why did he think he could try with her anyway? Why did he want to?

He groaned having no answer but whatever the reason it had him ignoring the blonde at the other end of the bar and thinking about a woman who wasn't there and for all intense purposes had no desire to be there. This was madness, he muttered even as his phone rang signaling an incoming call. Looking down at the annoying interruption he noted the number and smiled.

"Ello," he said dropping his 'h' and cursed he was drunker than he'd realized.

"Mr. Elwood, are you drunk?"

"A little," he admitted. "What can I do for you Robin?" he asked curious.

"I wanted to let you know I'm taking a few days off from the dig."

"What? Why?"

"I've got a lead on Excalibur."

"You do?"

"Yeah got a call earlier from some guy named Lance he claims he has the sword." Robin muttered.

"And you're taking him seriously?" Fox asked with disbelief.

"Yes, he told me It was drawn out of a stone in a cave somewhere in the Scottish highlands," Robin explained.

"You're not going alone," Fox stated.

"I'll be fine, Mr. Elwood."

"This guy could be dangerous," Fox argued.

"Fine he wants to meet tomorrow so you better be ready to go."

"I'm on my way back."

"I'm making flight plans now," Robin stated before she hung up.

Fox paid for his drinks and left the bar headed back for the hotel to pack.

88 Los Angeles, California

Dionysus lifted his head from his wife's breast as he became aware of another presence in his chambers. Artemis stirred as he rose from the bed.

"HECATE," he whispered in greeting not bothering to dress.

"Dionysus, forgive the intrusion but I have news I thought you'd be interested in."

"I'M LISTENING," the wine god assured her as he poured himself a glass of wine.

"This news does not come free," Hecate muttered.

"WHAT DO YOU DESIRE LADY?"

"A word with your bride," Hecate answered.

"YOU'LL HAVE IT," the wine god assured her as he led his guest out of the bedroom.

"Hermes has discovered the secret of the mantles, his attempt last night to steal it was to strip you of your powers. He is a genuine threat to you…however there is a means to negate his efforts and I'll share it with you," Hecate murmured.

"AND FOR THIS KNOWLEDGE ALL YOU WANT IS A MOMENT WITH MY WIFE?" Dionysus asked.

"That's right cup bearer all I want is a chance to speak with her and your guests," the woman answered.

"YOU'LL HAVE IT," he assured her.

"This is what you have to do," Hecate began with a smile as she whispered the secret for him alone to hear.

"THANK YOU MY DEAR, I'LL NOT FORGET THIS GIFT."

"You're welcome now, if you'll excuse me I've got words to share with your pretty princess," Hecate whispered. She watched pleased as the wine god dressed before walking off.

89

"What do you want witch?"

"To warn you against trusting the wine god to much, his influence is a powerful one, the taste of his blood a drug that few can resist once tasted. Many have surrendered all they hold dear to feed that thirst."

"What's your point?"

"The thing you guard, that he craves is your father's crown…"

"I won't be giving it to him…"

"Ah, but consider carefully the matter huntress giving him the crown maybe less dangerous than if Hades gets to it."

"My uncle can't reach it, I've sealed it beyond his reach."

"You are mistaken girl, your father's key is not the only one to the underworld nor is the door in the lost city the only one out there. Hades has his key and is searching for the lock. Hermes will soon seek another. Better your husband reach the crown before either of them," Hecate suggested before she turned and left

90

Lance froze in his research and looked up as he became aware he was not alone. Part of him had hoped it was Catharine standing behind him but he'd known better. His ice blue eyes went cold at the sight of the woman behind him, knowing that the clever agent, Blackwood was no more. The figure who stared back at him was Hecate.

"Detective, I see you've not yet surrendered the war god's sword. A wise choice, Hades would rip your sweet Serenity to pieces if he had the chance."

"What do you want witch?" Lance muttered, having no interest in his uninvited guest, the last time their paths crossed she'd thrown him into the damn dream world and made him hurt Catharine, only to bed her and find it was not Catharine in his arms but the witch.

"I come with two purposes, the first concerns your little hunt," Hecate teased, as she skimmed her fingers over the key board of the laptop.

"WHAT ABOUT IT?" Ares voice asked intrigued.

"I know many of the fallen's old secrets, one of those is where the missing gem lays in wait," Hecate revealed.

"WHAT DO YOU WANT IN RETURN FOR THIS GIFT?" Ares requested weary. Hecate was not a voice he trusted. The others indulged her, seeking to win her favor but the war god knew better. She was a schemer and a threat, if left unchecked.

"Help me to slow down Hermes. He's found the secret of the mantles. He's moving to strip the others of their power. You alone now are beyond his reach. If he succeeds, no one will be able to keep him from the crown."

"WHY DO YOU CARE WHO GETS THE CROWN, WHAT'S IT TO YOU?" Ares questioned.

"I've no desire to see Him in the seat of power, we both know he's not worthy of it nor is he capable of it," Hecate whispered, as she brushed her fingers against his cheek.

Ares resisted the impulse to flinch having no desire for physical contact with the woman, knowing she was only looking to manipulate him. "I'LL DO WHAT I CAN TO SLOW THE MESSENGER DOWN," Ares vowed, having no interest in serving yet another of his brethren.

"Thank you, the stone you seek lies in the bottom of sea," Hecate whispered.

"YOUR OTHER PURPOSE HERE?" Ares prompted.

"I'm aware of your host's current troubles with Hades and the wine god, I thought perhaps I could ease him," Hecate murmured as she ran her fingers down the side of his face.

"Don't touch me witch," Lance snapped outraged as he once more took control.

Hecate laughed at the change. "As you say detective, but if you change your mind..."

"I won't."

Hecate turned and left headed in the direction of the door without another word and Lance drew a breath. Glad she was gone, as he tried to sort out what had happened in the moments leading up to Hecate's caress. He found he didn't know.

"What did she want?"

"MY HELP WITH HERMES," the war god answered.

"What did you get in exchange?"

"YOU'LL FIND OUT SOON," Ares assured him before falling silent.

91

Catharine jolted at the sound of her door opening and closing, turning she looked up to see not Lance as she'd feared but worse, Hecate.

"You're not welcome here witch…"

"Relax, Serenity my visit is not malicious in nature, nor is it meant to cause trouble. I'm here because of what Hermes is up to."

"Why?"

"You know why you wrote it," Hecate said amused.

"You hate him, you want him to fail."

"That's right."

"Okay then, what is he up to?" Catharine asked. She sat and listened as Hecate explained.

"What about the horn, won't he need it?"

"Yes, he'll need it, most of all to ensure his power remains after he steals the others."

"Then Anna and Sam are in danger," Catharine whispered.

"I'm afraid so, but there is a way to keep him from hunting her."

"How?"

"I'll tell you, if you answer my questions first," Hecate offered.

"What questions?"

"Simple ones really, about your detective."

"You want to know about Lance?" Catharine asked confused.

"Yes, I do?"

"Why?"

"Curiosity. How do you think he's holding up against the sword?"

"I think he's doing okay, it would be easier without Dionysus playing with him I suspect," Catharine answered.

"He scares you at odd moments doesn't he?"

"Yes," Catharine confessed.

"I thought as much, and you should be scared; the war god is moving in secret. What will you do if he takes control?"

"I don't know…"

"Why do you linger?"

"I won't leave him, the moment I do, he'll be lost to Ares for sure," Catharine whispered.

"You're welcome then," Hecate said with a smile.

"For what?"

"I gave you what you wanted, I gave you Lance instead of Kurt as the war god's flesh," Hecate laughed.

"I don't want Ares, I want the detective," Catharine muttered.

"Sweet Serenity, so naïve, no one ever escapes the war god, once he set his eye on you; he'll hunt you forever. This way at least you'll still have what you desire as well," Hecate quipped.

"Enough, witch you got your answers now give me mine!"

"One more, do you love him?"

"I don't know what I feel where he's concerned, it's all mixed up after being lost to the wine of Dionysus," she admitted.

"Indeed. But know this, his wine does not create lust; it only enhances what's already there. Nor can it create love; it only draws out an emotion and heightens it."

Catharine nodded. "How can I help my friends?"

"By helping Hermes to seal his power, if they perform the task then they need not worry about his jumping hosts to save himself and they eliminate his need to locate them."

"How?"

Catharine listened as the witch walked her through the task at hand then asked one last question.

"If he can't jump hosts does that mean he can be killed?"

"Yes, but only by the weapon of another god," Hecate whispered, before she turned and left. Catharine blinked, then grabbed her phone and punched in Anna's number and waited for the other woman to answer.

92 Great Falls, Montana

Anna was just finished packing when her cell phone rang. She pulled it out.

"Who is it?" Sam asked, as he set his bag down by the door.

"Catharine."

"Put her on speaker phone," Sam requested.

Anna pressed the button to connect the call and then for speaker phone.

"Hello,"

"Anna, I've news on what Hermes is up to."

"From who?" Sam asked.

"Hecate. She said Hermes is trying to steal the other's powers, if he can get their mantle in a mortal's hands…"

"The whole thing starts again," Anna whispered with insight.

"Yes."

"But won't he be stripped of his power as well?" Sam asked.

"Yes, which is why he'll be coming for the horn, unless you take steps to keep him from needing to," Catharine replied.

"What steps?" Sam demanded.

"Hecate said there is a way to seal his power. Once it is done the fallen can no longer switch hosts at will or by force."

"They can be killed," Sam said with excitement.

"Yes."

"Why would Hecate tell us all of this?" Anna asked.

"She hates Hermes, more than anything, she wants to see him fail," Catharine stated.

"But she's not just giving us Hermes, this gives us the others as well, the question is why? What is she playing at?" Sam wondered aloud.

"Does it matter, this will keep Hermes from your door?"

Catharine replied.

"Okay, what do we have to do?" Sam relented.

"Take out the horn and each of you put a drop of blood on one of the sapphires. Once that's done, remove the tainted gem and destroy it," Catharine revealed.

"Okay, thanks for the tip," Sam said.

"How's Lance?" Anna asked.

"He's struggling, but still in control for now. The wine god is complicating matters."

"You might want to get out of there," Sam advised.

"I can't leave him alone, if I do he'll be lost," Catharine said with certainty.

"Be careful," Anna requested.

"I will," Catharine assured her.

"Keep us posted on any changes," Sam demanded.

"Of course," Catharine answered, before she disconnected the call.

"What do you think, should we do what she said?" Anna asked as she put her phone away.

"I don't know, Zaharrah said that Hecate was more dangerous than the fallen, if she's letting us know this, I hesitate to act, there is no telling what consequence the act will have. Even if it works, what is it she gets out of the exchange?"

"But…" Anna prompted seeing he was conflicted.

"If it's true it would give us one less thing to worry about and a way to kill these bastards," Sam muttered.

"Perhaps we should pray about the matter and sleep on it. The answer may be clear with daylight," Anna suggested.

"All right, let's get out of here, we'll worry about this tomorrow," Sam agreed and the pair left the hotel together it was time to get in the air and on their way.

93

Los Angeles, California
Tuesday
9pm

Catharine turned back to her laptop, ready to get back to work but Hecate's words rang in her mind, Ares was moving in secret. She wondered if it were true as she speculated on what Lance might be up to. She hadn't seen him since they left the film shoot.

Rather than worry about him, she reasoned she could knock and check on him, but pushed the notion aside quickly. He was fine, she assured herself even as she admonished herself for letting Hecate get to her. Having set the matter aside, she reasoned she'd see him at dinner and went back to work on the novel.

94

Lance listened to the exchange next door and wondered what Hecate had wanted with Catharine. As he contemplated the matter, Ares became agitated warning that he should not trust the witch. The war god nudged him to check on the pretty writer and make sure she was okay. The detective was ready to ignore him when it occurred to him just how devastating being faced with Hecate might be to her.

The witch was wearing the face of the woman Catharine had been forced to watch Kurt torture and rape. It was only a few days ago Catharine had been so desperate to forget that nightmare, she'd contemplated giving into Dionysus's offer for aid to escape them. Lance crossed the floor to the door to knock but as he got near it his mind flashed to what Catharine had said earlier.

"I heard you at the door last night," Catharine blurted out.

"I didn't open it."

"You wanted to and he wanted you to I felt his presence."

Lance blinked, as he recalled all too well standing in front of the door, struggling against Dionysus's influence and Ares nudging. Seeing again the fevered dream that had started the whole bizarre incident.

In his mind he'd pictured crossing to the door, sliding the key in the lock and opening it. He'd seen her sitting in front of her laptop, lost in her story; oblivious to his presence.

"Not for long," he'd vowed. Telling himself she'd ignored him too long that day already. He'd crossed the threshold and moved into her room to stand behind her. He'd reached over her and closed the screen with a snap. She turned her blue eyes full of irritation and outrage. Lance silenced her objection to his action by drawing her out of her chair and into his arms. His mouth slanted over hers claiming it with demand.

Lance cursed as the memory became more intense and he felt his body begin once more to stir as the wine god pressed his mind with power.

Her lips came alive under his answering his intensity, with a hunger all her own. Her arms wrapped around his neck and he eased his grasp upon her, indulging in the need to touch her. She gasped, startled and then moaned with delight as she arched toward him her body craving more.

"Yeah, now I've got your attention," he breathed before he kissed her again. His hands fisted in her clothes and he drew back, heart pounding wildly. "Tell me to go now Serenity," he murmured, aware if she didn't, he wouldn't be able to draw back later.

"I don't want you to go detective," she whispered before she grabbed him by the shirt and drew his mouth back to hers and kissed him.

Lance's hands tore her shirt off of her, tossing it aside with disinterest before moving to remove her slacks. He wanted her naked in his arms. Wanted to see the body he'd been dreaming of. She trembled against him thrilling in the feel of his hands on her as he stripped her. Hungry eyes settled on her form only to growl in frustration at finding his view was barred by her underwear.

He reached for her bra, his intent to remove it but instead he shoved it aside to indulge in the feel of her under his hands, it wasn't long before touching her wasn't enough to satisfy him. His mouth fell on her breasts to her pleasured cry as his hands slid down her body and inside her panties to torment more excitable erogenous zones with the promise of what was yet to come.

He felt the bite of her nails on his scalp as she begged for more and groaned to find her wet and ready. When he pressed inside her, she cried out as her body trembled with her first release. His eyes locked with hers to find her pupils wide with her arousal, no fear lingered in her gaze and he closed his eyes overwhelmed by the raw need in hers. Lance drew his finger out of her only to press it back in harder deeper. She moaned at the sensation, as his touch built the next wave of her passion.

His other arm wrapped around her waist as his mouth left her breasts to kiss down her belly. As his tongue darted into her navel he could smell her desire and he felt an overpowering need to taste her. He played her body now with more urgency adding a second finger pushing her over the edge. As her body quaked, he drew out of her and brought his fingers to his lips to satisfy his own rising hunger. The beauty before him watched transfixed as he indulged in his first taste of her.

Lance's eyes fell shut as he licked his fingers unable to meet her gaze. The taste tore through him like a hurricane and he pictured removing her panties to really taste her, could feel her nails biting his skin, hear her desperate sounds of pleasure as he did so. He groaned as his jeans became uncomfortable and contemplated shedding them but knew the moment he did that he wouldn't be able to hold himself back. The thought of shedding his clothes had his mind filling with images of pressing inside her to take her. Different places, various ways.

It was as he pictured bending her over her damn desk to have her from behind, his eyes flew open.

Reality crashed in on him once more to find he was standing beside the door. His skin burned as before with desire for the woman on the other side. He wanted to open it now not to check on her as before but to have her. He wanted to feel her under him, body trembling with her passion, wanted to look in her eyes and find no fear, hungered for a taste of her.

He lowered his hand to his side struggling against the mental attack, even as Ares began to whisper for him to open the door and take what was his. Reminding him of how she'd wanted him. Lance argued that she hadn't been herself, that Dionysus had caused her desire and the war god laughed.

"IS THAT WHAT YOU THINK THAT NONE OF IT WAS REAL?"

"Yes," Lance admitted with hurt and regret.

"SHE WANTED YOU DETECTIVE, SHE STILL DOES, DIONYSUS'S POWER DOES NOT CREATE EMOTIONS OUT OF NOTHING HE SIMPLY INTENSIFIES WHAT'S ALREADY THERE BY REMOVING INHIBITIONS," Ares said amused.

"She's not ready for this; ready for me," Lance muttered knowing it was too soon after all she'd endured.

"IF YOU GO TO HER NOW SERENITY WILL YIELD TO YOU, YOU HEARD HER, SHE KNEW YOU WERE THERE AND DID NOTHING, MERELY WAITED FOR YOU TO MAKE YOUR MOVE. SHE WANTS YOU, WHEN YOU TOUCH HER SHE'LL BE READY FOR YOU," Ares assured him.

At the words, unbidden the image from the dream flitted back to the surface, he watched as his hand slid under her panties to touch her, fantasy shifted to memory as he recalled the night he'd touched her for real to find her as the dream suggested, hot, wet and ready.

Lance pressed a heated cheek against the wooden door, cooling his flesh as he fought against the impulse to take the key out of his pocket and open the door. As he drew a breath and struggled for control Dionysus's power pressed against him, again wrapping him further in the net of lust he'd cast about him. Lance's mind fell back into the dream he'd run from.

Lance opened his eyes as her body shook in his embrace. He gave her body a parting lick as he lifted his head and got to his feet. Scooping her up in his arms he lay her down on the bed and watched as her lashes fluttered to look up at him as he began to undress.

He watched transfixed as she sat up and took hold of his jeans freeing his aroused flesh from its confinement, warm hands wrapped around him and he cursed, his eyes slamming shut as her warm mouth wrapped around him to taste him.

Lance's eyes shot open once more turning away from the dream; he had to stop this, he told himself aware it was trouble but found he didn't want to, he wanted the dream wanted her whatever way she was willing to give herself, but he wasn't about to go there if she wanted no part in it. At the thought Ares words ran through his mind again.

"SHE WANTED YOU DETECTIVE, SHE STILL DOES, DIONYSUS'S POWER DOES NOT CREATE EMOTIONS OUT OF NOTHING HE SIMPLY INTENSIFIES WHAT'S ALREADY THERE BY REMOVING INHIBITIONS," Ares said amused.

Lance reached in his pocket and took out the key to look at it. It burned in his palm and he slipped it in the lock.

"OPEN THE DOOR DETECTIVE, OPEN THE DOOR AND YOU'LL SEE I SPEAK THE TRUTH," Ares whispered.

Lance turned the key and pressed the door, opening it a crack, just enough to see her within. As he'd pictured, she sat at her laptop, fingers poised over the keys but she didn't move. Her body was tense and he knew in that moment she was aware of him watching her, was waiting to see what he would do. Experimentally he nudged the door open further to gauge her reaction. She simply went back to typing as if his watching her didn't bother her. When she said nothing, he was emboldened and stepped across the threshold wanting to get a rise out of her but none came; she simply kept working.

"YOU SEE, SHE'S SUBMISSIVE, EVEN GIVEN YOU YOUR FANTASY SCENARIO, SHE WANTS YOU," Ares said amused.

Lance stood and watched her for a couple minutes longer and imagined crossing to the desk closing her laptop as he had in the dream, making it real but when he pictured moving to kiss her the image shifted to the reality of what had happened the last time he tried to kiss her.

Lance closed the last few inches between them and kissed her. His hands fisted in her hair pulling lightly, tilting her head back so he could get a better taste.

Catharine gasped startled and eased back. He looked at her his blue eyes held questions and confusion. "I'm sorry Lance, I just..." she began unable to explain the mix of emotions running riot inside her.

"Too fast," he whispered with understanding. She nodded sheepishly.

Lance blinked as if coming out of a daze and cursed, mentally feeling ashamed for the thoughts that had been running round in his brain. She wasn't ready for any of it and he knew it. His flesh cried out in protest as he turned away from her retreating back into his own room. He slammed the door shut and locked it before retreating into the bathroom.

He turned on the shower as his mind again threw him back into the maddening fantasies that had been plaguing him throughout the day.

Ares laughed as the detective stepped under the freezing cold spray of the shower, clothes and all in a bid to combat his raging libido.

When he closed his eyes, he groaned as the shower did nothing to cool his lust.

Catharine knelt before him naked save for a disheveled bra, her mouth warm and wet wrapped around him bringing him dangerously close to release.

"Serenity," he cried not sure what it was he wanted from her in that moment. His passion divided between the desire to have her finish and the hunger to lay her back on the bed and finish what he'd begun. He pictured her now under him arching up to meet him as he filled her depths with his body and made his choice. Drawing back from her mouth, he eased her back on the bed.

"No more," he breathed before crawling over her moving in to claim what he desired most. His lips met with hers as he slid inside her slowly savoring the sensation of her body wrapping round every inch of him. He drew out again in the same manor only to drive back in hard and all at once. She tightened round him at the shock of pleasure and he groaned as he struggled to wait her out.

When her body stilled, he began to move, racing now towards his own climax. His lust crazed mind playing out other ways he could have her when they were done here. He felt his body strain with the coming release and pressed harder increasing his pace. When she went over again he followed.

Lance blinked as the fantasy shattered and he cursed to find he was in his damn shower. Icy water pelted him through drenched fabric. His body strained, painfully aroused within its confinement and he groaned. When did it stop?

"IT'LL STOP WHEN YOU GO TO HER," Ares whispered.

Lance snarled at the fallen in warning before his mind tried to fall back into dream. His eyelids lowered and for a moment he saw her laying back over her desk him standing over her moving inside her driving them both wild with the pleasure of it.

His eyes flew open and he tore at his sodden clothes, needing to be rid of them. He pressed a cheek against cool tile at the ease he found for burning skin, his eyes fell shut only to fall into another image. Once more she was stretched out over her desk. Only now her back was too him and he was taking her fast, hard without quarter, she was begging for more, nails biting his ass as she drew him closer still.

Lance's eyes shot open and he realized his hand which had been working to peel off drenched clothes was now wrapped around his aroused flesh moving to silence the storm tearing through him. He blinked. God, what was he doing? He didn't want this, he wanted her but not like that, she wasn't ready for any of that, for that matter neither was he.

"Help me," he muttered, as he sank down to the shower floor with disgust at his actions, he was behaving no differently than a damn stalker. Reaching up Lance turned off the water and sat silent as his blood finally began to cool. His stomach rolled with disgust as guilt crashed through him for his behavior and then anger flared within him.

"You said you wouldn't interfere."

"AND I HAVEN'T," Ares snapped in hostility. "I HAVE NOT ONCE FORCED YOUR HAND," he reminded.

"You've been pushing…"

"NO, I'VE BEEN GIVING YOU INSIGHT INTO MATTERS YOU DON'T UNDERSTAND."

"I don't want your opinion on the matter so from now on shut up," Lance muttered.

"AS YOU LIKE DETECTIVE BUT MY SILENCE WILL DO LITTLE TO CHANGE WHAT HAPPENS. THE WINE GOD'S INFLUENCE GROWS STRONGER WITH EACH DAY THAT PASSES. THE NIGHT OF THE BAUCCHAE DRAWS NEAR."

"What?"

"YOU SAID YOU DIDN'T WANT MY THOUGHTS ON THE MATTER SO I'LL SAY NO MORE, FIND IT FOR YOURSELF," Ares quipped, before he fell silent, leaving Lance to his own thoughts.

Lance rose from the shower and dried off. Moving into his room he pulled on a pair of pants and slipped into bed. He'd had enough of the fallen and their games for one night.

95

Catharine pressed the save button on her laptop before closing the lid her hands shook for a moment involuntarily with the memory of the image of Lance stepping into her room standing over her silent, watching her.

She still couldn't believe he'd come in. Had been afraid that whatever he'd been tempted with, she'd soon know but in the end he'd turned and left closing and locking the door. She'd soon after heard the shower and had little difficulty imagining what he might be up to now.

What startled her was her reaction to knowing he was watching, while she'd been frightened at first, part of her had soon wanted him to stop staring and make his move. She wanted him. Not the mindless longing she'd felt under Dionysus's spell but the mild desire she knew as her own. She blinked as she tried to understand the ramifications of what that wanting might mean for them if he did cross the line, from looking to acting out his fantasies. It was a dangerous line she was walking now and she knew it, one wrong step and they both would be lost to the war god.

96

Robin woke to the rhythmic sway of her hammock rocking in a familiar sea breeze and smiled knowing instantly where she was, she stretched lazily not yet ready to get up.

"MAY I JOIN YOU ROBIN," a familiar voice questioned and her violet eyes opened to meet with blue-green eyes, ones she knew well. They gleamed with excitement at the sight of her and her heart began to race.

"Sei," she breathed his name with wonder, as many times as she'd dreamed of this place and him he'd never been there when she woke, she'd always had to seek him out. Here he was asking to share in her resting place. She licked her lips nervously as she recalled his question when last they met. His words echoing in her mind. "PRETTY ROBIN, WILL YOU LET ME LOVE YOU HERE?"

She understood that something had changed between them that night. He was asking now for permission to share her bed. Robin hesitated, unsure if she wanted to change the dynamic of their relationship. He was her comforter here, a shoulder she cried on in secret when the world around her became too much. Though he was but a dream she cared for him deeply and she didn't want to lose that closeness.

Robin contemplated getting up, following him back down to his manor but as she did the sea breeze stirred. It whipped through his golden hair. The spiky and wild shoulder length mane danced on the breeze, longer bangs curled at his ears in the humidity.

Robin bit her lip as she recalled the feel of the heat of his golden sun kissed skin pressed against her back as he held her close. The wonderful sensation of his fingers skimming over her skin. "Of course, welcome," she answered.

"THANK YOU," he breathed. She felt the hammock sink as he

settled down beside her. She closed her eyes as his arms drew her back against his chest.

Somewhere overhead seabirds called as the hammock swayed lazily beneath her. She felt his fingers skim down her shoulder and along her arms and smiled, this was heaven, she mused as she lost herself in Sei's caresses.

97

Poseidon reveled in the feel of Robin's body so near his own. He'd waited for this. When they first met in the dream she'd been like a wild bird frightened and timid, wounded even. He'd led her slowly in his seduction, where his brothers would have forced her. They were fools, they'd never understood women.

He'd learned in his time among mortals that women did not respond well to force, they were far more enjoyable when they came willingly. He'd sought her while she was vulnerable and had been leading her since. At their last meet he'd asked her if she would let him love her in this place. It had not gone as he'd hoped. While she'd not refused him, she'd not consented either. She still wasn't ready and he knew why.

FOX. Despite how the mortal had hurt her, she still cared for him. Wasn't ready to move on yet. Poseidon mentally cursed at the reality that the man was looking to reconnect with her. Was beginning to realize he loved her. The lord of the sea was running out of time.

Poseidon's gentle caress ran back up her arms and then changed course to trace along the strings holding her suit top in place. His fingers skimming from her neck to the swell of her breasts.

"Sei," she breathed his name with contentment and he smiled.

"DO YOU LIKE THAT PRETTY ROBIN," he asked gently before he brushed a kiss on the side of her neck.

"Yes," she said her voice lazy revealing her relaxed state.

"CAN I TOUCH YOU?" He requested as his fingers slid along the perimeter of her suit top. Enticing her flesh with the promise of the pleasure she could know if she let him.

"Sei," she began in refusal as her eyes popped open.

"NOTHING MORE ROBIN, I JUST WANT TO TOUCH YOU," he assured her as his hands brushed over her covered breasts giving her a taste of what he was offering. She stretched like a cat under his caress and he thrilled knowing he had her. She said nothing, simply nodded before settling back down against him.

The sea god kissed her shoulder as one hand untied the strings to her top. He folded the teal fabric down revealing her breasts to his hungry gaze and drew a breath seeking restraint, he had to go slow with her or she'd run. His hands wrapped around her flesh cupping it as the suit had, fingers teasing the peaks to aching awareness. He leaned over her, lowering his head toward a straining peak aware she was ready for his next move.

As his mouth wrapped around a hardened nipple, his hands slid down her belly to introduce her to the sensation. He wanted her to get used to the idea of him touching her so, wanted her to desire it.

He watched as violet eyes flew open and cursed as the reality of what he was doing to her crashed in on her.

"Sei…"

"SORRY, GOT CARRIED AWAY, PRETTY ROBIN, YOU OVERWHELMED ME," he admitted feigning embarrassment. He fixed her top knowing he'd taken her as far as she'd allow. He kissed her shoulder and squeezed her in a reverse hug, letting her know the encounter was over.

'It's okay, that was amazing, I'm just…"

"NOT READY, I KNOW. I DON'T WANT TO PUSH YOU," he stated.

"Yeah."

"NO MORE TONIGHT, THEN, COME WE'LL GO BACK TO THE MANOR HAVE A MEAL, PERHAPS WALK ALONG THE SHORE," he suggested as he rose from the hammock giving her the space he knew she needed. He drew her up and when she got to her feet, he brushed a tender kiss on her lips before turning to lead her in the direction of his home within the dream realm.

"Thank you," she said gratefully.

"PRETTY, ROBIN I LOVE YOU, I DON'T WANT TO DO ANYTHING THAT WOULD HURT YOU," he whispered. His words were rewarded with her moving to his side, allowing him to wrap an arm around her waist. As he walked, he let his fingers skim along her hip.

"Sei, about what you asked before," she said nervously.

"YES," he said his voice casual.

"I think that I can, but…"

"NOT YET," he finished.

"Yes."

"I CAN WAIT," he assured her as they came to his patio. He sank down on one of the deck chairs and was pleased when she sat down in front of him. Sinking back against his chest once more. He again let his fingers skim down her arms and then up her legs. She shivered and he watched as goose-bumps rose on her skin in his wake. Again her eyes fell shut as she relaxed under his touch.

He traced the path of the cord of her top, skimmed along the perimeter of the suit top and then moved lower. The tips of his fingers slid down her belly with the lightest of touches, careful to not startle her again. Then rubbed along the waistband of her suit bottoms. Before heading back up to safer territory.

"Sei," she murmured his name with contentment and emboldened he untied her suit again and his hands brushed over her skin slowly, avoiding getting to intimate with his exploration too quickly. Allowing her to discover on her own what he'd done.

98

Fox watched as Robin's smiled in her sleep, she let out a familiar little sigh that set his blood humming and had the image of her stretched out on the bed naked reveling in his touch fill his mind.

"Are you dreaming about me then Dr. Chase," he whispered amused as a smirk curved his lips it changed to a scowl when her lips parted and instead of his name she whispered another.

"Sei…"

Fox blinked; who was Sei he wondered as her lashes fluttered and parted. Violet eyes opened wide with desire.

"Pleasant dreams, sleeping beauty?" he teased.

"Fox," she gasped startled and he watched as she blushed.

"Sure now you remember my name," He muttered.

"What's that supposed to mean?"

"Who is Sei?" Fox demanded his voice cold with jealousy.

"Sei? He's a character in a romance novel I read after you left," she stated in a rush.

"Oh really? So what's got you dreaming about a fantasy guy?"

"Fox…"

"Come on Doctor Chase give, you have no idea how jealous I was for a minute there," he said with a laugh.

"Not that your ego needs a boast Mr. Elwood but he kind of reminded me of you," she said with shrug.

"Then you were dreaming about me," he said with a smug grin.

"Maybe," she relented.

"I don't want any maybes today, Robin," he whispered before he closed the distance between them and lowered his head to claim her lips. He thrilled as Robin yielded to his kiss and his hands sank into her auburn tresses pulling lightly as he took more. He laughed with victory as her hands fisted in his clothes to tear at them. His hands slid out of her hair to trail down her body. Aware he had her right where he wanted her.

Then without warning she pushed him away.

"No, you can't do this to me again Fox, I won't let you."

"Robin…" he began in protest.

"I'm sorry Fox, but this isn't going to happen…I can't…"

"You can't what?" Fox asked wanting to understand why she was now denying what he knew they both wanted.

"Nothing…just let me go Fox."

"Robin, honey, talk to me, help me to understand this," he requested.

"I can't Mr. Elwood, do us both a favor and once we land just go."

"Damn it, Robin, I told you I'm not going anywhere."

"Stop it Fox. We both know…"

"Don't…don't you act like you know what I'm thinking, feeling; I missed you Robin. I haven't thought of anyone but you…" Fox began but she cut him off coldly.

"You had your chance Fox, you left," Robin said bitterly before she rose from her seat and headed in the direction of the privacy of the bathroom. Fox blew out a breath, mending the bridge he burnt with her might prove harder than he'd originally figured. She was holding a grudge and he had to wonder why.

99

Robin resisted the urge to scream as she locked the bathroom door to ensure he didn't follow her in. The man was impossible. What was wrong with her? She'd just been dreaming of Sei. He was an amazing man and yet she'd been kissing Fox Elwood ready to let him lead her right back into his bed was she nuts? Had she forgotten the pain he'd left her in when he walked out. Why couldn't she get her hormones under control around him…Oh shit!

Robin blinked as a startling fact slid into place in her mind. The night she'd back slid into his bed they hadn't used protection…

"No, Robin, you didn't… not twice," she muttered with irritation. As the reality began to sink in. She wiped her hands over her face. How could she have been that careless again? Hadn't she endured enough? She asked herself disgusted as unbidden memories she'd tried to forget filled her mind. A hand ran down to her abdomen as she recalled a time it had been swollen with the promise of a new life and her tears began to fall.

"Sei, I wish you were here," she whispered her heart breaking all over again. As her eyes closed, she fell once more back into her dream.

100

Fox turned and looked in the direction of the restroom and then down at his watch. He cursed noting how much time had passed. "What's taking her so long?" he muttered in frustration. How could they get through this if she refused to talk to him? Why was she so upset? It couldn't be just that he'd left if it was Israel would never have happened. No there was something else here.

If he was going to get anywhere in his efforts of reconnecting he was going to have to find out just what had happened to her after he left.

101 Hilo, Hawaii

Sam led Anna off the plane and through the airport in Hawaii headed in the direction of the rental car terminal. The two said nothing while in the midst of the crowd of tourists but as soon as he was behind the wheel and the door was shut she spoke.

"Sam."

"Yeah."

"What do you want to do about Hermes horn?" She asked reminding him of their conversation with Catharine the night before.

"I want to go ahead with removing the jewel like Catharine said." Sam admitted.

"You do?" She asked surprised.

"Yeah, as much as I'm not fond of the idea of helping Hecate along with whatever plan she has in motion I'd still rather ward off another encounter with Hermes."

Anna nodded her understanding.

"What do you think we should do?" he asked her.

"I agree with you. I don't want to cross his path if I don't have too." She confessed

"Okay then, once we get settled in I'll get out the horn and we'll see about taking care of the matter," Sam said, the decision made.

102 Los Angeles, California

Dionysus toyed with a lock of his wife's hair as he tried to relax but Hecate's warning kept playing through his mind. It made enjoying his cup a little bit harder.

"Is something wrong my lord?"

"No, just thinking," he assured her.

"What about?"

"Hermes…He tried to steal my cup."

"He's gone, if he comes back he'll have my wrath to contend with," Artemis vowed.

"You're amazing huntress do you know that. You've done an amazing job as Serenity."

"Thank you."

"I hate to ask anymore of you…"

"But," she prompted.

"I need your help in preventing Hermes or the others from taking my power."

"I…"

"I realize that our marriage was not your choice and protecting me is of little interest to you princess, but you must realize that if Hermes succeeds in his efforts to strip me of my power you will be vulnerable both to him and Hades attacks but beyond that these mortals you care for will be as well." Dionysus murmured as he rubbed her back.

"Very well, you'll have my help in this my husband," Artemis vowed.

"Thank you," the wine god said with relief before he kissed her and turned toward her to indulge once more in the taste of her passion.

103 Hades Fortress, Cayman Islands

Hades trembled at the feel of the weight of the large emerald he'd just removed from his candle. The scent of blood still lingered in the air and his green eyes moved from the jewel to the woman whom had made it possible.

Brooke. Ares parting tribute before he betrayed him. The pretty geneticist was now his. The loss of Zaharrah had been a blow to his ego but that was no matter. Now with the destruction of the gem in his hand, he could ensure his power was secure. He could begin once more to hunt the crown and seek his vengeance.

Hades closed his fist around the emerald and using his power crushed it. Green dust fell between his fingers onto his map.

"My lord, come to bed," Brooke requested as she brushed her fingers through his black hair. Hades turned into her caress and leaned down to kiss her. When his lips parted hers, she was dazed and under his spell.

"SOON MY DEAR," he vowed before turning back to his map. He listened to the sound of her footfalls retreating before he focused his power on the dusted map.

"Show me where Dr. Gallagher is," he breathed and focused on the map but nothing happened and he cursed in fury. It seemed Anna's location like the location of the door was being hidden from him. He drew a breath and tried to calm himself recalling his pretty wife waiting for him. "IT IS OF LITTLE MATTER, I CAN STILL FIND ANNA BY OTHER MEANS, ALL I HAVE TO DO IS WAIT FOR HER TO DREAM," he reminded himself, before he turned away from the map in the direction of his chambers to seek out his lovely lady to thank her properly for her help.

104

Robin's violet eyes opened to find she was resting in Sei's arms, still sitting in the deck chair. His fingers brushed over her warm skin in lazy circles.

"WELCOME BACK MY DEAR, TELL ME, WHAT TROUBLES YOU?" he entreated as he used his hands to sooth her.

"Sei, I'm scared," she whispered as she sank back against his chest.

"WHY?"

"The night in Israel…"

"WHEN YOU LET YOUR MR. ELWOOD PAST YOUR GUARDS," he whispered letting her know he knew what she was referring to.

"Yes, I really screwed up."

"HOW SO?"

"I wasn't careful," she muttered.

"IT'LL BE OKAY," he assured her, before he kissed the side of her neck.

"What if…"

"DON'T WORRY ABOUT IT PRETTY ROBIN, IT WILL BE FINE," he whispered before he kissed her. Robin felt a spark of hunger tear through her at his kiss and her mouth came alive under his. His light touch became more demanding; that set her body to aching for more of him. His lips left hers and she fought for air as he peppered her skin with kisses.

A jolt of pleasure tore through her at the feel of his mouth wrapping around her nipple. Her eyes flew open to the sight of his golden head at her breast. Her hands fisted in his hair nails biting his scalp as she urged him on.

"Sei…"

He lifted his head, kissing her racing heart before meeting her gaze. "RELAX, ROBIN, I'M NOT GOING TO HURT YOU, I COULD NEVER HURT YOU AS HE DID. I LOVE YOU, YOU ARE MORE PRECIOUS TO ME THAN ANYONE I'VE EVER KNOWN. I DELIGHT IN OUR TIME TOGETHER HERE AND TREASURE EVERY MOMENT WE GET."

"Sei…"

"LET ME FINISH DARLING?" he requested. Robin licked kiss swollen lips and relented.

"I'VE BROUGHT YOU ANOTHER GIFT. I HOPE YOU'LL ACCEPT IT AND MY LOVE," he murmured before handing her a small box.

Robin opened the lid to find a set of six golden bracelets with dolphins on them that matched with the rest of her jewelry he'd given her. "They're beautiful," she murmured touched.

"COMPARED TO YOU MY SWEET THEY ARE NOTHING," he whispered before he brushed a kiss on her brow. Robin blushed, flattered before she pulled them out of the box to show she was accepting them.

Sei took the first two and secured them around her ankles. He kissed her foot and her knee eliciting a pleasured sigh. When they were secure, he wrapped the next two around her upper arms sliding them into place, his lips brushed her shoulders and then he put the last two around her wrists. He brushed a kiss on her palms and smiled pleased at the sight of her.

"Thank you Sei, for everything. Being here always brings me peace, but why do you want my love when you know it can't last or be real. This is but a dream. When I wake I'll be with him and I…"

"HUSH LADY, NO NEED TO BRING HIM HERE. IN THIS PLACE HE IS THE DREAM AND WE ARE ALL THAT IS REAL. HERE YOU ARE THE FAIR PRINCESS THAT I SEEK TO WOO. LET ME LOVE YOU ROBIN AS HE NEVER COULD."

"Sei…" she began overwhelmed.

"YOU NEED NOT ANSWER NOW, ROBIN, JUST LET ME HOLD YOU FOR A WHILE AND THAT WILL BE ENOUGH UNTIL YOU ARE READY," he assured her, before he kissed her again. Robin melted into his kiss as he held her close. Robin wondered why he would want her, knowing she might be carrying another man's child. His lips parted hers as his hands skimmed over her body.

"Tell me a story Sei, like you did when we met," she requested as she tried to relax allowing him to do as he'd asked. "VERY WELL, I

SHALL TELL YOU THE STORY OF THE SEA KING AND HIS BELOVED," Sei whispered before he kissed her shoulder as his hands skimmed over her body.

Robin lost herself in the sound of his voice. The deep baritone voice was soothing and hypnotic, his words were in another language she didn't understand and yet as he spoke she found she understood him. His words stirred her blood with the desire for him to touch her further. Made her want him.

105

Poseidon thrilled in the feel of Robin's body under his hands at last. He was touching her now in a way that he'd hungered to since that first night they'd met and was confident that the touching would soon give way to more. As his one hand tormented her straining breasts the other slid down her abdomen unerringly toward the waistband of her suit. He traced the line for several moments letting her get used to the feel of his hands in this region of her body before dipping it inside the suit to touch her directly.

Poseidon watched as her eyes darkened with her passion and licked his lips as he reached lower seeking the part of her he desired most. She moaned as he pressed a finger inside her and drew in a breath seeking calm and restraint.

She was so ready for him he wanted to end the seduction here and take her but knew not to rush her, he needed her to want this as much as he did. So rather than strip her bear and fill her he drove his finger deeper into her using his hand to drive her wild.

"Sei, " she cried out, both with pleasure at her fast approaching release and with alarm at just how far he'd taken his touching, aware she was losing herself to him; that soon she wouldn't be able to deny him anything.

"EASY, MY LADY, JUST LET GO, I DON'T WANT YOU TO BE LEFT FRUSTRATED," he whispered as he increased his pace. He reveled in the feel of her body quaking with her release. He waited her out, his hand pulling away the rest of her suit leaving her naked in his arms. Before she came back completely from her dose of ecstasy he began to move again.

Robin eyes flew open as he kissed her and she turned in his embrace pressing her naked body against him. Poseidon smiled as he took hold of her hips and pulled her down against him letting her feel what she'd done to him.

Her hands slid down his body and inside his trunks to touch him. Poseidon groaned at the feel of her hands on him and knew their seduction was at its end; after this meeting she would be his. His mouth met with hers as he used his power to shed his trunk.

Robin's body arched like a bow as his initial entry had her trembling with release, her eyes flew wide as her arms wrapped around him holding him close. Her pleasured cry died out as her mind fell out of the dream. Poseidon groaned to be denied her at the last moment.

106

Robin's eyes shot open and she lifted her head from her hands to look at herself in the airplane's bathroom mirror. She was mortified to find her skin flushed with passion. Her body dangerously aroused from the dream. She bit her lip at the bizarre and wonderful sensation of still feeling Sei moving inside her.

She sighed reveling in the feel and smiled as she wondered why she'd waited so long to indulge so in her dreams. Sei was amazing and not for the first time, she found herself wishing he were real. Her hand moved off her abdomen recalling his request she not worry and she splashed cool water on her face to try and level out her system. Once she was confident she was no longer in a state that might be embarrassing she unlocked the bathroom door and headed back to her seat.

Once more she kept her focus away from her seatmate respecting Sei's previous request of her. Treating Fox as if he wasn't there. Vowing that this time they were really over. As she settled into her book once more, the pilot announced their decent into LAX and she smiled. Soon she'd be out of her seat on the ground and away from Fox Elwood for good. Taking out her cell phone she punched in the buttons to call back Lance Roman.

"Hello."

"Mr. Roman."

"Yes. This is doctor Chase I'll be landing in LAX in less than an hour did you still want to meet?"

"Yes."

"Okay my colleague and I will be headed to the nearest coffee shop, we'll be waiting to meet you," she said before she disconnected the call and settled back in her seat as the fasten seatbelt light came on.

107

Los Angeles, California
Wednesday
12am

Lance hung up his phone and grabbed his keys heading for the exit, he looked back at the door that joined his room with Catharine's and he froze. Leaving her there alone was not a good idea, but he couldn't take her with him, she'd just worry. So what was he supposed to do?

As he contemplated the matter Ares spoke for the first time since they'd fought.

"YOU CAN PROTECT HER BY WARDING THE DOOR AGAINST THE WINE GOD," Ares muttered.

"How?"

"LEAVE IT TO ME," the god of war whispered and was pleased as Lance relented, allowing him to take the reins to protect the pretty writer from the cup bearer's influence. When the task was done he gave control back to the detective and the pair left to meet with Dr. Chase as they left, Lance again asked Ares what the night of the Bauccaei was.

108

Catharine blinked at the sound of Lance's door opening and closing. She heard his footfalls retreat down the steps and was stunned. He'd left her alone with Dionysus after what the wine god had done to her. As she reeled at his abandonment Hecate's warning circled round in her mind.

"Ares is moving in secret."

Unable to silence her fears, Catharine rose from her desk and pulled the key she'd found on her dresser from her pocket and opened the door that joined their room. Catharine flipped on the light and cursed at what she found. The detective's laptop was open to reveal multiple web sites dedicated to the Arthurian legend and Excalibur.

"Son of a bitch, Hecate was right, Ares is moving behind closed doors," she muttered as she began to hunt for the sword to take it. She groaned at finding no sign of it.

"Damn it Lance, be careful," She whispered before crossing back to her room and switching off the light. Closing the door she secured it before sinking down on her bed to rest. Her heart and mind were weary and sleep soon overtook her

109 Hilo, Hawaii

Sam secured the door for the hotel room before he pulled out the horn of the god of knowledge and set it down on the desk.

"You ready for this?" he asked his fiancé as he produced one of his knives.

Anna nodded and offered him her hand. Sam sliced her finger drawing blood and allowed a drop to fall upon one of the larger sapphires that adorned it. He then pried the gem loose separating it from the mantle and sealing its power. He set the jewel aside he'd sort out how to get rid of it later, first he wanted to tend to her.

Sam cleaned the injury then bandaged it with care. Once the task was done he kissed her hand. Anna brushed her hand against his cheek in response and enjoyed the caress. His hands slid over her cheeks as his fingers sank into her hair. Sam kissed her, thrilling in the ability to do so without Dionysus's influence tainting it. Her mouth came to life answering him with a hunger that was all her own. When his lips parted hers she was breathless.

"You're amazing, doc, do you know that?" he murmured.

"Sam…"

"I love you," he whispered before he kissed her forehead.

"I love you too, Mr. Abrams," she said playfully knowing he didn't like it when she addressed him so formally.

"Anna…" he muttered in warning.

"Yes, Sam," she said sweetly.

"You're maddening, do you know that?"

"No one's ever called me that before," she answered with a laugh. "Maybe, Zaharrah was right and you are a bad influence on me."

"I like you this way," he admitted.

"I think I like me this way as well," Anna confessed.

"I'm glad, it will make being married to you interesting," he whispered before he kissed her again.

Anna melted into his kiss, losing herself in it and his touch, as well as the reminder of his off the cuff proposal. When she was ready, they would wed. She blinked as she wondered how she'd gotten there from where she'd been. Her parents would be disappointed to learn she'd left Ian for good, and more so with her choice in Sam, but she found she didn't care; everything inside her told her that this was right for her.

Unbidden the image of Hades face flashed before her eyes and fear washed through her as she wondered if Sam would still want her if he knew what the lord of the underworld had done to her. She didn't know and the not knowing made her heart ache. As their lips parted, he spoke again.

"What's wrong?"

"Nothing, just bad memories."

"Ian?"

"Yes." She lied not about to get into another discussion about Hades. He'd never hear any part of it from her

"Tell me?" he requested.

Anna nodded and he held her close as he waited for her to speak.

"Well, you know why I left, but that wasn't the end of it."

"It wasn't?"

"No, he used the dig to try and reconnect and I was doing just fine at refuting him until I found Sodom."

"What happened?"

"It was my birthday and he took me out to celebrate, we talked, we ate, I had too much to drink, one thing led to another and the next thing I knew I was waking up hung-over to find myself in his arms."

"I'm sorry," he whispered and he kissed her hair. "He took advantage, that wasn't right."

"He thought that the night before just changed everything and we'd go back to the way it was before Ithaca. He didn't understand when I pushed him away."

"He didn't want you back for the right reasons," Sam muttered.

"I know, I pricked his ego when I left and he…"

"No, need to say more doc, I get it. I can understand why you play prim and proper with strangers, you push them away to avoid getting hurt. It must have really stung that day you found me in the kitchen with Pamela." He said with regret.

"It did, but it's okay now, no need to dwell on it or him," she whispered before she kissed him again. When their lips parted she smiled. "Sam," she whispered.

"Yeah, doc."

"I love you," she murmured and she closed her eyes as she enjoyed his embrace.

110

Los Angeles, California
Wednesday
1am

Lance stepped through the door of the coffee shop, his blue eyes scanned the crowd looking for Dr. Chase. He spotted her in a corner sitting with a man with red hair. He stood and studied the two for a moment and noted a closeness between them and yet it was strained.

Lance made a mental note of the observation then began to cross the room. He watched as the other man lifted his head and green eyes met with his. He smiled whoever the guy was he was quick.

"Dr. Chase?" Lance asked as he approached the table.

"Mr. Roman?" The woman answered.

"Yes, I apologize for the rush on this but I'm glad you made it," Lance stated.

"We were curious," the man stated eyeing him with speculation.

"And you are?" Lance questioned.

"Mr. Elwood is an associate of mine, he insisted on coming along," Robin answered.

"Fair enough."

"You claim to have Arthur's sword," the man prompted.

"That's right."

"May we see it?" Robin asked wanting to get right to the matter.

"Of course, I only ask that you not allow Mr. Elwood to touch it," Lance muttered.

"Okay."

"Follow me," Lance requested as he turned and headed for the door.

"Where are we going?" Fox questioned.

"I left it in the trunk, can't exactly carry a sword in public without raising eyebrows or questions."

Lance watched with satisfaction as the pair moved to follow him. Good he had their curiosity piqued. He unlocked the trunk and pulled out Ares sword still in the sheath.

“It’s magnificent” Robin murmured as she gawked at it.

“It’s missing a gem,” the man muttered with mistrust.

“Yeah, that’s the problem…”

“You say you found it in a cave in the Scottish highlands,” Robin questioned.

“Not personally no, I acquired it from a man who got it there.”

“Acquired it how?” Fox questioned with suspicion.

“It’s complicated, I’ll explain it shortly, but I need to find out where the missing piece is.” Lance stated.

“Robin head back to the hotel and get started on that research,” the man stated.

“Fox…”

“Go, Dr. Chase I’ll finish things here with Mr. Roman.”

“Fine,” Robin muttered before she turned and left.

“Fox?”

“Yeah.”

“Things seemed strained between you and Dr. Chase.”

“What of it?”

“Can you handle working together?”

“We’ll be fine, Mr. Roman so forget your concerns you’re not sending me out of here.”

“Why is that Fox?”

“I’m not about to leave Dr. Chase alone with a complete stranger.”

“Relax, Mr. Elwood I’ve no intent of harming Dr. Chase I’m a cop.”

“A cop? If that’s the case detective then tell me how you came by that sword.”

“I got it from a suspect he was using it to kill women.”

“Oh, hell.”

“Yeah, now you understand why I hesitated to speak of it with your Dr. Chase present.”

“All right detective we’ll help you with your sword, but I want you to help me figure out what happened to Robin in this past year.”

“I’ll help you Mr. Elwood but you may not like what I find.” Lance warned.

“I don’t care, she ran from me and the not knowing why...”

Lance nodded his understanding, then closed the trunk and shook the other man’s hand before getting in the car, he watched as Fox Elwood left before starting the car and heading back for the house.

111

Robin sat in the lobby of the hotel trying to sort out what she was doing there. She was furious with herself. Fox had said go and she'd left like an obedient dog. Why? He was nothing to her. Their relationship was supposed to be purely professional now. As she thought it, she groaned realizing the answer. Fox was in charge of the hunt and he'd used that boss tone as opposed to the casual conversational one.

Now she was sitting here waiting for him to get back so she could give him a piece of her mind. She was aware that he was probably at the moment giving Lance Roman the third degree about himself and the sword and where did he get off playing overprotective lover. They'd had sex; one night, it hadn't changed anything! She knew that better than most. She wasn't so naïve as to think it meant he would stay.

She had wanted him from the first time she saw him, despite knowing his reputation; had been naïve enough at the time to think maybe she could change him. Now she knew that had been a foolish sentiment born of pride.

She'd hurt him as well with her ideas, had known his reputation and passed judgment on him same as everyone else but had never bothered to learn why he ran from true intimacy. Now she was punishing him for what she'd known he would do and was acting all wronged after their latest encounter when she was the one who had left him.

She said it was because she didn't want to feel that pain again but part of her knew it had been in some need to hurt him as he'd hurt her. She'd let him get close and now she was punishing him because she was expecting him to leave and yet he hadn't. He was staying. He'd been trying to get close to her since then and she was pushing him away.

What was with him? For that matter what was wrong with her? She had what she'd wanted a year ago, Fox staying and she didn't trust it. Her temper faded and she headed for the elevator. No longer having any desire to face him. Feeling a terrible mass of conflicting emotions. Needing a distraction Robin headed back to her room to get started on her research.

112

Lance stepped through the front door of James Hardagen's home and moved up the steps to his room. Upon walking through the door he froze. His instincts buzzed telling him someone had been in the room. At first he suspected his host but as he looked about, it became clear to him that it wasn't the wine god who'd invaded his turf but the pretty writer next door.

Lance glanced over at the door that divided their room with interest, how had she gotten in? He figured he had Dionysus to thank for it. Lance closed his eyes trying to quiet his mind and he pictured her as she'd been earlier sitting in front of her laptop lost in her work. He crossed to the door and opened it to confront her. His plans derailed as he opened the door to find her not hard at work but sprawled on the bed lost in sleep.

"WAKE HER," Ares urged with agitation wanting the trespass addressed immediately. Lance didn't budge, he instead stood silent and watched her. Pleased to see her resting peacefully, it hadn't been too long ago she was avoiding sleep like the plague for fear of nightmares, it seemed that when Dionysus released her mind the nightmares had faded along with the lust.

Lance closed the door and locked it once more. He wasn't going to disturb her rest. He'd confront her in the morning for now he'd see about the man Fox Elwood's request.

113

Fox Elwood sat in front of his laptop running a web search on Detective Roman. He was pleased to find that Lance's claim checked out, he was indeed a cop, though not based in LA. Lance Roman was a homicide detective out of DC. Fox wondered what the other man was doing in Los Angeles, until he hit a news article concerning the Fury Killer. It seemed the detective was there originally to catch a killer, though why he was still there, Fox didn't know. He'd worry about it later. Now that he was satisfied that Lance Roman's claim was legitimate he had work to do.

With a little luck he or Robin would soon find the information the detective needed and he would learn why Robin was holding a grudge.

114 Somewhere in the Hawaiian islands

Sam stood on the deck of a ship alongside Anna at the rail. They'd been touring the Hawaiian Islands for hours. Looking for a coastline that matched the one Anna had seen in her vision, but so far she'd seen nothing. As the waves crashed below he dropped the sapphire he'd removed earlier into the sea below.

Anna blinked at the feel of its power swelling and spreading out. As it radiated a second power pushed back and she gasped.

"Doc?"

"It's here," she whispered with certainty.

"Okay, we'll go ashore when we stop and see about a hotel on Kauai."

"Right, after we're settled in, see about locating the cave." Anna prompted.

"We've got some time yet Anna, let's head back to the cabin out of sight until we make land."

"Okay." Anna relented and she allowed him to lead her away from the rail and below deck back to their cabin. As they walked she felt the faint echo of another power and swallowed, Ares power laid somewhere in the bottom of the sea as well.

115

Anna cursed as she opened her eyes to find herself naked in a vast open expanse of parched earth. The ground beneath her was grey in color the soil cracked and breaking. Vents of heat rose through the cracks and where she stood her bare-feet cried out in pain, as the soil broke to become blistering hot muck.

The only focal point beside the burning sun above was a dead tree that loomed before her in the distance. Its branches were like gnarled fingers that she knew, from previous visits to this godforsaken corner of the dream realm, if she got too close to them they would tear at her flesh or ensnare her limbs.

Hades.

He was back.

"ANNA MY DEAR, SO GOOD TO SEE YOU AGAIN. I ENJOY OUR LITTLE VISITS SO, I HAD HOPED TO MEET WITH YOU DIRECTLY AGAIN AS WE DID IN HERMES PALACE, BUT I'VE NOT BEEN ABLE TO LOCATE YOU. HOW HAVE YOU MANAGED THAT LITTLE FEAT?" Hades asked as he drew her back against him.

"I'll never tell you anything." Anna said vehemently as she stepped out of his grasp, just because she'd inadvertently given him an open door to her, didn't mean she was going to accept him.

"I THINK YOU WILL," he said as he caressed her cheek. Anna flinched as she turned away. "I THINK IF GIVEN AN ADEQUATE PUSH YOU'LL TELL ME ANYTHING," Hades murmured, as his hand slid down her neck.

"Stop," she demanded.

"I'LL STOP WHEN YOU ANSWER ME, DR. GALLAGHER," he promised as his hand fondled her breasts and then moved lower to grope the part of her he enjoyed tormenting most.

"Hades…" she cried the name desperate to stop him.

"ANSWER ME ANNA AND IT'LL BE OVER," he assured her before taking his game to the next level crossing the line between touch and molestation as icy fingers clawed inside her.

Anna wept, but did not speak. Irritated Hades withdrew from her and his hand took hold of a whip. He rubbed the lash against her cheek in a twisted caress before letting go of the coil.

Anna screamed as the lash tore her skin, but didn't utter a word.

116

Hades cursed at his prisoner's refusal to answer him, even as he beat her. Her body here was broken bleeding and yet she uttered no words and he knew on the other side bore no scars. He couldn't reach her out there. The way was not clear. The path barred by the power of the Creator.

"WHERE ARE YOU ANNA? JUST TELL ME NOW AND YOU'LL FEEL NO MORE," he entreated as his lash licked the back of her legs. Her body gave out and she screamed a new as she fell to the broken earth, and cracked the crust, scalding her wounded flesh with the heat of the mire below. He dropped the whip and stepped on her back, pressing her deeper into the filth of the earth, coating her in it.

Still she said nothing and he roared in rage as he lifted his foot from her back and kicked her in her side. She turned to her back and cried out again as the muck covered the rest of her. He knelt at her side and once more his hand brushed her cheek, his icy fingers making her cry as they chilled her burning flesh.

Hades drew his hand away from her face and stared at his fingers with disgust. "LOOK AT YOURSELF DR. GALLAGHER, YOU'RE COVERED IN THE DEATH OF THIS PLACE, YOU'RE MARKED WITH MY PRESENCE FROM HEAD TO TOE. DO YOU THINK YOUR SILENCE CAN SAVE YOU FROM ME FOREVER? IT SEEPS INTO YOUR FLESH AS I HAVE, AND WILL,I'LL PRESS INSIDE YOU AND FILL YOU WITH MY LUST. JUST ANSWER ME AND IT WILL END, I'LL LEAD YOU TO MY GARDEN WHERE YOU CAN WIPE AWAY THIS GRIME AND COVER YOUR SHAME WITH A GOWN BEFITTING YOUR BEAUTY." He whispered as his hands slid down her body to torment her once more.

"No," she whimpered in protest to his hands fondling her once more.

"I'LL PUT SANDALS ON YOUR BLISTERED FEET. I WILL GIVE YOU EASE AND REST AND YOUR SHACKLES WILL FALL AWAY AS I'VE NO ILL WILL AGAINST YOU. I'VE SET MY EYE UPON ANOTHER YOU KNOW THAT, I'D MUCH PREFER TO HAVE HER HERE,THAN A SUBSTITUTE. TELL ME WHERE TO FIND THE DOOR AND I'LL LET YOU GO ANNA. TELL ME WHAT I WANT TO KNOW AND I'LL SEE YOU AND YOUR SAM ARE PROTECTED FROM MY BRETHREN'S REACH." Hades vowed using his best offer to entice her and still she spoke no answer.

"SO BE IT, DOCTOR BUT KEEP IN MIND THAT ALL YOU NEED DO TO MAKE THIS END IS TELL ME WHAT I WANT TO KNOW," he hissed before he leaned over her to capture her lips with his own. Kissing her split and peeling, muddy lips as he prepared to complete his torment of her. Even as he pressed her down into the muck with the weight of him over her he cursed. His best move wasn't working, he'd need to rethink his strategy for manipulating Miss Gallagher. She was not going to break here.

117

Sam jolted awake to the sound of Anna screaming. He rose from his bed gun in hand and made his way to her room. Pushing open the door he scanned the dark room but saw no danger. Flipping on the light he found her thrashing in the bed. Sheets wrapped about her soaked in sweat and cursed.

Nightmare.

He set his gun on the nightstand and he sat down on the edge of the mattress and drew her into his arms. His eyes skimmed over her flesh and was relieved to find no mark upon her. Whatever her dream it wasn't reaching her here. Sam kissed her sweaty brow and whispered words to sooth as he prayed for her to wake.

Hazel eyes flew open wild with alarm until they locked with his blue ones.

"Sam," she breathed with relief as her arms wound round his neck.

"Easy," he whispered as he rubbed her back to comfort her. "You okay?"

"Better now," she said with a weak smile.

"What's wrong?"

"Hades is back. He's sealed his power and is looking for the location of the door again."

"He was hurting you."

"Yes, trying to make me talk."

"How?"

"Sam…"

"Answer me doc."

"He beats me," she admitted.

"That's not all of it though, is it?" Sam muttered.

"Let it go, Mr. Abrams," she demanded.

"Anna…" he began, hurt, she'd resort to using that tone when she knew how much he disliked it.

"Please…I can't…" Anna began as she moved to separate herself from him.

"I'm sorry," Sam whispered as he drew her back against him not ready to let her go.

"It's not your fault Sam, I shouldn't have said it like that I don't want to hurt you," she murmured as she rest her head against his chest.

"It's okay doc, I pushed you too hard, too soon, when you're ready," he assured her, before he kissed her brow and let her go, moving to leave.

"Sam…"

"Yeah."

"Can you just hold me for a little while?" Anna asked not wanting him to go.

Sam nodded before he drew her back into his arms, he sank down on the bed beside her and closed his eyes as he ran his fingers through her hair. Anna sank down against him and closed her eyes, it wasn't long before he heard her breathing level out as she fell back to sleep once more. He whispered a prayer that her rest be undisturbed as he too fell asleep.

118 Hades Fortress, in the Cayman Islands

Hades eyes flew open and he roared in rage as Anna's mind moved beyond his reach. His pawn was out of paly. The game would have to change. Looking to his map, Hades smiled. "Show me Sam," he muttered.

He watched as the green dust gathered over the Hawaiian Islands and smiled. His former host's old foe was his way to the door. He'd bluff his way to the crown.

119 Los Angeles, California

Fox Elwood lifted his head at the sound of his phone ringing and cursed. The distinctive tone told him that the one calling was his employer and that he was running out of time in his hunt. Dr. Broody expected results and he didn't like delays.

Fox had hoped for another couple days before the boss man started asking questions, it seemed he was out of time. Pressing the button to connect the call he drew a breath.

"Mr. Elwood, how goes the dig?"

"Things are progressing nicely we've unearthed Camelot and have begun the search for Excalibur."

"That's wonderful news. I look forward to touring the site soon."

"I think sometime next week should be possible," Fox offered.

"Perfect, as soon as you have anything more, contact me directly. I'm on the move at the moment but hope to get back to the main project soon after. There will be an extra seat open with Dr. Lynch gone."

"I'll be looking forward to that opportunity sir," Fox said thrilled.

'With this find Mr. Elwood, you'll have earned a spot," Dr. Broody assured him before disconnecting the call. Fox put down his phone and ran his fingers through his hair. He hoped he'd have answers to deliver when Broody dropped in at the dig. They needed to solve the detective's mystery before the week was out.

Rising from his bed Fox moved to the mini fridge and pulled out an energy drink, he cracked open the can and drank a sip before wincing. The things tasted awful but he didn't know anything better for waking up in the morning.

He crossed to his work station and saved the research he'd been working the night before, then punched in Robin's number and waited for her to pick up. To his frustration it went straight to voice mail and he cursed before it beeped.

"Robin, it's me, I wanted to find out how the research was going, when you get this give me a call," he requested before he hung up and sighed as he wondered how she was doing.

120

Robin's eyes opened to find she was laying on the deck chair beside the pool in front of Sei's home. She blinked as she became aware, his arms were still wrapped around her, their legs tangled. She watched as her lover stirred and brushed his fingers through her hair.

"Sei," she whispered his name with surprise and delight.

"WELCOME BACK, MY DARLING, I HOPE YOU'RE REST WAS PLEASANT."

"He won't leave," Robin groused.

"I'M SORRY."

"I don't understand it. Fox doesn't linger…"

"YOU'VE WOUNDED HIS PRIDE, HE WANTS YOU BACK TO PROVE HE'S STILL IN CONTROL," Sei reasoned as he rubbed her back to sooth her.

"He told me he missed me…"

"HE'S JUST TRYING TO GET PAST YOUR GUARD AGAIN. YOU CAN'T LET HIM ROBIN. HE'LL ONLY HURT YOU AGAIN. IF YOU WANT HIM TO GO YOU HAVE TO TELL HIM ABOUT US," Sei whispered as he rolled her onto her back so that he leaned over her.

"How can I, this is only a dream?" she muttered with dismay.

"DOES THIS FEEL LIKE A MERE DREAM PRETTY ROBIN?" He asked as he slid inside her. Robin hissed with pleasure overwhelmed by the feel of him.

"No, it's so real," she admitted.

"I AM REAL ROBIN, AND SOON WE WILL MEET; YOU WILL KNOW ME IN THE FLESH," he vowed as he began to move inside her. Robin wrapped her arms around him and drew him closer as she breathed his name; wanting his words to be true, for him to be more than a fantasy. "WAIT FOR ME PRETTY ROBIN, DON'T

LET MR. ELWOOD GET PAST YOUR GUARD AGAIN," he requested.

Robin's lips parted and she vowed to wait as he asked. Her lover kissed her and she lost herself in the wave of pleasure that swelled around them.

121

Robin's lashes lifted to look upon her hotel room and she sighed, aware she was once more in the real world. Her blood still hummed with the echo of Sei's passion. She blinked, as she noted her phone was blinking with the message of a missed call. Picking it up, she noted the number and groaned.

Why wouldn't he just leave her alone? She deleted the missed call and the message, having no desire to face him. Rising from the bed she changed and packed up her gear, she was getting out of the hotel room and as far away from Fox as she could. With this goal in mind, she shouldered her laptop bag and left, her heart set on one destination.

122

Dionysus rose from his bed and dressed for the day, as he was buttoning his shirt, Artemis stirred.

"GOOD MORNING MY LADY, ARE YOU READY FOR THIS," he asked as he set his cup down beside her. Artemis nodded as she sat up wrapping the sheet around her.

The wine god took her hand in his and kissed her palm, then her fingertips. Before pricking her ring finger with his fang. He watched as the blood bubbled and pooled and his eyes began to glow faintly red as the thirst stirred within him. He let her hand go and watched as his bride smeared her blood on the largest Amethyst on the cup. "With the mortal blood in my veins, I seal this stone and break the power that binds my lord to this cup," Artemis murmured. The gem pulsed and swirled with an inner light.

Dionysus took a letter opener and pried the jewel free of his goblet. "IF YOU WOULD DO ME THE HONOR MY DEAR," he requested as he handed her the gem.

"I'll keep it safe," she vowed as she accepted the Amethyst.

"THANK YOU, PRINCESS," he murmured, before he kissed her fingers once more sipping her blood to quiet the thirst. He wanted more but now wasn't the time they had to get to the set soon, there was a film to finish shooting.

123

Lance woke with a curse to find himself hot, sweaty and aroused. He didn't remember what he'd been dreaming but hand no doubt who he'd been dreaming about. As he threw off the sheets and sat up Lance made plans to grab a shower but his thoughts were derailed as the war god laughed. A deep dark rumble of delight that chilled the detective to the bone.

"What is it?" Lance asked curious and frightened.

"I FELT IT."

"Felt what?"

"THE MISSING GEM FROM THE SWORD."

"You did? Where?" Lance asked surprised.

"THE WITCH SPOKE THE TRUTH, IT'S IN THE SEA," Ares said with shock.

"You didn't believe her?'

:THE WITCH IS FAR FROM TRUST WORTHY. ALWAYS PLAYING AT HER OWN GAME. MY BROTHERS GIVE HER TOO MUCH FAITH. SHE IS A DANGER DETECTIVE, YUOU'D DO WELL TO REMEMBER THAT."

"Right. So, what exactly did she tell you?'

"SHE SAID THE STONE LIES IN THE BOTTOM OF THE SEA."

"The sea, that's less than helpful." Lance muttered. "The sea is huge, I need more to go on than that," Lance said with exasperation as he moved in the direction of the bathroom.

"IT'S A START DETECTIVE BE PATIENT."

"We're running out of time and you know it," Lance snapped, as he peeled off his sweaty clothes and stepped into the shower stall. He turned on the water and rinsed off. He was pleased when Ares said nothing more to him. He'd needed a few minutes to himself.

Once he was clean, Lance turned off the water and stepped out of the shower. Grabbing a towel, he dried off before getting dressed. He turned his focus once more to the task Mr. Elwood had given him, in exchange for his assistance in locating the rest of the sword.

As he looked back through Dr. Chase's financial records, he found an entry from the time Fox indicated, for a large purchase at a baby supply retail store and blinked.

Interesting.

Lance clicked on the mouse prepared to look into the matter deeper when Ares spoke again, startling him.

"I THINK DETECTIVE, BEFORE YOU LOSE YOURSELF IN THIS, YOU HAD BETTER SPEAK WITH YOUR PRETTY WRITER BEFORE SHE LEAVES FOR THE DAY."

Lance blinked at the comment, recalling the fact she'd entered the room the night before without his being there. Knowing what he did about the house, he couldn't let it happen again. Rising from the desk, he crossed to the door to confront her.

124

Catharine stood before the vanity brushing her hair, trying to get ready to go. As she set down her brush, the sense of being watched struck her. Turning she found Lance standing in the doorway watching her.

"You were in my room while I was gone." He said, his voice was cool and hinted of temper.

"I was," she admitted, figuring honesty was best given the circumstances. She didn't want him angry, didn't want to give Ares any chance to slip his leash.

"You had no business…" Lance began in temper and she blinked with disbelief.

"Don't…" she snapped cutting him off. "If you're going to scold me for invading your privacy, then you better turn that pointer finger around and direct it at yourself."

"When I left, I took precautions to ensure our host couldn't disturb you. When you left this room you made yourself vulnerable." Lance stated, ignoring her interruption completely.

"Fine, I'll stay out of your space, so long as you stay out of mine," she snapped!

"What's that mean?"

"Don't play dumb detective, you've opened this door on multiple occasions now and stood there watching me…"

"The two situations are completely different. I'm talking about you're entering my space when I'm not around. You were here…"

"You weren't invited!"

"Like hell I wasn't." Lance snapped, as he crossed the threshold into her room, closing the distance between them. "You knew I was here and said nothing to make me leave." He challenged as he moved closer. "You were waiting for me to make up my mind," Lance accused as he came to stand in front of her so that they were face to face.

"I was waiting," she admitted, "because I wanted to believe your claim that you're in control and not Ares, but you're not. He's got you chasing down information on the sword; looking for something."

"No, he doesn't; I'm in control; not him. I'm trying to learn as much about the sword as I can to avoid trouble. I'm doing everything I can to protect us."

"Lance…"

"I'm not going to let anyone hurt you Serenity," he whispered as he brushed her hair away from her face. Catharine's heart began to pound as he leaned in. she felt the air around her move as he drew in a breath and bit her lip nervously as she wondered what he would do next. His hand then lifted her chin so that their eyes met. "I'm not going to hurt you," he assured her, before he kissed her.

Catharine gasped, stunned, aware that he'd just taken in her scent like an animal and after picking up on her fear, had tried to quiet it. Ares power was growing but at least for now Lance was in control as he claimed. Catharine's eyes fell shut as she let herself get swept away by his kiss.

125

Fox finished the page he'd been reading and glanced to the clock on the screen. He blinked to see how late it was. Glancing at his cell phone, he cursed, noting Robin hadn't called him back. Fine, he'd take a few minutes to go down and speak with her directly.

Getting up from the desk, he grabbed his key and stepped out of the hotel room. He moved down the hall to her room and knocked.

"Robin," he called, to gain her attention, if she was busy at work. He waited a moment then knocked again harder this time. "Damn it Robin, let me in," he snapped irritated by her lack of response! He turned to go but stopped when he spotted a maid just down the hall.

"Excuse me ma'am can you help me?"

"Sir?"

"I've lost my key card and my wife is asleep I can't get in," Fox said giving her his best sheepish grin.

"I'm not supposed…"

"I'll be ever so grateful," he stated, interrupting her as he pulled out his wallet.

"I guess…"

"Thank you," Fox said with relief, as he led her back to Robin's door. He watched as the maid stuck the keycard in the lock and opened the door. He gave her a fifty for her help and then slipped inside closing the door behind him.

Fox cursed again to find the room empty. Looking about he found that Robin's phone was sitting on the night table beside the bed.

"Where is she?" he muttered, as he turned away from the phone and began to pace. He turned his thoughts to what he knew of her. She'd no doubt been wanting to get out of here and away from him to clear her head, but where had she gone? She wasn't familiar with the area.

Fox saw the image of Robin standing on the hillside in Camelot staring off into the distance at the crashing waves below and smiled. He knew where to find her.

126

Robin stood on the seashore staring out at the crashing waves. The tide rolling in, swept over her bare feet and she laughed. She wasn't getting much done this way, but damn, had she needed this. She drew in the sea air and sighed. "Sei," she whispered the name wishing he was there.

"Who is he?" Fox's voice questioned from behind her. His tone held hurt and accusation. Robin jolted at his voice and turned to meet his stare. His green eyes said he knew she'd lied to him.

"I don't know."

"What do you mean you don't know, you've called his name twice now with a longing that speaks of more than friendship, he's important to you, you love him," Fox snapped betrayed.

"I've never met him; he's a dream," Robin whispered and blushed embarrassed."

"A dream?"

"Yes."

"But you love him?"

"Yes," she admitted.

"And me?" he asked as he drew her close to him.

"Fox…" she began in protest as she tried to get away.

"Answer me."

"I don't know Fox, there are a lot of conflicted emotions where you're concerned," she confessed.

"Why did you leave that night?"

"I needed space Fox. When you left it really messed me up. I didn't know if I could go through it again."

"I wasn't going anywhere Robin," Fox assured her, as he rested his forehead against her brow.

"So you say, but how can I believe that," Robin asked as she turned away from him.

"You'll just have to trust me," he murmured as his hands skimmed down her body.

"Fox… stop it, you're not fighting fair."

"Still like that, then," he teased, knowing he was turning her on.

"Maybe," she answered noncommittally.

"Maybe? I'm not looking for a maybe," he muttered as he touched her more intimately.

"Fox…" she breathed his name, the tone spoke of desire and passion.

"There, that's the Robin I know," he murmured and then kissed the side of her neck.

"No Fox, I won't let you do this to me again," Robin stated as she pulled his hands off of her and walked away from him. She grabbed her bag and left.

127

Fox blinked as he watched her go. Pain washed through him and confusion clouded his mind. What the hell?

"I lost her," he whispered with disbelief. Fox laughed with disgust. "Lost her to a damn dream," he muttered. Turning Fox walked back up the beach in the direction of the street. As he came to the road he reasoned he'd need a cab but he didn't see any. His eyes scanned the area but nothing was in focus. "I need answers," he told himself as he looked around again. His eyes settled on a pub and he sighed.

"I need a drink," he said, weary as he made his way across the street.

128

Lance felt his blood heat as Catharine's mouth came alive under his kissing him back. He felt his lust swell and cursed knowing it was time to go. He broke the kiss, breathless and hungry for more.

"Lance…" Catharine whispered his name in question.

"Get away from me Serenity," he demanded his voice harsh.

"What? Why?" she asked hurt and confused.

"I'm not safe." He replied, fear in his own voice.

"Lance…" she began, her intent to sooth him.

"Don't. I'm not okay. I can feel my control slipping. Ares and Dionysus are wearing me down," he confessed.

"You'll be fine," she assured him.

"No, I won't. I stood here and watched you like a damn stalker. I wanted to …"

"Whatever you wanted; it wasn't you, it was Dionysus's influence." Catharine assured him.

"You're wrong, Serenity, they're my desires, my hungers, they're just…"

"Out of control…if the sword is taking you then let it go." Catharine urged.

Lance considered the matter but the second he reached for the sword, he saw a mental flash of Hades, the lord of the dead, he advanced in their midst, took hold of the blade, plunged it in Catharine's heart. Lance watched as she slipped into death with despair and then looked on in horror as the god of the underworld breathed her name calling her back.

When her eyes snapped open, she gasped and her arms wrapped about the keeper of the lost souls and drew his mouth down upon her own.

Hades eyes gleamed as he kissed her, his fingers skimmed over her clothes and they fell away from her as if they'd aged. "NOW SERENITY WE ARE ONE," he whispered, before he lowered her to the ground and trapping her beneath him he pressed inside her and took her.

"IS THIS WHAT YOU WANT?" Ares asked with disgust.

"Of course not," Lance snapped outraged.

"I DIDN'T THINK SO, BUT THIS IS EXACTLY WHAT WILL HAPPEN IF YOU GIVE UP MY SWORD AS SHE'S ASKING."

"How do I know you're not just making it up?"

"WHAT YOU JUST SAW IS ONLY A GLIMPSE OF THE THREAT HE'S BEEN SENDING, SINCE YOU KILLED HIS PET."

"Sending?"

"WE CAN SPEAK WITHOUT WORDS, OUR MINDS ARE CONNECTED. HE'LL TAKE HER THE SECOND HE THINKS I AM NO LONGER HERE TO DEFEND HER."

Lance put the sword back in its sheath. "I can't...if I do you're in danger, but more than that whoever picks it up next won't be able to control it. I won't let it be used to hurt another person."

"Lance…"

"I need space Serenity…I need you to go, get far away from me."

"No. I'm not leaving Lance, the moment I do he'll take you."

"If you stay…" Lance began in warning, but she cut him off.

"I'll take my chances, detective," she answered.

"Why? After what happened to you, why would you linger?"

"Because, I love you,' she breathed, before she kissed him. As he drew her against him, holding her close, she prayed she wasn't making a terrible mistake.

129

Robin sat in her hotel room in front of her laptop reading through yet another version of the Arthurian legend. Normally she enjoyed the tale but today she couldn't get into it. Her thoughts kept drifting back to the beach and what had happened there.

Fox had looked devastated when she'd walked away. She wanted to go back, but her thoughts kept drifting back to Sei and his request. She promised not to let Fox Elwood get past her guards again and that had kept her walking. Now she worried she'd made the wrong choice after all, Sei was nothing but a dream.

Robin sighed, as she turned her attention back to what she was supposed to be reading. As she read, she couldn't help but feel a little like Guinevere caught between two men. But which was Arthur and which Lancelot, she didn't know nor did she care to think further on it. As she read this latest version of the tale, Robin laughed, here was what she was searching for. Picking up her phone she punched in Lance Roman's number, with a little luck she'd be done with this job and on her way. Leaving Fox Elwood in the past where he belonged. As the phone rang Robin wondered if it was really what she wanted.

130

Lance froze, as the sound of his phone ringing registered in his mind. He let Catharine go as he broke their kiss.

"Hello," he said as he connected the call.

"Mr. Roman, I found your legend."

"I'm listening Dr. Chase."

"The tale suggests that the lost piece of Excalibur is in the deepest part of the sea."

"Nice work doctor, what's our next move?"

"I guess we'll need a ship," Robin muttered.

"Set it up, I'll meet you at the docks," Lance said before he hung up.

"You're leaving?" Catharine asked with hurt and disbelief.

"Yeah, it looks like they found what I'm after," Lance revealed.

"Lance, don't…"

"I have to go. With everything that's happened this is the only way to protect you," Lance stated, before he kissed her on the forehead.

"Then I'm going with you."

"What about the film?"

"The film is coming along fine, I can work on the book there and check in to learn about its progress. I'm sure it will be fine. Artemis is doing great with the part."

"You're sure?" Lance asked, surprised.

"Yes. You wanted me away from the wine god and now you've got it."

"Right, then we best get packed," Lance muttered, before letting her go, to return to his room.

131

Catharine drew a deep breath to calm herself once Lance was gone. Her heart was pounding in her chest. She'd just made arrangements to ride along while Lance completed Ares sword. Was she insane? The second the war god's power was fully reached Lance's ability to hold him back would be nonexistent.

What had she done?

She'd kissed him and in that moment she'd felt that same jolt of hunger for him as she'd felt before while she was under Dionysus's influence, just less violent. She'd wanted him. Maybe some of what she'd felt for him while under that spell had been real. Catharine blinked, as she contemplated the matter. She moved to pack and then cursed.

What had she said?

He'd asked her why she would stay and she'd told him she loved him.

Did she really?

Catharine wondered now at the validity of the statement. But found she couldn't deny it, somewhere in the middle of all this madness, she'd fallen in love with the detective and because of that she wouldn't, no, couldn't leave him

Catharine questioned, if under the circumstances what she was about to do was wise. Lance was struggling against Dionysus's influence upon him and losing, she could see it. If she went with him now as she said she would, she was giving him access to her. Inviting him even, maybe.

Catharine didn't know if she was ready for the possibility of things getting physical between them yet, but what she did know was, she wasn't going to let him be alone with Ares. If she did, she feared that Lance would lose the battle of wills.

132

Lance finished packing his things and moved to save the data he pulled on Robin. As he was working, he picked up the phone and dialed Fox Elwood's number. He figured the other man might be able to shed some light on the strange transaction.

"Ello," Fox Elwood slurred.

"Mr. Elwood, I've got a few questions regarding Dr. Chase for the project you gave me," Lance began, skipping a greeting.

"Forget it detective, I don't care about it anymore."

"Why not?"

"I lost her to a damn dream," Fox muttered.

Lance froze at the words and blinked." What?"

"She's mooning over some dream guy she met named Sei. How am I supposed to compete with that?"

"You can't just walk away from this. Your Dr. Chase maybe in serious danger."

"What? How?"

"There are fallen among us, upon their waking they begin courting a bride, the way they do this is in their dreams. There's a good chance your lady friend's dream guy is one of them and if he is, her life is in horrible danger."

"Fallen?"

"It's complicated, I'll tell you more when next we meet." Lance stated before he broke the call and shouldered his bag. He crossed to the door connecting his room to Catharine's and knocked on it. "You ready?"

"Almost, I'll meet you downstairs," she called back.

"Okay," he answered, before turning and leaving the room.

133

Fox sat at the bar, his phone still in his hand, the bizarre conversation he'd just had with the detective still running around in his mind. Fallen? What the hell was the man going on about? He was crazy. Had to be. Fox blinked, trying to clear his head as the phone rang again. He cursed and then felt something inside him ease as he saw the number.

"Ello Robin," he said in greeting.

"Fox, are you drunk?"

"A little," he admitted.

"Well you better sober up, I found the information for the missing piece."

"You did?"

"Yep, it's out in the Marinas Trench."

"Okay, then I'll arrange for a boat," Fox said.

"Fox, about earlier…"

"Don't Robin, I know I hurt you…I just wish…"

"I'll see you at the dock," she stated, cutting him off before she hung up.

Fox sighed, before hanging up on his end and punching in the number for his employer to make arrangements for the boat, he'd need clearance from Broody.

134

Robin put her phone down and closed out her laptop. She powered it down then packed it up. As she worked, she wondered if she shouldn't skip the boat ride and just go. Her part of the job here was done. She wasn't needed for the recovery of the missing piece. Fox could handle it. She considered the possibility of just going now without a word but the opportunity was taken when a knock sounded and then Fox called her name.

Robin answered the door allowing him to come in though she knew it was a mistake.

"Hello again Mr. Elwood," she muttered.

"Dr. Chase, I've secured a ship for our hunt. It looks like we'll be at sea for the next several days."

"I know, I can't wait," she confessed.

"You like the sea don't you Robin," Fox murmured.

"Yeah, I do. I don't know why but there's something about it that draws at my heart. My mother joked, I was a mermaid living on the land."

"Well, you're about to get a major dose of it," Fox stated, before he moved in the direction of the door. Robin followed after him.

135

Catharine stepped out of her room and made her way down the hall to the stairs, as she walked she heard the approach of her host and paused.

"CJ?"

"Good morning, Mr. Hardagen, I'm going to be leaving this morning with Mr. Roman I trust you'll be fine with the filming in my absence."

"Yes, I'm confident we can see your vision for the film completed," he stated.

"Good, I'll be calling once a week to check in on your progress and be in contact via text the rest of the week."

"Be careful out there Miss Nichols," Artemis requested.

"I will," Catharine assured her.

She then descended the stairs to join the detective.

136

Dionysus gave his wife a kiss and bid her start breakfast without him.

"Where are you going?"

"I FORGOT SOMETHING UPSTAIRS I'LL BE RIGHT BACK," he assured her, before moving back in the direction of their room.

After closing the door, he crossed the room to his cup and picked it up. Turning his thoughts to Pamela Walsh, he called her and was pleased when her mind answered with a hesitant yes.

"I THOUGHT YOUR MASTER WOULD BE INTERESTED TO KNOW THAT THE DETECTIVE AND MISS NICHOLS LEFT THE HOUSE THIS MORNING FOR PARTS UNKNOWN. I WOULD ASSUME HE'S LOCATED THE MISSING PIECE OF THE SWORD."

"Thank you, I will let Hades know." Pamela's mind answered.

Dionysus set his cup down as Artemis walked back in the room.

"What's taking so long?"

"ALL DONE PRINCESS," he assured her.

As he moved to join her, Hermes came out of the shadows and snatched the cup.

"GO AHEAD BROTHER, TAKE IT. IT WILL DO YOU NO GOOD. I'VE BROKEN THE CURSE OVER IT. MY POWER IS BEYOND YOUR REACH," Dionysus gloated as he poured his power out into the cup. He watched with amusement as Hermes tipped back the goblet and gulped down its contents. The wine god watched as his brother's eyes blazed with lust.

Dionysus grabbed Artemis and pulled her against him, kissing her with passion in front of the other fallen, as Hermes had flaunted Pamela in the throne room. The lord of knowledge dropped the cup and moved to depart. Dionysus's lips parted from his wife's and he laughed.

"CAN'T TAKE HIS OWN MEDICINE." The wine god mocked. He watched with satisfaction as Hermes tried to open the door and cursed finding it wouldn't budge.

"LET ME GO CUP BEARER!"

"I WILL UNDER ONE CONDITION."

"NAME IT."

"THE LOCATION OF APOLLO."

Hermes snarled at the demand, no doubt aware of what he was up to.

"FINE." Hermes said, desperate to get away from the lust filled temple. Before pressing the information in his brother's mind. With the answer given the seal on the door broke and Hermes left.

137

"My brother?" Artemis questioned?

"A GIFT TO YOU FOR ALL YOU'VE GIVEN ME."

"I am humbled. Your gift exceeds mine. What can I do to thank you?"

"LEAD ME TO YOUR FATHER'S CROWN, PRINCESS MAKE OUR UNION OFFICIAL," he requested.

"I cannot my lord…"

"YOUR UNCLE HAS HIS KEY, IT'S ONLY A MATTER OF TIME BEFORE HE FINDS THE DOOR. HERMES IS SEEKING POSEIDON'S. DO YOU WANT TO SEE ONE OF THEM GET IT?"

"No, of course not…"

"THEN TAKE ME TO IT; BETTER ME THAN THEM."

Artemis blinked at his words, they echoed what Hecate had said to her. "I need to think about it."

"TAKE YOUR TIME, I'LL NOT ASK YOU AGAIN THIS WEEK," he vowed.

"Thank you."

"YOU ARE WELCOME MY LOVE." Dionysus whispered, before he kissed her, drawing her deeper under his spell.

138

Robin followed Fox up the gangplank onto the deck of the Odyssey. She stared out at the water for a moment, before trailing after him down the stairs into the hold below. He opened a cabin, as she walked past him into the room. The door closed behind her and she turned to find him standing by the door.

"What are you doing?" she asked with mistrust.

"There are only two cabins, this one and the other across the hall. The detective has a guest, we have to share this room."

"Oh."

"Relax, Dr. Chase," he muttered as he put his bag down.

"Right, no problem. I just need a minute," she stated, as she set down her bag. She drew a breath, then walked out of the room headed back for the deck to clear her head. As she stared out at the water, her mind drifted once more into her dream.

139

Poseidon thrilled in the feel of Robin's acceptance of him. She was ready and finally they would meet. He couldn't wait. Soon they would be together in the flesh and when they were he'd be within reach of his key and the door. It was only a matter of time before he took his rightful place on Zeus's throne and when he did he would have a bride truly worthy to be called the queen of the gods.

140 Hades Fortress, the Cayman Islands

Hermes stormed through the door into the main hall of Hades fortress. The lord of the underworld glared at him in warning.

"WHAT DO YOU WANT IN THIS PLACE MESSENGER," Hades hissed.

"I seek passage to Miss Walsh," Hermes muttered.

"WHY SHOULD I GIVE YOU ACCESS TO YOUR FALLEN BRIDE, AND MY BEST WHORE?"

"I have news of the wine god's movements, I will give you it in tribute," Hermes offered, his eyes gleaming with the effects of tasting from Dionysus's cup.

"SPEAK PLAINLY BROTHER."

"He is wooing the huntress to obtain her father's crown; time is running out."

"THE NEWS IS A SUFFICIENT PAYMENT, GO SHE IS YOURS TO ENJOY," Hades muttered, pointing in the direction of Pamela's chambers. Hermes moved down the hall and stepped into the room without a word. Pamela rose from the bed at the sight of him and he grabbed her by the arm drawing her against him. His mouth fell upon hers, hands fisted in her golden hair pulling it, taking greedily.

His hands tore at her clothes and he threw her down on the bed. She gasped, overwhelmed, as he drove the proof of his desire in her and began to move. His thrusts were hard and deep, coming at a pace so fast she could do nothing but endure.

"My lord," she breathed his name, with both fear and desperate need as his lips parted hers to bite her neck. He licked the wound, tasting her blood, lost to the wine god's power.

"Hermes," she cried frightened, as his nails tore her flesh marking her. He paid her no mind, caring nothing for her discomfort, fear or even her pleasure, his only interest here was to quench this wretched thirst the wine god had woken in him.

Once his body was spent and his lust slaged he slid out of her and rose from the bed dressing to go.

"You'd leave me?" she asked, hurt and confused at his rough treatment of her and his lack of care for her pleasure.

"OF COURSE, A GOD TAKES A MAIDEN FOR HIS QUEEN, HE DOES NOT ELEVATE HIS WHORE OR ONE OF HIS BRETHREN'S WHORES TO SUCH A STATION." Hermes said as he moved toward the door.

"But you came back…" she began as she moved to get up.

"I PAID A TRIBUTE TO BE HERE PAMELA, I DIDN'T COME HERE TO CLAIM YOU."

"You married me, I'm your bride."

"YES, YOU ARE AND YOU'VE WALLOWED IN THE FILTH OF MY BRETHREN'S EMBRACE. HADES AND DIONYSUS HAVE BOTH DRANK FROM YOUR CUP," Hermes said with disgust.

"But you said…"

"I SAID YOUR PASSION WHEN GIVEN AS A SACRIFICE IS PLEASING, WHEN IT IS INDULGED IN MERELY TO SATISFY YOUR OWN DESIRES IT IS REPULSIVE, ESPECIALLY WHEN IT IS GIVEN TO ONE OF THEM. NO PAMELA, YOU BEAR THE MARKS OF THE WINE GOD, IT IS TO HIM YOUR FLESH NOW BELONGS. ON THE NIGHT OF THE BAUCCHAE YOU WILL KNOW WHAT THAT TRULY MEANS," Hermes warned, before he left without even a second look back.

141

Pamela dropped her head in her hands and cried bitter tears at Hermes rebuff. She couldn't believe what he'd just done to her. How could he speak of love and treat her so? These gods were far worse than any man she'd ever known. As she wrapped the sheet about her, she wondered what the lord of knowledge had been talking about and flipped on her laptop.

Typing in the words night of Baucchae she ran a search and felt her stomach churn with disgust at what she found. Fury burned in her blood as well to find she was no better than a damn concubine. "Hecate. Get me out of here," she breathed and watched with shock as the woman appeared before her.

"Miss Walsh what troubles you?"

"I want nothing more to do with these petty gods," she snapped with disgust.

"I can give you that Pamela, that and more, I can take you out of this pit they've cast you in and elevate you back to the heights you were reaching for. I can give you all you deserve."

"How?" Pamela asked curious.

"Invite me in Miss Walsh, and you will have the power to crush them all," Hecate promised.

"I want that. I want to bring them low as they've made me, I want them to grovel at my feet and beg for the right to touch me or any other mortal again. I want them to suffer!" Pamela raged.

"Then ask me in, Pamela, ask me to help you and I will give you all you desire most. I can give you back your Sam, I can make him forget the upstart Anna, I can even give you back your detective if you wish it, whatever your heart desires, I'll make it so," Hecate bargained.

"Hecate, goddess of the chaotic night, help me, I am your humble servant," Pamela murmured. The moment the words left her lips the woman before her fell to the floor weak and helpless, as Hecate's power left her. Pamela cried out in a wild burst of ecstasy as Hecate's power poured into her. She felt fire wash through her and pain ripped at her flesh as the marks of Dionysus were burned away.

She blinked and her whiskey colored eyes became black as coal.

"Hecate, no you promised me…you can't leave me here like this," Gail Blackwood whimpered in protest.

Hecate ignored the other woman as she opened a pathway of shadow and departed for the lost city, leaving Gail Blackwood to face Hades wrath.

142 Kauai, Hawaii

Anna stood beside Sam, her eyes scanned her surroundings, as they waited for their turn to arrange a room. Her gaze moved to the coastline and she gasped as she spotted Hades standing at the rail of a ship in the process of docking.

"What's wrong?"

"Hades, he's here."

"Shit. How?"

"I don't know. We've got to get out of here if he sees us…"

"Yeah, I know, come on," Sam said as he took her hand to lead her away.

"Wait."

"What?"

"We can follow him."

"What, why?"

"Find out where he is and steal the key."

"Anna this is not a good idea."

"It's better than letting him reach that door," Anna argued.

Sam sighed not liking the idea but knowing she was right. "Okay, we'll do it but not until after we're settled in," Sam muttered, as he stepped up to the desk to get them a room.

143

Port of Los Angeles, California
Wednesday
6pm

Lance and Catharine stepped out of a cab in front of the port of Los Angeles, they made their way down the docks to the birth for the Odyssey and walked up the gangplank. Once they were on board the crew lowered the gangplank and began the task of casting off. The pair moved across the deck to the stairs leading to the cabins below.

As Lance opened the door to usher her in, one of the crew walked by.

"Your presence is requested along with our other guests in the dining hall for a dinner with the captain."

"We'll be there," Lance assured the man, before he stepped in the room behind Catharine and closed the door. She set her bags down and went straight to unpacking her laptop. It seemed she wasn't going to waste a minute.

As he set down his own bag on the bed. he watched her flinch. He could hear her heart racing and cursed, she wasn't comfortable with this. He didn't blame her, he'd been less than stable of late and the idea of being in closed quarters with him probably was unsettling.

"Why don't I see if we can make a change of sleeping arrangements," Lance offered, not wanting to leave her regretting her choice to come along.

"That would be good," she admitted.

He nodded and grabbing his bag he stepped out of the cabin and knocked on the door across the hall.

"Detective?"

"I don't suppose you'd be willing to change up the sleeping arrangements."

"Why?"

"Catharine isn't too keen on the idea of sharing a room and I thought maybe you and I could share a cabin while Dr. Chase and she shared the other."

"I'd rather it stayed as it is but I think Robin would appreciate the change, so yeah let's swap it out," Fox muttered as he opened the door allowing Lance to step inside. The detective dropped his bag and grabbed Dr. Chase's taking it back across the hall.

"Well?" Catharine asked.

"It's all set. Robin will be staying with you instead, I'll be across the hall," he stated. "I'll see you at dinner."

"Right, thanks again Lance."

"No problem," he assured her before he left.

144

Catharine blew out a breath, relieved to be alone and grateful he'd adjusted their arrangements to ease her discomfort. It was yet another sign that the man she loved was still in control. Detective Roman was respecting her need for space. Maybe he wasn't as far gone as she feared.

Turning from her fears Catharine flipped on her laptop and opened the file for her novel; it was time to get busy.

145

Robin blinked as she came back from her dream to find herself standing at the rail staring off at the sea.

"IT'S BEAUTIFUL ISN'T IT?" a male voice asked from behind her, startling her out of her reveling as she became aware, she was not alone.

"Yes, it is," she agreed.

"YOU HEART POUNDS FOR IT, YOU LOVE IT DON'T YOU," he stated as he walked closer.

"Yes, I always have, there's just something about it that calls to me."

"IF YOU WISHED IT DOCTOR YOU COULD BE SWEPT AWAY ON ITS TIDES AND EMBRACED BY ITS WAVES FOREVER," he whispered as he came to stand at her side.

Robin smiled at the idea and then sighed. "It's a pretty dream, but my life is on the land,' she said with regret.

"IT DOESN'T HAVE TO BE MISS CHASE," the man answered at hearing her last name Robin turned to look at her visitor and gasped at the sight of him.

"Sei…" she breathed with disbelief.

"YES…"

"But how can that be you're a…"

"I TOLD YOU I WAS NO MERE DREAM," he whispered, as he ran his fingers through her hair.

"How…"

"I HAVE MY WAYS. I MEANT WHAT I SAID, IF YOU ASK IT OF ME I WOULD GIVE YOU THE SEA IN ALL ITS SPLENDOR," he murmured, and he brushed a kiss on her brow before he turned and left.

Robin drew a breath to quiet her racing heart. She felt a yearning inside for what he offered but something inside her hesitated to answer him. Instead she turned and headed below. When she opened the door to her cabin she found Fox and Lance were both inside.

"You're staying across the way," Fox stated.

Robin nodded and turned, stepping inside the other room. Within a petite redhead sat in front of a laptop typing away. Robin picked up her bag and carried it with her into the bathroom. Now that she was alone, she could deal with pesky questions and fears that were still troubling her mind.

For the second time in her life Robin took out a pregnancy test and went through the motions of taking it. She waited for the results and then tucked them away, not wanting to see them yet. She wasn't ready for the answer. Putting her bag on the bed, she walked out of the cabin and back up to the deck. Running from the answer.

146

Fox watched as his cabin mate tucked the sword away and recalled that the other man had wanted to ask him something about Robin.

"So what was it you needed to know about Dr. Chase?"

"Does she have any family or a friend that might have been pregnant?"

"Not that I know of why?"

"Because your lady friend spent a lot of money at a baby supply store during your year in question."

"She did?"

"Yeah, you ask me Fox… I think…"

"She ended up pregnant," Fox said with shock.

Lance nodded. "There's more…"

"I don't want to hear it detective, not from you," Fox said before he turned and left to find Robin.

147

Lance shook his head as the other man walked out of the room, he'd warned him he may not like what he found. It seemed he'd been right. He had to give the guy credit though for choosing to get the rest from Dr. Chase; rather than him.

He wondered how he'd have felt if Catharine had vanished on him for over a year and he'd learned during that time she'd been pregnant. Lance figured he'd probably feel numb at first, too much to feel all at once, he'd not feel any of it then, well he wasn't sure.

Lance figured it didn't matter because the whole thing was hypothetical anyway. He wasn't about to walk away from her, nor was he going to let her vanish on him. And the rest well, wasn't going to happen anytime soon, Catharine wasn't ready to let him in that deep.

He groaned at the thought, admitting his disappointment in having to switch rooms as they had. Fox had said he'd have preferred to keep things as they were and truth be told so would have he. Lance wanted her close, both for her protection and his own peace of mind, but he'd seen she was scared and he didn't want that. He knew the sort of relationships she'd endured in the past, was aware that his behavior the past few days had to be unnerving. He'd arranged the swap because he wanted her mind to ease. He wanted to earn her trust.

"YOU'RE WASTING YOUR TIME IN THAT EFFORT AND YOU KNOW IT DETECTIVE. TRUST FROM HER IS SOMETHING THAT CANNOT BE EARNED," Ares muttered.

"I think your wrong," Lance stated.

"BY LEAVING HER ALONE YOU'VE LEFT HER UNPROTECTED, DO YOU THINK THAT BEING OUT TO SEA KEEPS HER FROM HADES REACH?"

"No I know better than that, but she needs her space," Lance argued.

"YOU HUMANS AMUSE ME, ALWAYS STEPPING BACK FROM EACH OTHER AT THE WRONG TIME. WE ARE NOT ALONE HERE."

"What does that mean?"

"THERE ARE OTHER FALLEN AMONG OUR RANKS ON THIS SHIP," Ares warned.

"What?"

"YOU'LL SEE, I SUSPECT AT DINNER. IF I WERE YOU DETECTIVE I WOULD NOT LET YOUR WRITER OUT OF YOUR SIGHT," Ares prodded.

Lance pulled the sword from where he'd stowed it and walked out of the cabin. He lifted his hand to knock and the door opened.

"Catharine…"

"Lance."

"Can I come in?"

She stepped aside letting him walk past her and closed the door.

"What's on your mind detective?" she questioned keeping her distance from him.

"Ares says…"

"I'm not interested in what Ares says, and if he sent you over here, I'll ask you to leave," she said her voice crisp and cool.

"He didn't send me Catharine, I told you, he's not in control here," Lance snapped, irritated at her implication.

"I know, I'm sorry, I just wish you wouldn't bring that thing in here," Catharine muttered, eyeing the blade with both mistrust and fear.

Lance cursed, as he recalled the damn thing had not long ago held a different form, one that had been used to leave the wound that was healing under her eye. He lay the sword down tucking it under the bed. "I'm sorry Serenity, I need it right now. He says there are other fallen among us on this ship, he can feel them."

"Oh hell."

"Yeah, I just want you close for now," he confessed.

Catharine nodded. "Well, since you're here, did you want to read the rest of what I've got for the new book?" She asked.

"Sure," he said with a smile, accepting the distraction offered. Catharine crossed to her laptop and scrolled the text back to where he left off last time. Lance moved in behind her and took the seat as she vacated it.

His ice blue eyes settled on the screen as his ears followed her movements. He heard her footsteps retreat to the other side of the cabin. The sound of her sinking down on the bed. Pen on paper as she scribbled more notes. He felt the urge to turn and take the pad from her, to kiss her but instead he turned his attention to Dark Heart and began to read.

148 KAWAI, HAWAII

Sam slipped out of the hotel room leaving Anna secure inside. Once more he gave her his gun for her protection and prayed she'd not need it. As he descended the stairs, he worried that leaving her was repeating an earlier mistake and prayed for peace as he stepped outside.

His gaze moved to the ship that had just finished docking and watched as the lord of the underworld disembarked. Careful not to be spotted, Sam followed Hades at a distance from the ship to where the fallen was staying. Once he had obtained the room number of Hades hotel room, Sam left the hotel and started back for his own. Pulling out his phone he punched in Anna's number.

"Hello, Sam."

"I'm headed back. I've got what you wanted."

"Great."

"I still think this is a bad idea Anna," Sam muttered.

"It may be, but right now it's the best bad idea we've got," she reminded.

"I know, doc," he relented.

"When you get back we'll need to go look for the cave," Anna stated.

"Right," Sam agreed before he hung up. He walked through the lobby for the hotel and headed for the stairs. They'd look for the location of the door, but not immediately not it if he got his way.

149 Somewhere on the Atlantic

Fox emerged from below deck and spotted Robin standing near the rail staring out at the water. As he crossed the deck to her side she did not stir. He cleared his throat to let her know he was there, aware she was lost in her own thoughts.

Robin gasped, startled, then turned and visibly relaxed. "Fox," she whispered his name, glad to see him.

"Robin, can we talk?"

"Yeah, look Fox, I'm sorry for leaving before but…"

"No need, I understand honey. I'm sorry I left you like that it wasn't right. You deserved better…"

"Fox…"

"Why didn't you tell me Robin?"

"Tell you?"

"That you were pregnant."

"You took off after sharing one night with me Mr. Elwood I figured you wouldn't…"

"Wouldn't what? Did you think I wouldn't take care of you, or that I'd have told you to get rid of it?"

"I didn't know what to think."

"Robin I'd have…"

"It doesn't matter Fox, she died," Robin said with pain and regret.

"Oh, Robin, sweetie. I'm so sorry…" he whispered as he drew her into his arms to comfort her.

"So am I…" she murmured, on the verge of tears.

"Robin, you're shaking what's wrong?"

"I'm scared Fox, what if I'm…" she began unable to finish the question.

Fox blinked and cursed his loss of control. Recalling that the night they'd shared in Jerusalem he'd not been careful with her. "If you are then you won't be alone this time," he assured her.

"What if it happens again? What if I…"

"It won't," he whispered.

"You can't know that,' she said with temper.

"We'll do everything that can be done to prevent it."

"Fox, I don't know, not for sure."

"Did you take one of those tests?"

"Yeah, but I couldn't look at it. I got scared."

"Then we'll both take a look at it together after dinner," he said before he turned and lead her in the direction of the galley.

150

Catharine set down her note pad as Lance pushed the chair away from the desk signaling he'd finished reading. "So, what do you think detective?" She asked curious.

"It's really good Catharine, the perfect way to finish out the series. It will make the fans happy. It'll satisfy your publisher but it also redeems Serenity. Brings her full circle."

"You think so?" she said pleased.

"Yeah, but I'm curious, how are you going to end it?"

"I don't know yet, obviously they'll save her but where they'll end up I'm not sure," she confessed.

"You'll figure it out," he assured her.

"Thanks."

"Come on, it's about time for dinner, we should probably get moving."

Catharine nodded and the pair left the room headed in the direction of the galley.

151 Kawai, Hawaii

Anna smiled as the door opened and Sam stepped inside. She was relieved to see him and grateful to have not needed the gun he'd given her this time around. She rose from her seat and shouldered he purse ready to go. Sam crossed the room to her side and took the purse from her, setting it down on the floor.

"Sam," she began in protest.

"Hush, doc we'll go look for your cave but not now. I want to wait until nightfall, but beyond that I want a moment of quiet before things get crazy," he muttered.

Anna blinked at the request and relented. They'd taken very little time to rest since he'd rescued her in Athens. Running from one problem to the next. He was right a few minutes of downtime would be nice. "Okay, Sam, we'll wait a bit. I'll see about room service and we can sit and relax," she offered.

"That sounds wonderful," he said with a sigh.

Anna picked up the menu and picked a meal before grabbing the bedside phone and calling in her order.

"It'll be here in thirty minutes," she stated.

"Perfect, then I have a request."

"What's that?"

"Will you read to me for a bit doc?"

"I guess that can be arranged, anything particular in mind?"

"Something other than Greek myth," he requested.

"Mr. Abrams you've got a deal," she replied with a laugh. She pulled out of her purse an electronic book and flipped through her list of stored titles until she found one that she thought he might enjoy. Opening the file she began to read.

152 Somewhere on the Atlantic
Wednesday
7pm

Lance stepped into the dining hall of the Odyssey and took a seat at a round table beside Fox Elwood. Catharine sat down beside him and took a sip of her water.

"Catharine I don't believe you've met our shipmates yet, this is Fox Elwood and his associate Dr. Robin Chase."

"It's nice to meet you," Catharine said politely.

"IT IS A PLEASURE INDEED," a masculine voice murmured from behind. Lance turned and watched as the captain rounded the table to take the empty seat beside Robin. She blushed prettily at the comment and Lance wondered at the significance as Fox eyed the other man with mistrust and envy.

"LADIES, GENTLEMEN I WILL BE YOUR CAPTAIN WHILE YOU'RE ON BOARD THE ODYSSEY. I HOPE YOU'LL ENJOY YOUR STAY," he said, his blue-green eyes gleamed with amusement and the chef brought out their meal and set it on the table.

"IT'S GOING TO BE AN INTERESTING ADVENTURE," another man said with amusement as he approached the table from the opposite end of the galley. Lance cursed, as he came into focus. Dr. Ian Broody. Catharine flinched and Lance switched seats with her placing her between him and Fox to separate her from the fallen in their midst.

"Dr. Broody…" Fox began with alarm.

"YOU DIDN'T THINK I WAS GOING TO FOOT THE BILL FOR THIS LITTLE VOYAGE WITHOUT OVERSEEING IT DID YOU?" Hermes asked with disbelief.

"No sir, I just figured you'd be busy with other matters."

"I WAS, HOWEVER I FELT THAT THIS EXPEDITION REQUIRED MY PERSONAL TOUCH MORE THAN THE OTHER DIG," the god of knowledge stated.

"SHALL WE HAVE A TOAST?" the captain asked.

"INDEED," Hermes answered.

"What do we drink to?" Fox asked.

"TO THE QUEST, MAY WE LEARN ALL THE TRENCHES SECRETS," Hermes said lifting his glass.

"TO THE SEA AND ALL ITS MANY TREASURES," the captain countered.

"To the sea," Robin whispered as she lifted her glass.

"To life and its many adventures," Fox offered, as he lifted his glass and clanked it with Robin's.

"I think I'll pass on dinner if you don't mind, I'm not feeling that well," Catharine muttered, as she rose from her seat having no interest in a brush with another of the fallen.

"I'll see you later," Lance whispered. She nodded and then left. "To life," Lance said and Robin followed suit before the group drank. When the toast was done they began to eat.

153 Kauai, Hawaii

Sam sat and finished the last few bites of his meal as Anna read to him. She'd finished hers already and picked up the e-reader. He'd lost the thread of the story well before their meal arrived, having lost himself in her voice.

When he finished his meal Sam took the e-reader from her and kissed her. "Enough for now Anna, it's time," he murmured as his lips parted hers.

"To be continued then," she offered.

"I'd like that," he agreed.

Anna put the reader in her purse and the pair headed for the door; it was time to get back to work.

154 Somewhere on the Atlantic

Fox Elwood clenched his hand into a fist at his side as the captain and Robin spoke, the other man had been occupying her time throughout dinner, he kept touching her every now and again like he was now. Brushing her hair away from her eyes, his fingers skimming against her cheek and the shell of her ear. And damn her, Robin kept blushing as if she was enjoying it and the other man's attention. Who was this guy?

Something weird was happening here, before dinner they'd agreed to face whatever answer lay waiting within her cabin, now she'd barely noticed him since that damn toast. It was like she was under some sort of spell.

Fox watched as the captain leaned closer and whispered something in Robin's ear and felt the impulse to rise from his chair and pull the two apart. To tell the other man to back off; she was already spoken for, but knew that if he did Robin would be outraged and he'd only be pushing her closer to the captain. So instead he rose from the table, brushed a kiss on her brow and told her he was going to get some fresh air. She didn't respond and he felt his nerves begin to grow. There was something wrong here, but what he didn't know.

155

Lance sat eating his meal watching the others. He wasn't shocked when Fox left, he couldn't blame him. Understood how he'd have felt if another man was wooing Catharine in front of him. He'd want to separate them, make it clear she was claimed and no doubt with Dr. Chase that was the wrong thing to do, so Mr. Elwood had left before he did something to upset her.

The detective was not surprised either when the captain took the lady he was wooing by the hand and led her from the room, leaving him alone in the dining hall with the former Dr. Ian Broody.

"YOU KNOW WHY I'M HERE," Ares voice hissed out of him addressing Hermes directly.

"I DO," the lord of knowledge confirmed.

"IF YOU INTERFERE MESSENGER…"

"RELAX WAR LORD I'M HERE FOR POSEIDON'S KEY NOT TO STOP YOU FROM OBTAINING YOUR MANTELS FULL POWER," Hermes assured him.

"SEE IT STAYS THAT WAY BROTHER, YOU NEED ME AT FULL STRENGTH TO STAND AGAINST HADES AND WE BOTH KNOW IT," Ares warned.

"INDEED. I MUST SAY YOUR NEW HOST IS AN IMPROVEMENT TO YOUR LAST ONE BROTHER AND YOUR BRIDE…"

Lance grabbed the fallen by his shirt collar and drew his fist back ready to hit him. "ENOUGH!" Ares snapped, as he eyed the messenger god with contempt. "LET'S MAKE THIS CLEAR YOU STICK TO YOUR BUSINESS AND STEER CLEAR OF MINE. YOU'RE NOT TO GO NEAR HER. NOT HERE OR IN THE DREAM REALM. I'LL BE STANDING GUARD THERE, IF I SEE YOU THERE…"

"YES, YES," I UNDERSTAND NOW KINDLY GET YOUR HOST TO RELEASE ME," Hermes snapped.

"NOT YET, I'M NOT DONE. DON'T TALK TO HER, IN FACT IF YOU SO MUCH AS LOOK AT HER AGAIN; I'LL END YOU." Ares growled, as Lance released his hold on the other man shoving him away from him.

"RELAX WAR GOD I'VE NO DESIGNS FOR HER."

"GOOD, BECAUSE SHE'S OFF LIMITS," Ares stated, before his power receded and Lance once more took over.

"Stay away from us, fallen one," Lance stated, before he rose from the table and turned to go as he walked, he pulled out his cell phone and punched in Sam's number. He figured the spy might want to know what was transpiring here. Lance walked out of the galley, as he waited for the other man to pick up; leaving the schemer alone with his musings.

156 Kauai, Hawaii

Sam wiped sweat from his brow as the cave he and Anna had entered grew warmer. The dark passage into the deep of the earth was quiet and still and the air stunk of sulfur. They'd been walking for a while now and the only sound was that of their feet on the ground, the sound of their breathing and the pounding of his own heart.

This was it; he was sure of it. He could feel the hairs on his neck standing on end. He'd wanted to turn back satisfied but Anna had insisted they needed to know the layout of the passage, so that when they came back they'd know exactly where to go in case they were being chased.

Not for the first time Sam looked back the way they'd come, checking the shadows to be sure they weren't being followed.

"I found it," Anna called from somewhere ahead and he turned to face her. He swallowed as his lantern illuminated a vast opening that came to a dead end and there, where she stood was the indentation in the earth for the key their enemy now carried. Hades door.

Sam cursed, as his cell phone rang breaking the silence around them. He dug the offending object out of his pocket and noted the name on the caller id. "Lance," he breathed the name both with trepidation and relief, he hadn't heard from the other man for days and had begun to worry.

"Put it on speaker," Anna requested.

"Hello."

"Sam I've got news on the fallen front."

"What's up?"

"I'm on a boat right now bound for the Marianas Trench and I've got unwanted company in the forms of Hermes and Poseidon, unless I've missed my guess. Hermes claims he's here for a key and I figure Poseidon is as well."

"Ah hell, thanks for the news, but what are you doing there?"

"He's trying to complete the mantle," Anna said with disbelief.

"I am," Lance confirmed.

"Why would you do that, the only reason Ares hasn't taken you is that missing piece…" Anna began in warning.

"If I have it I can keep Hades at bay," Lance argued.

"If you have it; Ares will win," Sam warned.

"I can handle it, and if I can't, I've got a failsafe in place," Lance stated before he hung up.

"A failsafe?" Anna questioned.

"He's going to have Catharine kill him," Sam muttered.

"No, that's terrible. Why would he do this?"

"To protect her and us," Sam muttered.

"That's crazy," Anna said, with disbelief.

"So is proposing to steal the god of the underworld's key to hell, but that's what we're about to do. Come on doc, we've got to move. The clocks ticking and time's running out." Sam stated, as he turned and headed back toward the surface.

157 Somewhere on the Atlantic

Robin stood once more on the deck of the Odyssey staring out at the sea and the stars above. The captain had left her to get the gift he'd promised her at the table. She smiled at the thought. She could barely believe that this was real. He was real her Sei.

"Robin," a woman's voice called from behind, drawing her out of her musings. She turned to see the woman Catharine and greeted her. "I'm glad I caught you alone I wanted to warn you…"

"To warn me, about what?"

"Your captain, he's not what he seems, he's dangerous."

"Sei, isn't dangerous, he's been nothing but a friend to me and a gentleman," Robin snapped with temper.

"You've met him before?" Catharine asked with alarm.

"Yes, many times…"

"In your dreams," Catharine suggested, and watched as the other woman blanched.

"How did you know that?"

"I've met two of his kind the same way, and believe me there is nothing kind or safe about them."

"But he's been so…"

"It's a lie, for what your heart longs for, only to trick you into surrendering to him willingly. He's not a man Robin, he's a god. Being his is not a thing you should desire he is damned and he'll only hurt you," Catharine warned.

"A god? That's…"

"Crazy I know, but it's true, be careful and don't let him make you forget."

"Forget, what?"

"Who you are, what you love and that you're not alone." Catharine stated, before she turned and headed back below.

Robin blinked, trying to sort out the bizarre conversation. It wasn't long before her thoughts receded and she was once more lost in the beauty of the ocean and the night itself.

"Sei, where are you?" she murmured and as soon as the words left her lips, she fell into the dream realm.

158 Kauai, Hawaii

Sam sat beside Anna in the sand on the beach and watched the tide roll in. it was a beautiful night and he'd have liked nothing more than to be spending it with her but that wasn't in the cards. Instead he was going over the reckless plan they'd put together again.

"I still don't like this," Sam muttered, using her as bait to draw out the fallen was not a pleasant prospect but he knew she was right, it was the only way to pull this off.

"I'm not overly fond of the idea either Sam, but it's our best option. I'll draw him away from the hotel, you just concentrate on getting in there and grabbing that key."

"What if he has it with him?"

"He won't when I meet him in the dream realm, I'll tell him that if he comes near me I'll steal it. He'll not risk that…"

"I wish there was another way, leaving you exposed like this, unprotected…"

"I'll have your gun Sam and I'm a good swimmer, I'll be fine," she assured him.

Sam nodded. He drew her into his arms and kissed her hair. "I love you lady," he breathed as he held her close.

"I love you too Sam," she whispered. "Now get going we've got a key to steal."

"Not yet, I'm going to stay with you until you fall asleep," he whispered as he tucked her head under his chin. She sighed, and sank back against his chest and closed her eyes. As she slowly sank into sleep, he prayed she'd be safe.

159 Somewhere on the Atlantic

Poseidon crept down the stairs from the captain's quarters onto the main deck where Robin stood waiting for him, lost in the dream realm. In his hand he carried the gift he'd promised her, he couldn't wait to see the look on her face when she opened it. Having it here in the real world would complete their courtship. The upstart Fox Elwood would never be able to come between them again. After tonight, she'd forget he ever existed.

Poseidon closed his eyes for a moment as he came to stand behind her and indulged in another glimpse of their shared passion on the other side. She was naked beneath him in his bed within the castle by the sea. It was the first time she'd set foot within his domain and he thrilled to have her there knowing that for her tonight the dream was more real than any other, when he woke her she'd be ready for him begging for him.

The sea god opened his eyes knowing if he lingered, he'd not be able to hold back his true hunger for her. He'd tasted her within the dream but the blood in his veins burned with a need to be satisfied. He was straining to maintain the pleasant natured façade he'd wrapped himself in to woo her over the last year. The beast that lay under the mask was starving and impatient to be released. It wanted her and it wanted her now.

Poseidon set the gift down on a deck chair and moved closer to his prize. With gentle hands he drew Robin back against his chest and groaned at the feel of the heat of her pressed against him. He bit his lip as his hands cupped her shoulder, fingers meeting just above the swell of her chest.

He wanted to tear her clothes off then and there; throw her down on the deck and fuck her till she screamed his true name for all to hear, but instead he lowered his head and brushed a kiss against her neck pressing his power against her. She jolted from the dream, unseeing eyes blinked and she gasped at the feel of his hands on her.

"Sei," she breathed the name she'd been calling him for months and it was nearly his undoing. He turned her in his embrace and lifted her chin so that their eyes met. "No more dreams, my love, tonight will be real," he whispered before he lowered his head and captured her lips kissing her for real.

The taste of her was a shock to his system, one the dream realm could not prepare him for. His hands fisted in her auburn hair and pulled, drawing a startled cry from her as he dove deeper taking more. The beast beginning to feed. His teeth pulled at her lower lip bruising it. She panted wildly trying to catch her breath as his hands untangled from her hair.

"I'm sorry my dear forgive me, I wasn't ready for that, it was better than I ever dreamed it could be," he murmured as he drew back.

She blinked dazed and aroused but frightened. Here, come sit with me and open your gift," he entreated as he took her by the hand and led her over to the chair where her gift lay waiting. Robin sank down on the chair and he sat down behind her and drew her back against him as he had so many times before in the dream realm. She sank back willingly, her mind at ease at the familiarity of the embrace.

Poseidon ran his hands up and down her arms as she unwrapped the gift. Robin gasped at what she found tucked within the tissue paper.

"Do you like it?" he asked, before he kissed the side of her neck once more.

"It's just like what I wear in the dream," she said with disbelief.

"I had it made special for you," he murmured as his hands skimmed down her finger tips and along her legs.

"Sei, it's amazing!"

"Will you wear it for me?" he asked her.

"Of course," she whispered, and she picked up the necklace unfastening it with the intent to put it on first.

"Allow me," he offered, taking it from her hands. He pulled it up around her neck and fastened it closed. He lingered here adjusting the charm, his fingers skimming down her collarbone and towards her breasts sliding under her blouse. As he went to draw them out again knowing not to linger, the beast within him protested, nails marking her flesh as it tried to hold on.

Robin flinched and Poseidon cursed, wanting to skip this sweet seduction she seemed to need and to just take her. But he knew better than to do so, he needed her to come willingly to him. He couldn't force her here, if he did she'd not give him the heir he needed.

Instead he picked up the earrings out of the box and fastened the first to her left ear. He let his fingers skim along the lobe and as he secured the second one, his head lowered to nip at the first.

Robin moaned at the sensation and he licked the skin where the golden bobble pierced her skin. She trembled in his embrace and he smiled knowing her trepidation from the previous error was abating. He pulled out the bracelets and slid the first one up her arm as his mouth moved from one ear to the other, his intent to treat it to the same gentle tasting as the first but the beast within him strained against his leash and he bit her harder than before. Her eyes shot open and she cried out with alarm.

Poseidon's lips parted and he licked the abused flesh using his power to sooth it. She purred with delight at the sensation and sank back against him once more as he slid the second shoulder cuff into place. His fingers skimmed down her arms, nails scratching lightly drawing a contented sigh from her lips.

He slid the second set of golden bangles onto her wrists, his fingers skimming over her pulse point and down her palms and between her finger tips as his mouth left her ears to kiss her shoulders. He smiled, pleased when her violet eyes fell shut once more.

Poseidon drew the last set of bracelets from the box and slid the first around her ankle as his mouth moved to her other shoulder kissing it as well. As he slid the last golden bangle onto her flesh his teeth sank into her skin where neck and shoulder met.

She gasped at the sensation as his hands skimmed up her leg under her pant leg towards the part of her he craved most to feel. When he felt her body tense in his grasp the sea god drew his hand back out again, nails raking her skin as the beast protested the denial of what it sought.

His lips parted her neck and he took her hand in his and kissed her wrist. "Relax, Robin, I'm not going to hurt you he assured her.

"Sei..." she began, overwhelmed by the mix of sensations running through her.

"This is nothing more than we've done before," he murmured, before he kissed her fingers. He released the first hand and took hold of the other. Repeating the same caresses only to draw those fingers in his mouth and nip at the finger tips. Satisfied she was once more at ease, he rose from behind her and knelt before her to slide the golden sandals on her feet.

He kissed the tops of her feet, then rolled up her pant leg enough to kiss her ankles where his gems dangled. His hands slid up her leg rolling the cuff higher so the he could kiss her knee and he watched as goose flesh rose on her skin. He groaned inwardly, wanting her out of those clothes and in the suit still lying in the box, knowing it would give him more access to her flesh.

Poseidon sprinkled kisses down her leg and then rolled up the other cuff to treat her right leg to the same treatment. He watched with pleasure as she sank back in the chair, eyes closed and lost herself in the feel of his gentle ministrations. With care he wrapped his power around her and watched as her clothes vanished only to be replaced by the rest of his gift. As he kissed her knee his hands slid up her bare thigh and she jolted. Then blinked.

"How?" she began, startled to find herself wearing not her clothes but his suit.

His hands parted her legs and he kissed her inner thigh, the beast marking it.

Her eyes fell shut at the jolt of pleasure that tore through her and the question was forgotten for a moment.

"You know how," he breathed as he leaned over her to kiss her.

"Magic," she murmured, as she slid away from him frightened. "Who are you? What are you?" she asked as she rose from the chair and backed away from him.

"You know that as well," he assured her as he trapped her against the rail and kissed her

Below the sea swelled with anticipation.

"Poseidon," she gasped with disbelief as his mouth fell once more on her throat marking it.

"Yes, Robin that's it, see I told you, you knew me," he whispered, before his mouth captured hers once more. His hands took hold of her body and he delighted in the feel of her finally in his grasp.

160

Fox rounded the deck headed back for the dining hall only to freeze at the sight before him. At the rail near the front was Robin. Her body pressed against that of the captain's, their lips locked and his hands sliding down her curves. He watched as the other man took hold of her ass to press her more firmly against him. Robin gasped his name and Fox flinched.

She'd called him Sei.

This was the guy she'd claimed was a dream. He looked real to him. From the look of it Sei looked ready to tear her clothes off and have his way with her and Robin looked more than willing to follow. He turned to go and then stopped. No, he wasn't going to let this go uncontested. There was a good chance that even as she stood there kissing the other man his child was growing inside her and he wasn't going to give it or her up without a fight.

Letting his anger lead Fox stormed up the deck and pulled the two apart.

"Just a dream," he muttered with disbelief as he eyed Robin with mistrust.

"Fox," she breathed the name with disbelief, as she realized what she was wearing what it looked like.

"Yeah now you remember my name, what the hell is wrong with you, I thought we'd agreed to…"

"I'm sorry, I don't know what came over me. He's just so much like Sei..."

"I see."

"Robin my dear, I think we'll finish this another time," Poseidon breathed as he brushed a kiss on her forehead.

"Good night Sei," she murmured as relief began to set in.

"Sweet dreams doctor," he whispered and Fox watched as she

trembled at the parting comment.

"You okay?" Fox asked, seeing she was clearly upset.

"No, I'm scared Fox, he's not what he seems. Not what he pretended to be. That wasn't what it looked like. I…"

"Hush Robin, no need to explain, you're okay now, I'm here," he assured her as he drew her away from the rail where she was still leaning.

"Thank you."

"Come on, I'll take you below, get you to bed."

"No! I don't want to sleep."

"Why not?"

"If I do I'll dream, he'll be waiting…I'll find my way back into his arms and I don't…"

"Okay, let's go back to the cabin, we'll watch movies or something and if you do fall asleep I'll be there to wake you," he offered. Robin nodded, allowing Fox to lead her below out of the sea breeze that had turned cold.

161

Anna opened her eyes to find herself once more near the base of the dead and barren tree within the wasteland where Hades tormented her. She struggled to get to her feet and watched with dread as the lord of the underworld drew near her.

"HELLO AGAIN DR. GALLAGHER," he said amused, as he reached her side only to have her kneeling before him.

"Hades, please just let me go," she requested.

Rather than do as she asked he grabbed hold of her golden hair and drew her to her feet so that they were eye to eye. "GIVE ME WHAT I WANT ANNA AND I'LL GIVE YOU WHAT YOU ASK," he hissed, as he skimmed his fingers down her mud caked flesh, the filth crumbled under his touch falling away revealing her battered body to his heated gaze.

"Never. I'll never help you ascend to claim Zeus's throne. I'll die first," Anna snapped in disgust.

Hades laughed at the boast. "FOOLISH WOMAN DO YOU THINK DEATH CAN SAVE YOU FROM ME. I AM DEATH, IF YOU CAST YOURSELF IN THE SEA AS YOU'RE THINKING OF DOING I'LL BE THERE TO DRAW YOU FORTH AND CALL YOU BACK, THEN YOU'LL NOT ONLY TELL ME ALL I DESIRE TO KNOW BUT YOU'LL GIVE ME THAT PRETTY PINK FLESH WILLINGLY," he hissed, as his hands skimmed lower.

"That's not true. I'll be beyond your reach fallen and we both know it," Anna snapped as she took a step away from him. It was a terrible mistake in judgment as it brought her under the tree and the instant her back touched the trunk, root and branch alike wound about her limbs to hold her captive.

162

Hades walked toward her, his hands brushed through her hair, fingers caressing her temples and he laughed with delight as the wall that kept her location from him crumbled and he pictured her laying on the sands of the beach under the evening sky. He pressed her mind for the location of the door and the wall rose again thicker than before.

Infuriated, he produced the whip he'd used on her more times than he could count and let her feel the cool leather of the lash against her skin. He thrilled in the power that washed through him as she trembled in fear of it and him. He wrapped his power around her, tightening his hold on her mind drawing her deeper into the dream. He had her mind here, he wanted her flesh, wanted her to feel what he was doing to her. He lifted her chin with the whips handle so their eyes met.

"I HAVE YOU HERE ANNA AND THERE IS NO ESCAPE FROM THAT. GIVE ME WHAT I DESIRE AND YOUR SUFFERING WILL END," he breathed, as his eyes gleamed green with his power.

He watched as her cracked and peeling lips parted and roared as she denied him again. A curse flew from his lips as the lash landed its first blow.

Hades opened his eyes drawing half his mind from the dream realm. Her denial was not important, he knew where she was. The lord of the underworld set his key inside the safe locking it away and left the hotel room where he'd been resting to seek out the woman who held the secret that would give him Zeus's crown. So long as he kept her in the dream, he could get to her in reality before she did anything rash.

163 Kauai, Hawaii

Sam watched with disgust as Hades left his hotel and headed unerringly in the direction of the seashore where he'd left Anna asleep on the sand defenseless. He again prayed she be safe even as he slipped through the lobby doors and started up the stairs for the Fallen's room.

He was past the door and in the room with an ease that worried him and could feel his goal within the room, its evil pulsed from within the safe. Sam dusted the key pad with finger print powder and got the keys pressed for the lord of the underworlds code.

He typed the numbers in one way and cursed when it didn't give, then tried a second time knowing the safe only allowed for three tries and there were four other combinations still possible for the three digit code. On a hunch he pressed the numbers that spelled out his own name on a phone and cursed as the door gave.

Hades had known he was coming. Was aware of what Anna was up to. Shoving the key in his bag. Sam closed the safe, not bothering to clean it before he turned and ran, he had to get back to Anna before Hades reached her and he was already several minutes behind the fallen.

164

Somewhere on the Atlantic
Wednesday
8pm

Lance lay on his bed trying to rest but Ares kept nudging at him to go see Catharine.

"I thought you said you'd not interfere…"

"YOU MISINTERPRET MY INTENT DETECTIVE, I THINK YOU SHOULD WARN HER AGAINST PULLING STUNTS LIKE THE ONE SHE DID EARLIER BY LEAVING. IT'S NOT WISE FOR HER TO UPSET OUR HOST," Ares warned.

"Poseidon," Lance muttered the name with distaste. "He hardly seemed upset, he was too busy playing with Dr. Chase," Lance muttered.

"DON'T LET THE SEA KING FOOL YOU, HE IS THE CLEVEREST OF MY BRETHREN WHEN IT COMES TO THE FAIRER SEX, AND HE'S LEARNED THE WAYS TO WIN THEIR AFFECTIONS SO THAT THEY GIVE THEMSELVES WILLINGLY TO HIM. IF SHE SPURNS HIM HE WILL SEE IT AS A CHALLENGE," Ares hissed.

Lance rose from the bed and cracked stiff joints before crossing to the door taking Ares warning to heart. He lifted his hand to knock and the door once again opened before he touched it.

"Detective."

"I trust you're feeling better."

"I am," she said with a shrug.

"Good, though I wish you'd not left so abruptly."

"You know why I did," she said with irritation as she stood in the doorway, keeping him in the hall.

"I do, but it was not wise," Lance muttered.

"I suppose Ares said as much," Catharine said with disgust.

"He did."

"I wish you'd stop listening to him," Catharine muttered.

"I know it bothers you but he offers insight into his brethren and you shouldn't upset our host."

"Poseidon, he didn't seem all that threatening," she whispered.

"Which is why he is, he's good with manipulating women, setting them at ease. Don't challenge him."

"I won't but I did warn Robin against him."

"I did the same with Fox, but that's the end of it Catharine I don't want you doing anything to land yourself in his cross hairs."

"What does Hermes want here?"

"A key. So long as we stay out of his way he'll stay out of ours," Lance stated.

"That's good, I guess," Catharine breathed, as she stepped aside allowing him to come in.

"Relax, Serenity, this will all be over soon," he whispered, as he stepped inside and closed the door.

"I know, I just can't help but worry that it will end badly. What if Ares…"

Lance closed the distance between them and pressed a finger to her lips. "Shh, I'm fine Catharine," he assured her.

"At the moment, but for how long? Dionysus is chipping away at your control with his power."

"I won't hurt you Catharine. I could never hurt you," he breathed, as he rested his head against hers. His hands sank into her hair as he took hold of her chin. Lifting her head so their eyes met.

"Lance…"

"I hope you know that."

"I do," she admitted, as she trembled against him.

"I won't let him hurt you either. I'd die first," Lance murmured.

"I know, and that's what scares me," she confessed.

"Why?" he asked, as he rubbed his nose against hers.

"I don't know what I'd do if you were gone," she whispered, letting him know just how much he meant to her.

"I'm not going anywhere," he assured her before he closed the last few inches between them and kissed her.

165 Kauai, Hawaii

Anna woke with a scream as her mind fell out of the dream realm, she drew a breath, relieved to be free but she was cautious in her stirring aware that Hades was nearby.

"HERE YOU ARE DR. GALLAGHER SO GOOD TO SEE YOU IN THE FLESH AGAIN," he whispered, as he came over the sand dune.

Anna got to her feet and drew Sam's gun. "Stay away from me," she snapped in warning, as she took a step back toward the waves.

"COME NOW DOCTOR, SUCH THREATS ARE NOT NECESSARY. WE BOTH KNOW YOU LED ME HERE SO YOUR MR. ABRAMS COULD STEAL MY KEY. TELL ME, WHAT DO YOU INTEND TO DO WITH IT ONCE YOU HAVE IT?" Hades asked, as he closed the distance between them. Anna pulled the trigger, the bullet hit its mark piercing his chest and the lord of the underworld laughed, as his magic swelled. The wound sealed before her eyes and the bullet fell into his hand.

"OH ANNA, YOU'RE DELIGHTFUL," he taunted, as he moved closer. Anna took another step back so that the tide lapped over her feet before firing again, this time the bullet tore through his head and the lord of the underworld hissed as his power again repaired the damage.

"DAMN YOU ANNA THAT HURT, PLAY NICE," he hissed, as he grabbed her by the arm and drew her toward him. Anna pulled the trigger a third time shooting him in the temple at point blank range. He released his hold on her and she turned and fled into the rising water.

166

Sam heard the crack of a third shot as he raced over the sand dune that led back to where he'd left Anna sleeping. As he reached the top, he spotted his enemy on the shore staring at the surf, blood marked his flesh, making it clear Anna had hit her target. Good girl.

"COME NOW ANNA DEAR, THIS ISN'T AMUSING ANYMORE," Hades hissed, as Sam crept closer. He spotted the gun in the sand where she'd dropped it and picked it up.

"Back off Fallen one," Sam hissed in warning, as he raised the gun to fire.

"SAM WE BOTH KNOW YOU CAN'T KILL ME WITH THAT," hades said amused.

"Maybe not, but I can hurt you a bit and give her a chance to get away," Sam countered.

"ALL I HAVE TO DO IS THREATEN YOU AND SHE'LL COME BACK," Hades retorted.

"You won't and we know it, you need one of us to show you the way to that door and she won't, I won't either but you can't risk ending me because Hermes is closing in on claiming Poseidon's key."

"YOU LIE."

"No, I got it from Lance earlier. He and Poseidon are on a boat bound for the Marinas Trench," Sam stated.

"FINE MORTAL GET YOUR BELOVED AND GO, ENJOY HER WHILE YOU STILL CAN BECAUSE AS SOON AS HERMES GETS THAT CROWN HE'LL BE COMING FOR HER." Hades warned, before he turned and left.

Sam drew a breath and lowered his gun, relieved to have gotten through that unscathed. He called to Anna letting her know it was clear and as she came out of the surf he drew her into his arms.

"You okay?"

"Yes, I got away clean," she assured him, as he turned and led her back up the beach. "What about you, did you get it?"

"Yeah, it was too easy, he knew I was after it. Wanted me to take it though why I'm not sure yet. We need to get moving. I suspect he intends to follow us."

Anna nodded and they left the beach behind.

167 Somewhere on the Atlantic

Fox opened the door to Robin's room for her and she blushed at the sight within. The detective had his arms wrapped around Catharine and their lips were sealed in a kiss that made his blood warm as he thought of kissing the woman at his side so. Rather than give into the temptation he cleared his throat announcing their presence and watched as Lance let go of the woman in his arms.

"Sorry," Robin said with embarrassment.

"No need it's your room too," Catharine assured her as she looked past the man whom she'd been kissing to the pair.

"What's wrong?" she asked, seeing Robin looked uneasy.

"Our host scared her," Fox muttered.

"I see, I'm sorry to hear that," Catharine murmured, her eyes held sympathy.

"I'm going to take her next door so we'll be out of your hair we just need a few of her things," Fox explained.

"Of course."

Fox grabbed Robin's bag and carried it out of the room, careful to lock the door as he left to prevent the couple within from being interrupted again. He opened the door to his room and issued Robin inside. Once within he closed the door and flipped on the TV.

168

Catharine bit her lips at the sound of the doors lock clicking home. Aware that she was once more alone with the detective. "Well, I guess that means you're staying with me," she whispered, as she smiled at him nervously.

"It would appear so," Lance murmured, as he closed his eyes and drew in a breath filling his lungs with her scent before he kissed her forehead. "Do me a favor tomorrow."

"What?"

"No matter what happens, stay below deck."

"Lance…"

"Please Serenity, I'll feel better knowing you're safe."

"All right, but promise me you won't try to stand against the others."

"I'll do my best," he vowed.

"Thank you." Catharine whispered, satisfied she brushed a chaste kiss on his lips and wished him good night.

169

Lance watched as Catharine moved away from him, her intent on ending the moment of closeness they'd been sharing before Fox opened the door and cut it short. Lance's temper flared and his eyes flickered from blue to orange then back again as his hands fisted at his side.

In his mind he pictured grabbing her by the arm, halting her departure and questioning the abrupt dismissal in temper before pulling her back into his arms and capturing her lips once more demanding her surrender.

He imagined getting it; felt the heat that he had before they were interrupted, as his hands skimmed her body to touch her as he had done while they stayed in Dionysus's palace, his first visit to LA. He fantasized that when he opened his eyes to look into hers there was no fear in her gaze as he made his move to take her.

Lance blinked, as reality crashed in on him, his heart pounded wildly under the strain against the lust the wine god's power had stirred inside him.

"REACH FOR HER DETECTIVE, SHE'LL BE RECEPTIVE TO THE ADVANCE, SHE WANTS YOU I CAN SMELL IT ON HER," Ares mind whispered, as he nudged at his host to act upon his desires.

Lance clenched his hands tighter as he fought against the impulse. He didn't want the war god anywhere near her and was aware that now that they were outside Dionysus palace the wine god could press him harder to act without fear of reprisal from Hades.

The deal they'd struck was Ares would not get a taste of her so long as he was under the wine god's roof. Ares was no longer under that roof and if Dionysus wished it he could push them together so that he too might revel in their passion. Lance's efforts to keep his hands to himself had him drawing blood.

He drew a breath, filling his lungs with the metallic scent and Ares power swelled within him as his mind receded.

170

Catharine froze at the feel of Lance's hand wrapped about her arm at the elbow, the grip was strong and cold. He pulled turning her to face him and she gasped as her eyes locked not with blue but orange.

"GOOD NIGHT?" He questioned, his voice cold and brimming with impatience; hard with frustration. He drew her back toward him so that once more there were mere inches between them.

"You promised him," Catharine breathed, as their eyes locked.

"THIS IS WHAT HE WANTS," Ares whispered, as he brushed his cheek against her brow.

"If it's what he wants then let him take the lead," Catharine challenged.

"VERY WELL, BUT KNOW THIS, A TIME WILL COME SERENITY WHEN YOU NEED ME," Ares breathed, before he sank back into the confines of his blade and gave control back to Lance.

171

Lance blinked, startled to find he'd actually drawn Catharine back. Her blue eyes studied him with question as he tried to make sense of what had happened.

"Are you oaky?" she asked, her voice thick with concern.

"Yeah, I'm sorry, I just wasn't ready for you to go," he admitted.

"I noticed," she said, with a nervous laugh.

"Ares…" he muttered with irritation.

"Yeah, but nothing happened… I reminded him of your deal," she assured him.

"He's getting stronger," Lance confessed.

"We must be getting close to the rest of the sword," Catharine reasoned.

"I guess," he muttered.

"I wish you'd forget this. I don't want to lose you to him."

"You won't…"

"How can you be so sure, he just…"

"I won't let him win," Lance vowed.

"You can't fight a god with your will," Catharine warned.

"Watch me."

"I don't want to Lance, just let it go."

"I can't. I'm doing this for you. The second I let it go, Hades will destroy you."

"You don't know that."

"I do, I've seen it," Lance stated.

"What do you mean, you've seen it?" Catharine asked curious.

"The fallen, they communicate with each other without words. They send their thoughts. Ares showed me just a slice of the crap Hades has been threatening to do to you once he eliminates me as a threat. I won't let that happen."

"Lance..."

"I can't, if anything happened to you I'd be lost," Lance confessed, as he ran his fingers through her hair. Catharine blinked, stunned by his words, but he saw in her eyes she knew they were true.

"What do I do if you lose?" She asked, giving voice to her growing fear.

"Kill me," he breathed, without a second of hesitation.

"How can you ask me to do such a thing? Do you think I could?"

"Better that than the alternative," Lance muttered.

"Damn it Lance, you're asking for too much," she said, as tears pricked her eyes.

"I don't want to be the puppet of a blood thirsty god Serenity, and I especially don't want to watch you become his bride while I'm powerless to stop it. If I turn you'll be the only one who can stop me and him."

"Lance..." she whispered his name again. Lance was unsure what else she was going to say and the words never came as his lips met with hers ending the discussion.

172

Catharine moaned, as his kiss tore through her, leaving her weak with need of him and desperate for more. Her hands sank in his hair and she drew him closer as she kissed him back with a hunger that frightened her.

Lance groaned into her kiss as his hands slid down her body to take hold of her hips pressing her against him making clear his intent. She let go of his hair and took hold of his ass pressing him more firmly against her. As she breathed his name.

His hands slid up her side to take hold of her shirt and pull it free of her slacks. As he dipped his head to kiss his way down her neck. Catharine trembled at the heat of his hands as they brushed over her belly, under the shirt, reaching for her breasts. When he found her bra he cursed in frustration.

Catharine laughed at his frustrations and then gasped as he grabbed the shirt and tore it open with his impatience. He folded down her bra exposing her breast before she could react and his mouth was on her. She cried out with delight at the feel and her hands fisted in his hair in reflex as she fought for more.

She felt her bra loosen as he unhooked it and peeled it off before his head lifted. Their eyes locked and he breathed her name before he lowered his gaze once more to taste her other breast as his hands slid down her body making it burn with want as he touched her. She bit her lip as his hands pawed at her slacks covered thighs teasing her with the promise of more.

Catharine cried his name with need as her hands slid down his body letting him know she wanted to touch him and to be touched.

173

Lance lifted his head and kissed her as his hands slipped under the waistband of her slacks to skim over her underwear. Using the friction of the fabric to turn her on further and teasing her more giving her a taste of what she wanted but not all. He traced the band for a moment allowing her system to level out aware she'd been close to bliss.

Catharine cursed him for leaving her unsatisfied and he laughed at her curse. Satisfied she was more than ready for him, Lance slipped his hand inside the cotton garment to touch her directly, his fingers raked through feminine curls to find her wet and ready. He pressed a finger inside her and watched with pleasure as she went wild in response. Her blue eyes slammed shut as her teeth sank into his shoulder, muffling her cry of completion as her body trembled with release.

Lance froze, waiting her out and watched as fiery lashes lifted and blue eyes opened to meet his gaze. He smiled to see no fear in her eyes, only desire.

"I want you Serenity," he murmured as he pressed his finger deeper inside her making her ache for him as he ached for her.

"Lance…"

"Catharine let me make love to you," he breathed, as he drew his hand out of her slacks leaving her aroused. Making it clear that touching her was not enough to satisfy him.

"Lance I want this, want you but…" she began with trepidation.

"I won't let him get that close to you again," Lance whispered, to reassure her that he was indeed in control and the war lord would not get near her again. He kissed her as his hands played over her body, stirring her with hunger once more as he unbuttoned her slacks; to finish undressing her.

Catharine brushed his hands away and he bit back a curse, thinking she meant to refuse him, she gave him a wink and Lance watched with bated breath as Catharine brushed her slacks off her hips and stepped out of them. He reached for her panties and she brushed his hands away again.

"Not yet detective, you're still wearing too much," she breathed, before she pressed her hand against his chest and pushed him in the direction of the bed.

She pulled off his shirt and ran her fingers over his bare skin. Lance sank down on the mattress at the feel of her hands as they slid down his body to cup the part of him that wanted her most through the confines of his jeans. She knelt down in front of him pulling off his shoes and then unfastened his jeans, lowering the zipper with care, her hands fisted around denim and peeled it away from his body. His eyes screwed shut with pleasure and his head fell back as she ran her hands up the inside of his legs toward his boxers. Then her hands were gone and he groaned in frustration to have her tease him so.

His protest died on his lips as he opened his eyes to see her shed her panties. He gasped as she sat down on his lap slowly pressing her naked body against his.

Her mouth found his and she kissed him as he fell back on the mattress overwhelmed by her. She lifted her hips and pulled his boxers down. Warm hands wrapped around his aroused flesh and he groaned, his eyes closed and again she went still.

"Catharine…" he groaned in irritation.

"Look at me detective," she demanded. He opened his eyes and ice blue met with her cobalt blue eyes. "Stay with me Lance, because I don't want this if it's not you," she breathed as she took him in her hands once more and positioned him to take what he'd requested. He watched as she lowered herself onto him and his hips lifted straining to fill her quickly.

She sank down so that their pelvises touched. His hands closed round her hips as he drew her closer, pressing in deeper still. She cried out with shock at the pleasure that crashed through her and Lance came alive beneath her. his head lifted to taste her breasts as his hands lifted her drawing him partially out of her before pressing her back down again filling her all at once eliciting a desperate plea that might have been his name. Her arms wrapped round his neck and he turned the tables on her taking back control as he began to make love to her as he'd desired.

174 ATLANTIS, SOMEWHERE IN THE BERMUDA TRIANGLE

Hecate descended the passage from the hall of feasting into the throne room below, she reached out and touched the wall where the huntress had used her father's key to open the door and watched as the image of the tree pulsed with power and the door slid open. She threw her head back and laughed with victory as she stepped through the threshold to begin the decent to the crown, if her lord was still with her everything would unfold tonight according to her design.

175 Los Angeles, California

Dionysus thrilled in the power he felt flowing through him as the detective bedded his pretty writer. He reveled in the sensation until a warm hand ran down his body to squeeze his straining manhood.

"Forget the mortal, my lord I am here and my body is yours," Artemis whispered as she pressed her naked body against his back letting him feel the heat of her.

"MY HUNTRESS," he murmured with a thrill, as he turned to embrace her. As his body filled her she bit him, drawing blood and feeding. "SO THIRSTY PRINCESS, WHY SIP WHEN YOU CAN GULP," he murmured, as he bit his own wrist and let the blood flow into his goblet, he offered it to her and watched as she lifted it to her lips and tipped it back pouring the red liquid into her mouth.

She trembled in his embrace as the mix of the draught and his passionate exertions sent her to a powerful release. He did not still, simply pressed her harder, making her ache for more, not letting her find ease.

"Bacchus," she cried in desperation as the moon- light poured through the window. She stared up at the moon with shock as it began to turn red.

"YES, PRINCESS TONIGHT THAT IS MY NAME, IT IS MY NIGHT," he breathed, as the man became a beast, building her passion but not letting her enjoy it.

"Please my lord, I need…"

"YES, I KNOW, LITTLE HUNTRESS AND WHAT TRIBUTE WILL YOU OFFER ME YOUR LORD AND HUSBAND ON MY NIGHT, FOR WHAT YOU WANT," he growled, as he poured his power into his blood making it boil inside her, bringing her need to an unbearable blinding point that had her weeping for want of ease.

"Anything he desires," Artemis breathed, desperate for his blood desperate for him to finish and feel her passion break. Trembling with a hunger, she worried would drive her mad if not satisfied. A thirst she feared if quenched might kill her and yet she didn't care. She had to have him would not be right again until she got it.

"ANYTHING?" he asked with interest.

"Yes, anything," she said without hesitation.

"TAKE ME TO YOUR FATHER'S CROWN PRINCESS, LET ME TAKE MY PLACE AT YOUR SIDE AS THE RIGHTFUL KING," he breathed, as he used her own body against her to get what he desired.

"Oh, heaven, you're a devil," she cried with disbelief and he laughed as he pressed her harder still.

"YOU VOWED ANYTHING" he reminded."

"I did," she agreed.

"THEN SWEAR YOU'LL TAKE ME TO IT," he demanded, as he tripled his pace driving towards his own release.

"I will," she whispered, aware he intended to satisfy his own craving and leave her starving, while he sought his pleasure elsewhere.

"YOU'LL WHAT?" he asked demanding she say it. So there was no loop-hole in their verbal agreement for her to slip through.

"I'll take you to father's crown."

"WHEN?"

"Tonight after we're done," she answered.

"A DEAL," he breathed, and with that he lifted his wrist to her lips. She took the offered blood and drank deep her eyes went white as he pushed her over the edge and finally stilled letting the tidal wave of pleasure he'd denied her crash through her all at once.

The wine god stroked her body as he waited her out, talking her through it in his native tongue, not allowing her to slip into unconsciousness as her body sought to do. As she leveled out he began to move again and she cried out, her flesh so sensitive to him, his every entry had her crashing into another pool of bliss and his retreat left her begging for him to fill her again. When he finally found his own release he drew her to her feet and used his power to dress them both.

"COME MY DEAR YOUR FATHER'S CROWN WAITS," he whispered, as he drew her into his embrace, he wrapped his power around them and they vanished into the night.

176 Somewhere on the Atlantic

Robin looked over at her roommate as the credits for the film began to roll. “Fox you awake?”

“Yeah, I’m a wake” he said as his head lifted from the couch with a jolt leading her to suspect he’d been dozing.

“Movies over,” she stated.

“Right, what do you want to watch next?” he asked pressing the button for the guide to see what was on next.

“Um how about we let the movie wait and take care of our personal business,” she muttered.

He blinked, then nodded as he recalled they’d made plans earlier to look at her pregnancy test results together.

Robin pulled the opened box out of her bag and reached inside to pull out the little wand she shoved inside earlier that night.

The two stared at it for a moment and then violet and green met.

“That’s good news right,” he asked, not sure what she’d been wanting the test to reflect.

“Yes, yes, it is it’s a little scary but it’s good,” she answered as she blinked back tears.

“Robin, sweetie don’t cry,” he requested as he drew her into his arms. “We’re going to have a baby, it’ll be fine.”

“How can you say that, look at me? I’m dressed in his arraignments for me; I nearly let him…” she began with shame.

“But you didn’t, you walked away, you’re here with me,” he reminded.

“I’ve given myself to him in my dreams Fox, he can get to me if he wants, all he has to do is wait for me to fall asleep, he’ll be able to lead me back to him. He’ll finish what he started.”

“No he won’t Robin, he’s just a man,” Fox whispered not wanting to believe what the detective had started to tell him about the man she called Sei.

"You're wrong Fox, he's the god Poseidon, the sea king and he wants to make me his bride."

"He can't have you Robin, you're already spoken for," Fox muttered in temper, before he kissed her forehead. When his eyes opened he saw the other man's mark upon her and reasoned if she didn't like the sight of it then he'd do her the favor of removing it.

Fox pulled the combs holding her hair in place out first. Unpinning the wild mane setting it free. The next pieces to go were the earrings, he pulled the golden dangles free then licked the bare ear lobes making her tremble in his arms. He tossed the golden trinkets aside without care and took her hands in his; sliding the golden bangles off her wrists, followed by her shoulders. They joined the other discarded pieces on the floor and he scooped her into his arms.

"Fox," she cried his name with surprise and then laughed as he dropped her unceremoniously on the bed. When she looked up to ask him what that was for he was at her feet pulling off gilded sandals and ankle bracelets. He dropped both to the floor before sitting down on the bed at her side. He unwound the scarf covering her arms and then reached for the clasp on her necklace.

It fell away from her throat and he kissed her bare flesh. "Your beautiful Robin, always have been, you don't need all these trinkets to make you desirable," he whispered as he unwound the knot that held the sheer white skirt closed, leaving her in only the teal suit.

He reached for the knot that secured the upper part of her top and pulled the cord lightly, unraveling the bow a bit but giving her the chance to stop him if she wanted. Fox grabbed the other end and pulled it as well, the top fell loose but did not reveal her to him. As he reached to fold it down his eyes met with hers again asking silently for permission to continue.

Robin's answer was to kiss him as she shoved the scarf aside and kicked the skirt off the bed, making it clear she wanted him not the finery that Poseidon had tried to seduce her with. Fox smiled as his fingers untied the lower knot on the top and tossed the teal scrap of fabric away from them both. Robin lifted her hips and peeled off the bottoms she sent them flying across the room as well and Fox laughed.

"Finally got you naked and all to myself," he whispered as he skimmed his fingers down her frame.

"I catch you smirking Fox Elwood and I'll take off your shirt and leave you here by yourself," she muttered in warning.

"Oh, you want my shirt," he said with a gleam in his eye before he shed it and threw it at her.

"Fox," she said with exasperation.

"I suppose you'll want my pants to go with it," he muttered.

"Mr. Elwood," she snapped, stopping him from throwing them as well.

"No pants, okay, fair enough," he whispered, before he leaned over her to kiss her. Robin giggled as his lips parted hers and brushed light kisses down her face.

"You're crazy, do you know that," she whispered.

"Only with you," he murmured, before he lay down on the bed beside her.

Robin picked up his pants and began rummaging through them.

"What are you doing lady?" he asked puzzled by the strange behavior.

"I'd think it would be obvious to you," she teased.

"I'm afraid it's not."

"For a guy who likes to get in a girls pants I'm surprised you don't recognize the signs of a girl trying to get in yours," she said with a laugh as she tossed them at him.

"And you think I'm crazy," he said with disbelief and then rather than kiss her, he tickled her.

"Fox stop," she cried in protest as she laughed. When he did he was leaning over her. He drew her hands to his hips. "You want to get in my pants Dr. Chase," he murmured as he watched her.

"Yeah, Mr. Elwood I did, can't wait to get my hands on your butt," she teased.

"Really Robin, maybe I didn't have sex on the brain when I dropped you here," he whispered, as he lifted the waistband on his boxers, giving her what she'd said she wanted.

Robin reached inside and grabbed hold of his ass, nails bighting the skin and he groaned as he lowered his hips so that they rested against her bare ones.

"In that case maybe I'll just have to talk you into it," she whispered playfully, enjoying the strange role reversal. She moved her hands from his backside to his front, her fingers wrapped around his length and pulled gently.

"Okay, now you've got my attention lady, but I'm not convinced yet," he murmured.

"Then I'll have to try harder," she answered and to do so she reached lower to squeeze the more sensitive part of his man hood.

Fox groaned and then shed his underwear. "All right Dr. Chase you talked me into it, but next time I want to be wined and dined," he joked before he pressed inside her and began to move to both of their delight.

177 Thursday 6am

Lance woke as the sun rose to Ares buzzing in his ear. They were there, the missing piece of the sword lay beneath them. Lance looked over at the woman sleeping beside him and slid out of the bed careful not to wake her.

He'd made her promise not to come up on deck last night and he wanted her to keep that promise; knew her well enough to know if she caught him leaving, she'd go with him. So he dressed in the dark and crept from the room. He wasn't too surprised to find Fox and Dr. Chase wrapped together on the deck watching the sun rise.

He'd sensed a reconciliation coming when he saw them the night before. The tension between them he'd seen that first night he met them had been all but non-existent. No doubt Poseidon would be disappointed but Lance didn't care so long as the sea king kept his paws off Catharine.

"We're here, it's below us," Lance stated, breaking up their moment, ,part of him getting even for their busting up his with Catharine. He watched as the other man let Robin go and lowered the chain dropping the winch and the machine attached to it into the crushing black of the trench. They watched as the camera sent back images and waited for the missing gem to come into sight.

"This will take a while yet, you might as well go back to your room, we'll let you know when we've got something," Fox stated.

Lance nodded his acceptance of the offer, figuring he had a better chance of keeping Catharine in the room if he was there when she woke. Without a word he turned and headed back below, aware that as he went Fox moved back to where Robin stood by the deck and drew her back in his arms once more.

178 Atlantis, Somewhere in the Bermuda triangle

Artemis led her husband into the throne room and froze as she neared the door feeling the taint of another power within the chamber.

"Someone's been here," she muttered.

"WHAT?"

As Artemis placed her father's key in the lock, the power taint flared and she cursed pressing her power against it, the door gave way and she drew a breath. "Hecate is inside, we have to get to the crown before she can," Artemis warned.

"WE WILL," Dionysus assured her before they crossed the threshold together and entered the dark passage into the great prince's kingdom. They raced down the passage desperate to catch the old witch, neither sure what she was up to.

179 KAWAI, HAWAII

Sam led Anna back into the fiery cave of the volcano, his pace hurried and his eyes darted about more paranoid than before. Convinced that at any moment Hades would appear and strike.

They were walking into a trap, he was sure of it now, but just what trap and how he'd yet to determine. The lord of the underworld was playing them; he knew what they were doing somehow. He was using that knowledge to manipulate them into doing what he wanted of them.

He had to find a way to get them out of this mess alive and unscathed, but how it could be done escaped him. For now he pressed on and prayed he was wrong.

180 Marianas Trench

Robin stepped out of the circle of Fox's arms as the machine on their probe began to beep signaling it had located something. She crossed the deck to look at the screen and gasped, it seemed Mr. Roman had been right, it was there, she could see it, a huge citrine, which blazed orange and swirled in the light. She blinked as something else came into focus.

"Fox," she called with alarm.

He crossed the deck to stand behind her. "What is it?"

"I'm not sure there's something else there," she whispered with disbelief.

"YOU'RE QUITE RIGHT MY DEAR," Poseidon whispered as he joined her at the panel taking position on her other side.

"Sei?"

"THAT IS MY KEY," he whispered, as he flipped the switch, giving the machine the command to scoop up the two items and reversing the chain so that it brought both back to the surface.

"IT WAS YOUR KEY," Dr. Ian Broody's voice corrected. Robin turned to look at the new- comer but too late, a whip snapped from his side, its end coiled round her wrist and he drew her away from both the men at her sides.

181

Poseidon stared at the god of knowledge with outrage. That the other man dared to bring harm to his bride was unforgivable. Who did the fool think he was? Hermes was one of the weakest of their number, how had he managed to get to her.

"I'LL TEAR YOUR HEART OUT YOU INSIGNIFICANT LITTLE UPSTART," Poseidon roared in fury, as his eyes began to gleam aqua with his power. The scepter in his hand shifted to his trident of old as he readied himself for war.

"YOU'LL DO NO SUCH THING SEA KING IF YOU WISH YOUR PRETTY ROBIN TO STAY UNCHARRED, Hermes sneered, as he wrapped the whip at his side around her neck. The jewel of the sun god gleamed in the suns light and Poseidon cursed.

"WHAT DO YOU WANT MESSENGER?"

"GIVE YOUR SCEPTER TO MR. ELWOOD," Hermes demanded.

"WHAT?"

"Why, me?" Fox questioned his green eyes filled with confusion at the demand.

"WHAT OR WHY DOESN'T MATTER, JUST DO IT," Hermes ordered.

He watched with bated breath as the trident changed once more to the jeweled scepter. Poseidon reluctantly passed it over to the mortal.

Hermes laughed with amusement at the look of confusion and stunned horror that crossed the Sea god's eyes before the aqua glow faded reverting back to that of his host's natural color.

Russell York blinked, dazed and confused as he tried to sort out where he was and how he'd gotten there. The last thing he remembered was following Zaharrah Lynch in the desert. He'd found something golden laying broken in the sand and then nothing.

"Ian?" he questioned as he looked at the other man standing before him holding a woman he didn't recognize hostage.

"AFRAID NOT," Hermes replied, before he shoved the woman Robin at Mr. Elwood. He then cracked his whip. The long coil wrapped around Russell's neck before the fire opal began to glow, fire poured through the mantle to consume the mortal's flesh.

Hermes watched with satisfaction as the man fell to the ground dead as he unwrapped the whip around his neck. "THANK YOU MR. ELWOOD, I'LL TAKE THAT NOW," Hermes said pleased. He snatched the golden scepter from the treasure hunter's powerless fingers.

182

Robin gasped for air as Fox blinked relieved to see no mark was left on her flesh. "You okay?"

She nodded, unable to speak yet.

"What just happened?" He asked trying to understand what he'd just seen.

"HERMES STOLE THE SEA KING'S POWER," Lance answered, his eyes gleamed orange as he watched the intruder with disquiet. "How?" Robin questioned, as the chain bringing their find to the surface wound tighter. Whatever it was it wouldn't be long now until it broke past the surface.

"HE FORCED POSEIDON TO GIVE THE MANTLE TO A HUMAN. THE MOMENT HE DID SO HIS POWER WAS STRIPPED FROM HIM AND RETURNED TO THE SCEPTER," Ares answered.

"What power? What are you talking about?" Fox asked confused.

"IT'S OF NO CONCERN TO YOU MORTAL. IF YOU VALUE YOUR LIVES YOU'LL GET BELOW," The war god warned, as the last of the chain wound itself around the winch.

Lance was in the water in an instant, his fingers wrapped around the missing gem from the swords hilt and slipped it into place.

Hermes hissed, as the war god's sword blazed orange with his power. Lance groaned under the onslaught, aware he'd been tricked but could do nothing but obey the war god's voice as it ordered him to take the key as well.

"NOT SO FAST BROTHER, THAT'S MINE," Hermes challenged, as he snapped his whip snatching it away.

"HERMES YOU DARE CHALLENGE ME?" Ares voice boomed in fury as he rose from the water.

"EVEN YOU CANNOT CHALLENGE MY POWER WAR

GOD," Hermes crowed, as he transformed the scepter into the trident of old.

"WE'LL SEE," the war god hissed, as he drew his sword from its sheath and raised it for battle.

He heard the rush of footsteps as the mortals fled the deck. He heard the protest of his host at being possessed but heeded it not. Lance would fall into line if he wanted to live but particularly if he wanted Catharine to come out of this unscathed.

Orange eyes flickered back to blue as the mortal tried to take control but as Ares warning sounded in his mind Lance heeded it and once more his eyes blazed orange as fire as the god of war took control.

183

Hermes brought down the end of the trident like an ax aimed at Ares head. The war god blocked the blow turning the trident away from his flesh. He countered with a slash of his own slicing Hermes cheek as he changed the man Lance's clothes into his armor of old.

"YOU'LL PAY FOR THAT," Hermes roared, as he cracked the whip in his other hand striking Ares hand.

"YOUR POWER IS NO MATCH FOR CENTURIES OF COMBAT EXPERIENCE AND WAR STRATEGY. I'VE BEEN PRESENT AT EVERY CONTEST OF MEN SINCE OUR FALL. NO MATTER WHAT WEAPON YOU BRING AGAINST ME YOU CANNOT BEST ME," Ares mocked.

"YOU'RE A FOOL BROTHER, JUST LIKE THE OTHERS. YOUR BLOOD LETTING AND BRUTE STRENGTH IS NO MATCH FOR MY POWER," Hermes snarled, as his eyes gleamed with amusement.

Ares circled his prey moving in for the kill as a gasp sounded from behind him.

Orange eyes moved past his target to the woman who'd emerged from below deck. "CATHARINE GET OUT OF HERE," he roared in fury as he blocked Hermes next attack. Below the surface Lance pulled at the reigns of control for his mind, his need to protect her demanding he do something to get her clear of harm's way.

The war god hissed with pain as Hermes latest attack was deflected wrong and the spokes of the trident pierced his side.

"Lance!" Catharine shouted with alarm.

"GO!" Ares snarled again, orange eyes burned now with an inner fire that warned if she defied him again reprisal would follow.

"THE KEY IS MINE," Hermes crowed, as he threw his final volley in their duel. Drawing upon the tridents power he smashed a rogue wave into the hull of the ship behind Catharine sweeping the woman over- board.

The war god roared in rage. "THIS IS NOT DONE YET, MESSENGER," he barked, before the man Lance once more took command of his body. The sword was shoved back into its cursed scabbard and the detective dove overboard to rescue his beloved Serenity.

184

Hermes wiped the sweat from his brow as the trident reverted once more to a scepter. He picked up the sea king's key and tied the whip at his side. His prize in hand, he dove off the bow and plunged into the icy, black fathomless depths of the trench. To speed his decent he drew upon the scepters power, transforming his form into one of the great leviathan of old and swam unerringly in his course to the door below.

As it neared the bottom, the beast shifted, reverting to the human like form and Hermes hands out -stretched before him pressed the strange disk into the grooved lock. He watched with delight as the sea kings markers lit one after another and the door opened. Beyond was a great black chasm, void of any light. He swam through without hesitation, caring not for whatever danger might lay within, for at the end of the tunnel Zeus's crown waited.

185

Lance’s body cut through the water his eyes clamped tight to avoid the searing pain of saltwater in his eyes. His lungs protested his decent screaming for air. As the war god snarled at him to go after Hermes before he reached the door.

Lance ignored him.

He didn’t care about the damn crown, all he was interested in was finding Catharine. As he broke through the dark water to the surface above and sunlight his blue eyes scanned the waves about him.

“Catharine!” he called desperate for an answer.

“FOOL! ALONE YOU CAN’T HOPE TO FIND HER,” Ares hissed.

“Then help me damn you!” Lance roared in fury and the war god laughed.

This was why Ares picked him; all this raw emotion so easily turned to rage in his impatience. His need to protect and save those he loved so like the knights and warriors of old.

He was like young Paris willing to start a war for love of Helene, Mark Anthony defying Caesar and Rome for his beguiling Cleopatra or his namesake Sir Lancelot betraying all he knew and cared for to be with Guinevere. He was the best match Ares had found in his time roaming among men since waking from his stone slumber.

Ares had too much riding on this to let the fool go now. “I CAN’T IF YOU FIGHT ME,” the war god challenged and smirked, as he felt the man’s mind slip aside allowing him to once more take control.

Blue eyes gleamed orange as Ares dove beneath the water. He swam into the crushing black abyss of Poseidon’s sea. Drawing upon his power, he pulled his sword and used its glow to light his way. In the distance he spotted her. Her red hair burned like a flame in the light. Blue eyes wide with fear and desperation as her hand reached for his.

His fingers wrapped around her wrist and drew her back toward him. She froze with trepidation as she noted the unnatural glow in his eyes but the war god didn't let her retreat. His mouth slanted over hers passing the oxygen her body needed from his host's lungs to the woman knowing if she died here that all his efforts to gain a foot - hold over the man would be for not.

Ares felt a jolt of hunger he'd not known in years as he kissed her but pushed it aside, there was no time for such distractions now. He needed to finish the task before him.

Get the woman to safety and prepare for the backlash to come for his failure at gaining the key.

The war god eased back from her when he was satisfied she had sufficient air to hold her till they reached the surface. With the immediate danger having passed, he made his way for the surface and the ship that would get them out of there.

186 Kauai, Hawaii

Anna's heart hammered in her chest as she flew down the earthen passage blindly in the direction of the door. As she went, she prayed her gamble here would pay off. She figured the best way to prevent the fallen from opening the door was to open it herself and cast the key within.

So far they were clear but she figured Hades had to be close by. Ahead of her the corridor opened into a chamber and she knew her flight was near its end. The heat of the volcanic chamber had sweat dripping from her brow in her eyes. As she lifted her hand to swipe at it. The chamber before them lit with an unnatural green flame that chilled her to the bone. "Hades," she whispered the name with dread as she lifted her arm in reflex to shield her eyes against the light.

"DR. GALLAGHER, IT'S A PLEASURE TO SEE YOU AGAIN SO SOON," he breathed with amusement. "TELL ME MY DEAR, WHATEVER ARE YOU DOING IN SUCH A DANGEROUS PLACE AS THIS?" he asked feigning curiosity as he moved towards her.

Sam moved from her side to stand between them. "Back off fallen one, I'll not allow you to touch her," Sam snapped.

"MR. ABRAMS, PLEASE DO YOU HONESTLY BELIEVE YOU CAN STAND AGAINST ME. SUCH ARROGANCE EVEN FOR A MORTAL IS REFRESHING," Hades said with a laugh, "AND SHOWS JUST HOW MUCH OF A FOOL YOU ARE. I'VE FOUND YOU AT EVERY TURN IN THE ROAD; BEEN ONE STEP AHEAD OF YOU ALL THE WAY, HOW IS IT YOU THINK I'VE MANAGED THAT LITTLE TRICK," the lord of the underworld questioned.

"Hades," Anna snapped with impatience. She knew what he was up to with the question and she'd no intention of letting him use her as a sword against Sam.

"What's wrong Anna?" Sam asked stunned by her display of temper before the fallen.

"YES PRETTY ANNA, TELL HIM WHAT'S WRONG," Hades taunted

As he pressed his power against her mind. His eyes fell shut as his mind slid into the dream realm to torment her. Anna groaned at the feel of his unwanted phantom caresses as he tried to pull her mind from the waking world to that of dreams.

"Doc?" Sam questioned, with disquiet and a growing sense of dread.

"Sam," she breathed his name like a prayer as she fought against Hades demand.

Hades eyes popped open. His lips curled with a wicked smirk as the unnatural green met with blue. "ASK HER WHAT I'M DOING TO HER SAM? ASK HER WHAT I DID? NO, WHAT SHE LET ME DO, TO SAVE ZAHARRAH FROM MY WRATH," Hades said with amusement, before he pressed his power against her mind again with more force.

"That's enough Hades," Anna shouted with disgust. Tears stung her eyes as she fought against the mental attack. Splinters of an image of herself bound, broken and bleeding, marred with dirt pressed down in the mire began to bleed into her mind.

"NO, NOT QUITE," the lord of underworld corrected as he pressed her mind once more. Anna jolted as if struck by lightning; her body collapsed as her mind left the cave forced into the dream realm.

187

Sam caught Anna's limp body before she could hit her head against a stone. He cradled her against him, holding her close. She was still and cold as if dead and he fought for calm as fear tore through him like a razor.

"What did you do to her? " Sam demanded, his blue eyes locked with the Fallen's unholy green ones demanding an answer.

"I'VE TAKEN HER, MR. ABRAMS. YOUR SWEET LITTLE ANNALYNN DARCY GALLAGHER TRADED PLACES WITH MISS LYNCH TO SAVE HER LIFE AND IN DOING SO DIDN'T FULLY UNDERSTAND THE CONSEQUENCES OF HER ACTIONS. I'VE DRAWN HER INTO THE OTHER WORLD WHEN SHE'S ASLEEP AND YOUR FIANCÉ TELLS ME EVERYTHING I WANT TO KNOW ABOUT YOUR MOVEMENTS AND PLANS TO BE FREE OF ME. EVEN NOW MY MIND IS WITH HERS, TORMENTING HER, WHEN HER EYES OPEN NEXT SHE'LL GIVE ME THAT KEY," Hades boasted.

"You lie!" Sam roared with disgust and outrage.

"NO SAM IN THIS I SPEAK THE TRUTH. YOU CAN'T STOP ME FROM TOUCHING HER, I ALREADY HAVE. I'VE TOUCHED HER MIND AND CONTINUE TO DO SO AT WILL. NOTHING YOU DO CAN STOP IT," Hades taunted, and to prove it he pictured her as he had her in the dream realm and changed the nature of his torment upon her from a mildly unpleasant exploratory touch to cruel and invasive.

"No," Anna whimpered, where she lay and Sam flinched. Rage welled up within him but he pressed it aside, that was what the fallen wanted, his anger his hate.

"Let her go," Sam muttered.

"OH, I WILL MR. ABRAMS JUST AS SOON AS SHE GIVES ME WHAT I WANT," Hades answered with amusement, at the man's discomfort as Anna cried out in protest again.

"You've proved your point now let her go," Sam snapped.

188

Anna trembled as Hades icy hands clawed at her body leaving his mark upon her. As she lay in the filth she wondered which way he would hurt her this time. That was the worst part of this hell. She never knew what pain would come when he drew her here. She longed to be free of the chains that bound her but they refused to give.

She'd put them on willingly to save Zaharrah and like the Persephone of myth was now bound to him by her actions. She'd let him do his worst and given him an open door to her mind. Now all she wanted was for him to do whatever it was he intended and go. As she lay there beneath him, she wondered if when he left she'd get a chance to climb out of the muck and wash.

Morosely she questioned if she did manage to find water in this godforsaken place if she'd ever be able to get clean again.

"HE'S WATCHING US NOW, YOUR MR. ABRAMS, THIS TIME HE'LL SEE WHAT I'M DOING TO YOU AND WHEN IT'S DONE HE'LL BE SO APPALLED AT THE SIGHT HE'LL LEAVE YOU IN THE DUST WHERE YOU LAY AND THEN MY SWEET AND FOOLISH ANNA YOU'LL BE MINE," Hades taunted, as he lowered his head to lick salty tears from her cheeks.

189

Anna's eyes shot open as Hades released her mind from her personal hell. She swallowed as she looked over at the fallen in the flesh.

"WE MADE A DEAL ANNA," he reminded.

She nodded unable to speak.

"Anna?" Sam's voice questioned with concern and disbelief. She picked up the key and held it out for the lord of the underworld to take.

Hades snatched the key from her grasp his fingers stroking her palm in the process making her tremble with disgust.

"THANK YOU, MY LADY IT'S BEEN A PLEASURE WORKING WITH YOU, I LOOK FORWARD TO WHEN WE NEXT MEET," he whispered.

"You swore…" she began in protest. Her words fell off becoming a scream as he stabbed at her mind once more.

"SO, NAIVE AND TRUSTING FOR SUCH A BRILLIANT SCHOLAR," he mocked. "WHEN NEXT WE MEET I WILL BE KING OF THE GODS AND SUCH LAWS WILL NO LONGER TIE MY HANDS. SOON LITTLE ANNA YOU WILL KNOW ME IN THE FLESH," he vowed.

"Over my dead body," Sam roared, as he shoved the fallen away from her.

"I WOULDN'T HAVE IT ANY OTHER WAY," Hades stated with a laugh before he turned headed for the door.

"Anna…"

"Not now; Sam you have to stop him," Anna said.

Sam nodded then turned and ran after Hades. He entered the chamber in time to see the key placed in the lock begin to glow. He blinked as a bright light filled the chamber and when it faded a round cavern lay before the lord of the underworld leading into the darkness beyond.

Hades stepped through and Sam moved to follow but as he reached the door it slammed shut.

190

Sam punched the cavern wall with frustration as Hades vanished from beyond his sight. The door of the lord of the underworld having closed behind him; he was too late. Hades had reached the door and was, even now, headed down the dark passageway that would take him to the crown of Zeus.

No matter how hard they tried to get ahead of this mess they were always a step late, and now unless one of Hades brethren had reached Poseidon's door as well, the god of the underworld would claim the crown of the fallen.

Sam shuddered involuntarily with fear at the thought. Turning, he started back down the corridor in the opposite direction to seek out his fiancé. With Hades so near the goal of the crown Sam knew his time was short now, and he wanted to spend it with her.

191

Hades lit the corridor ahead of him to reveal a maze of caverns leading further into the earth. He drew upon his power, seeking first the location of the crown within the maze and then his brethren. He hissed in rage to find he was not alone within the labyrinth. Hermes was moving here as well as Dionysus. The wine god was the closest, but not for long.

Hades saw now his brother's game. While he and Hermes had been hunting for a key Dionysus had amassed enough power to gain influence over the huntress. The wine god had made His troublesome niece into his bride. He'd taken Zeus's daughter for his queen. Now the crown was within his reach.

"NOT FOR LONG," Hades growled as he poured his power into the earth itself. "SLOW HIS DESCENT," Hades commanded as he raced on.

192

Artemis cursed as the path she and her lord were on led into a dead end.

"WHERE IS HECATE? DID WE TAKE A WRONG TURN?" Dionysus asked confused.

"No, it's my uncle, he's here and he's using his power to try and stop you. Give me the cup," Artemis demanded.

"WHY?"

"I'll let him way lay me, you have to stop her," Artemis ordered.

The wine god nodded, handing over his goblet. He watched as his bride gulped down its draught. Her eyes gleamed red with the thirst and a moment later her teeth were at his neck feeding. She drew back and kissed him.

"Go!" she commanded, before racing off the other way. Dionysus waited until she'd vanished and watched the corridor change around him. Where the dead end had been it opened and he raced down the path. Until he spotted Hecate kneeling in the chamber ahead of him.

The wine god threw himself at her putting himself between her and the crown. Hecate roared in fury as she rolled in the dust to escape his grasp.

"YOU'RE POWER HAS DIMINISHED CUP BEARER," Hecate mocked as she easily overpowered him.

"THAT MAY BE SO, WITCH BUT I CAN STILL KEEP YOUR PRIZE FROM YOU," Dionysus hissed, as he kicked the crown beyond her reach.

"NO ONE WILL KEEP ME FROM WHAT IS MINE," Hecate snarled, as she wrapped her hands around his throat.

"YOU CAN'T KILL ME WITCH," Dionysus reminded.

"WHO SAID ANYTHING ABOUT KILLING YOU," Hecate mocked, as she snapped the clasp of a serpent band closed round his neck. Its amethyst eyes gleamed with power before its fangs sank into his jugular. Dionysus roared with fury and disbelief as his power was bound.

193

Hecate got up off the wine god and crossed the chamber to where the crown lay in the dust waiting for her. She picked it up with trembling fingers. Only to have it knocked from her grasp by the crack of a whip. She cursed, it seemed her scuffle with the cup bearer had given her troublesome ex-husband enough time to reach her.

"HERMES!"

"HECATE," he breathed the word with disbelief at the sight of her in his bride's flesh.

"ONCE YOU BOUND ME TO YOUR WILL OH LORD OF KNOWLEDGE, NOW I SHALL BIND YOU TO MINE," she snarled, before she reached once more for the crown. She felt the sting of the lash as his whip wrapped round her.

"SUCH ARROGANCE WITCH; WHEN WILL YOU LEARN YOUR PLACE HERE," Hermes snapped, as he drew her to him. His blue eyes locked with whiskey ones and he smiled as he ran his hand against her cheek. "YOU ARE MINE PANDORA, YOU ALWAYS WILL BE," he breathed before he lowered his head to capture her lips.

194

Hermes eyes fell shut as he lost himself in the taste of her. One he'd waited centuries to know. He felt her arms wrap around his neck as she kissed him back and thrilled in it. But his pleasure soon turned to rage and confusion as he felt the sting of cold metal pierce his flesh.

Blue eyes shot open to find a golden band like that of a serpent round his neck, its blue eyes gleamed with power and his was bound.

"I WAS NEVER YOURS TO BIND MESSENGER AND NOW IT IS YOU, WHO WILL DO MY BIDDING," Hecate hissed, as she turned from him to pick up the crown He watched with disgust as she set the golden circlet upon her head and its form changed, molding to her brow. Her eyes blazed gold and she smiled as her very form changed before him. Golden hair becoming black as night, streaks of crimson and others that mimicked that of flame. Her garment transforming to a blood red gown.

Power swelled around her and burst forth in flame. The band around his neck burned white hot and Hermes screamed at the injury. In the distance he spotted his brother Hades and growled, the only way he'd ever be free was if the lord of the underworld escaped.

"BROTHER RUN!" he shouted in warning and was rewarded with a second jolt that dropped him to his knees in the dirt. He watched as Hades turned and fled before he felt the lash of his own whip upon his back.

"FOOL! DO YOU THINK THERE'S ANYTHING HE CAN DO TO SAVE YOU? TO STOP ME? I AM YOU'RE NEW QUEEN; HECATE GODDESS OF THE CHAOTIC NIGHT. THERE IS NO FORCE ON THE EARTH OR IN IT THAT CAN STOP ME NOW," She crowed in victory as she held aloft a golden scroll that had once been sealed.

The Scroll of Chaos and the source of her power. From off its pages two other golden serpents slithered forth one with eyes of green the other orange they coiled round her wrists to await their time of use.

195

Sam cursed as the earth beneath his feet trembled and the volcano began to stir. Somewhere deep within the earth he imagined Hades had reached the crown of Zeus and placed it upon his brow. The end was drawing near now, he figured but he didn't care; his only thought was to reach Anna. He wanted to see her one more time before he died. To make sure she escaped this awful place and the new king of the fallen.

Blue eyes spotted her a short distance ahead and he raced to her side.

"Sam?"

"I was too late. He's gone. The crown..."

Anna gasped as power surged through her, a vision slammed into her mind with such force it had bloody tears falling from her eyes.

"Anna?"

"We have to find Lance," she whispered.

Sam nodded. Gathering her in his arms he made his way out of the cavern and into what should have been the noon day sun but outside the sky was dark the sun's rays blocked by a thick blanket of darkness.

"Is this death's power beginning to manifest?" he asked in stunned horror.

"No it's Chaos," Anna breathed before she lapsed into unconsciousness.

THE END

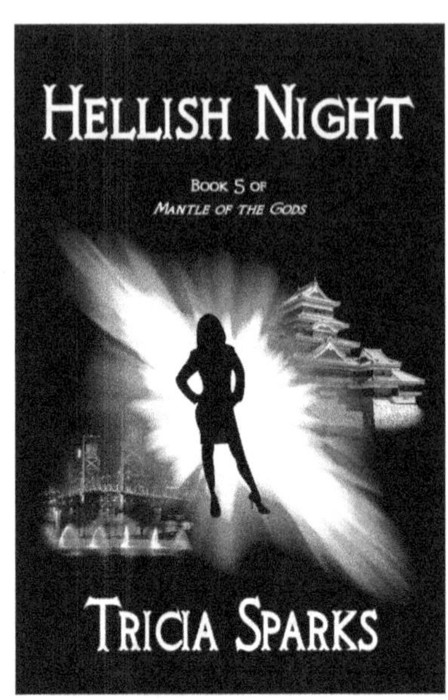

MANTLE OF THE GODS

BOOK 5

HELLISH NIGHT

BY

TRICIA SPARKS

The tables have turned...

Hades – for centuries, he'd stirred dread in the heart of mankind, a god among men that took whatever he desired. He feared nothing, but with Zeus's crown upon Hecate's brow and the band of Chaos in her possession the game has changed. The new Queen of Hell has two fallen in her control and moves to claim the others. As Hades flees before her, desperate to escape, his path will cross the most unlikely of ally.

The tides are shifting...

Ares has rescued Catharine Nichols from the unforgiving depths of the sea. Now he finds The Odyssey floundering, the sun shrouded by darkness. Flight is his first instinct yet neither his chosen bride or his host will allow him to abandon the mortals trapped onboard the ship. With no choice left to him, he sits in a lifeboat adrift at sea with the fury of a queen racing after him.

One left in the dust will rise...

Gail Blackwood lay in despair, broken and abandoned by the witch who'd tormented her. But she is not forgotten. Hades needs her to exact revenge upon the one that's wronged them both. All she has to do is steal a jewel suited for the Lord of the Dead's mantle. The job, however, means reconnecting with an old charge – a master thief she wanted only to forget.

...while another races towards the unknown...

Carrying the body of his fiancée Anna Gallagher, Sam Abrams sets out for Hilo Airport, unsure of his destination. The darkened sky above serves only to twist the knife of fear in his gut. He has to keep going, his steps guided by the last words Anna spoke before she lapsed into unconsciousness: to seek out the one man who can hold back the coming darkness.

A Queen has risen. Her wrath will follow as the darkness mounts.

Read on for a sample

1 Marianas Trench

Ares broke through the surface of the choppy water with his precious cargo held close. His orange eyes moved to the ship and he cursed. Hermes rouge wave it seemed had done more than just sweep Catharine off the deck; it had also managed to flood the ship.

The Odyssey was sinking.

The mortals Fox and Robin were already standing on deck looking for escape.

The war lord moved to seek safety from the sea as the sun overhead blackened. He cried out in agony as he felt the binding of the king's crown wrap around him. Someone had claimed the throne. The sighs pointed to Chaos but that wasn't possible he hadn't been in play at all.

Ares mind pressed against Hermes looking for answers and found blackness. He sought Dionysus and got the same. When he turned toward Hades he got a jumble of mixed images that had him cursing.

Hecate.

The witch had claimed the crown and Chaos's power for herself. She'd enslaved both Hermes and Dionysus to her will. She'd tricked the others into sealing the power of their mantles and had bound them to her will with Chao's scroll. He had to get out of there and as far away from anything connected to his image and the detective's life.

As he moved to secure a piece of the wreckage to carry them to safety Catharine cried out in protest.

"WHAT IS WRONG NOW?" Ares snapped with irritation this whole mess was her fault. If she'd just gone below deck when he told her to he'd have claimed Poseidon's key and have claimed Zeus's crown instead of the witch; now he, the god of war, was in danger.

"You can't just leave them there to die," Catharine sputtered with disapproval.

Ares was prepared to ignore the foolish comment but his host struggled against his grip the cop in him demanding he serve and protect the innocent. Ares cursed. "FINE," he hissed before he set her on the wreckage. "DON'T MOVE." He commanded before he sank back in to the water to do as she demanded.

The lord of war cut through the choppy current and boarded the scuttled ship. He made his way to the deck. "YOU, COME WITH ME," he demanded as he gave Fox a nudge the other man stood slack jawed for a moment dumb founded by what was happening before he blinked and moved to do as directed. With the mortal's aid Ares lowered a life boat from the deck into the water below.

He watched as man and woman boarded before moving below deck once more to gather any materials he could muster that might mean the difference between life and death. His host poked at him more than once to take certain things that he did not see as useful and to silence the man's struggle against his control he relented without asking too much of the nature of the thing he grabbed.

The last thing he took was the woman Catharine's laptop so that her work would not be lost. With the materials gathered he stowed them in the life boat before plunging back into the water once more. Ares drew Catharine from the debris where he'd left her and loaded her into the small vessel. Once she was safe aboard he joined her.

"WE HAVE TO MOVE," he muttered before taking a seat at the oars and beginning to row. His one thought to get as far away from the trench as possible before Hermes rose back from the depths to attack them.

2 Kawai, Hawaii

Hades raced back through the passage toward the volcanic cavern where his door waited. He had to get out of the mountain and clear of Hecate's reach. Back to his fortress to Brooke before the witch could reach her. He needed a way to fix his mantle and escape from the mess she'd wrought. He was DEATH he would not fall to the likes of her. Hades vowed as he reached the surface.

Around him the volcano stirred with fury as his queen raged at his slipping through her fingers. Let her rage; it would do her no good.

She would never catch him.

He was going to find the war god take his sword and drive it into her black heart. Then he'd take the crown from her brow and place it upon his own where it belonged. HE would be king and there wasn't anything she could throw at him that would stop him.

3 Atlantis, Somewhere in the Bermuda Triangle

Artemis footsteps carried her closer to Chaos's door and back to the lost city beyond. She could see it loaming in the distance when a pain strong and terrible tore through her. She cried out as it dropped her to her knees. Fingers fisted in the dust as her father's power left her.

Her eyes wheeled as fear gripped her. If Dionysus had reached the crown this would not be happening to her. Their bonding would have allowed her to keep her authority over the heavens. This horrible pain meant only one thing. Her husband had failed. Hecate had obtained the crown.

Artemis's gaze turned back the way she'd come. No matter she'd see to it this new upstart queen's reign was brief. Artemis told herself as she got to her feet and reached for an arrow with determination. Her mind set on slaying the old witch at last.

Any notions of striking down the vial woman died as the cup in her grasp heated the gold burning her hand. Artemis watched with disbelief as the wine within the goblet began to bubble and froth. Blue eyes looked on with dread as the contents boiled over. What was happening ahead? The huntress wondered as the cup spewed forth the blood red wine on to the dusty earth before her.

When it stilled the liquid within was no longer wine but water. She gasped with shock and fear tore through her. Something was wrong with Dionysus. Her mind ran wild with possible scenarios to explain the event and all of them were bad.

New pain shot through her belly where his child slept. Artemis hissed as she clutched her abdomen trying to quiet the infant. Artemis's mind turned to her lord seeking his mind through their bond and felt dismay to find he wasn't there.

The huntress closed her eyes fighting through pain and panic.

Desperate she sent a cry for aid and answers out through the god's channel and waited.

"THE WITCH TRICKED US ALL," her uncle's answer was vague and held a wealth of emotion behind it. Fury and fear. Artemis swallowed as she sank down in the dust. Her mind asked for further answers but Hades was quiet.

His silence was deafening and the huntress sat in it, head bowed aching with a pain she didn't understand. Her mind screamed at her to run aware that she was not safe where she sat but she found she couldn't move. Her body stirred with thirst for her lord's wine and blood. His cup offered her no relief its draught gone and the reality that the wine god may have fallen already crashed in on her.

Hecate's coal black eyes gleamed golden as her power pulsed through the bands upon her captives. She watched with fascination as the wine gods eyes turned blood red as the thirst that drove him tore through him only to be denied. His power repressed.

Her gaze wheeled to that of the fallen lord of knowledge and she laughed at the sight of him coiled on the dusty ground in a fetal ball as her power tore through him white hot with her fury at his vain attempt to warn Hades. It was time these upstarts knew their place. These vial Fallen who'd aspired to be gods so long ago.

Hecate crossed the floor of the cavern to where Hermes lay and released her power. The fool rose from the ground to stand before her and she pressed her power through him once more.

"INCOLENT DOG! How dare you rise before ME without MY permission? YOU are NOTHING NOW! YOU WHO ONCE DARED CALL YOURSELF A GOD ARE BOUND. YOUR POWER IS MINE! I CAN TAKE IT WITH A THOUGHT. YOU'RE ONLY ALIVE BECAUSE I WILL IT," Hecate hissed.

"My Queen," he hissed through the pain. "Hecate please," he cried wanting only for the pain to end.

"THAT'S RIGHT BEG FOOL, BUT YOU'LL NEVER BE FREE OF ME," she snapped before she kicked him in the face and dropped him to the ground once more. She knelt at his side and wiped his blood from his face before turning her focus back to Dionysus.

"LOOK AT YOU SO THIRSTY, SO WEAK…"

"My child…"

"YES YOUR CHILD AND YOUR, WOULD- BE, BRIDE BOTH SUFFER NOW BECAUSE YOUR POWER IS MINE. YOU WILL ONLY FEED WHEN I ALLOW IT. DO YOU WISH TO SAVE THEM?"

"Yes, my queen," Dionysus answered.

"SERVE ME AND YOU SHALL," HECATE VOWED.

"What is thy wish my queen?"

"RETURN TO YOUR PALACE AND FINISH YOUR MOVIES. SO LONG AS YOU DO I WILL SUSTAIN YOU BOTH," Hecate promised.

"As you will," the wine god answered and for the response Hecate pressed bloody fingers to his lips allowing him to sip Hermes blood. His eyes reverted back to their natural color with the taste and she smiled knowing his power was indeed bound.

"GO, COLLECT YOU WIFE SEE TO HER AND GET BACK TO WORK," Hecate ordered before turning her attention back to Hermes. The lord of knowledge wallowed in the dirt like a beast as her power punished him. She noted the gleam of power in his eyes had dimmed and that they too were now like that of a mortal mans. She eased her power and watched as he stilled.

"HERMES," she breathed the name and watched as he flinched.

"My queen," he murmured through bloody and split lips.

"RISE," she commanded and watched as he did so slowly careful not to look directly at her. She smiled with pleasure good he too was now hers to command. "GO, FIND ME ARES," she demanded.

"As you desire," he answered before he turned and left heading back out the passage he'd entered.

Hecate watched as he went before she turned to pursue Hades. The lord of the underworld would be the next of these fallen to be brought low.

Look for more in 2015

WANT TO SEE WHERE IT ALL BEGAN?

THEN CHECK OUT:

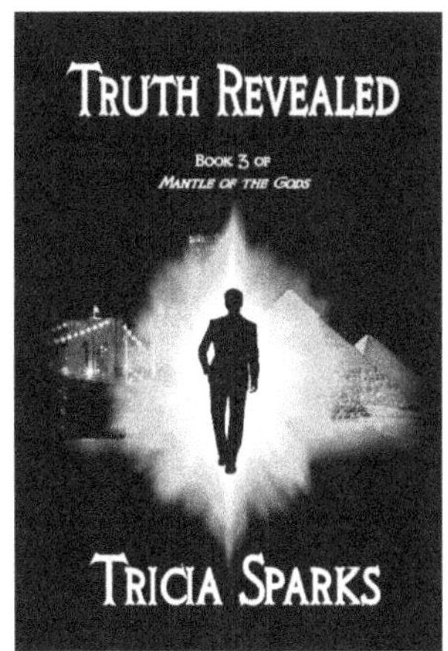

AVAILABLE AT AMAZON.COM

www.ingramcontent.com/pod-product-compliance
Lightning Source LLC
Chambersburg PA
CBHW071046250626
47159CB00002B/376

9781941426111